NIC™
THE HEDGEHOG
IMPOSTER SYNDROME

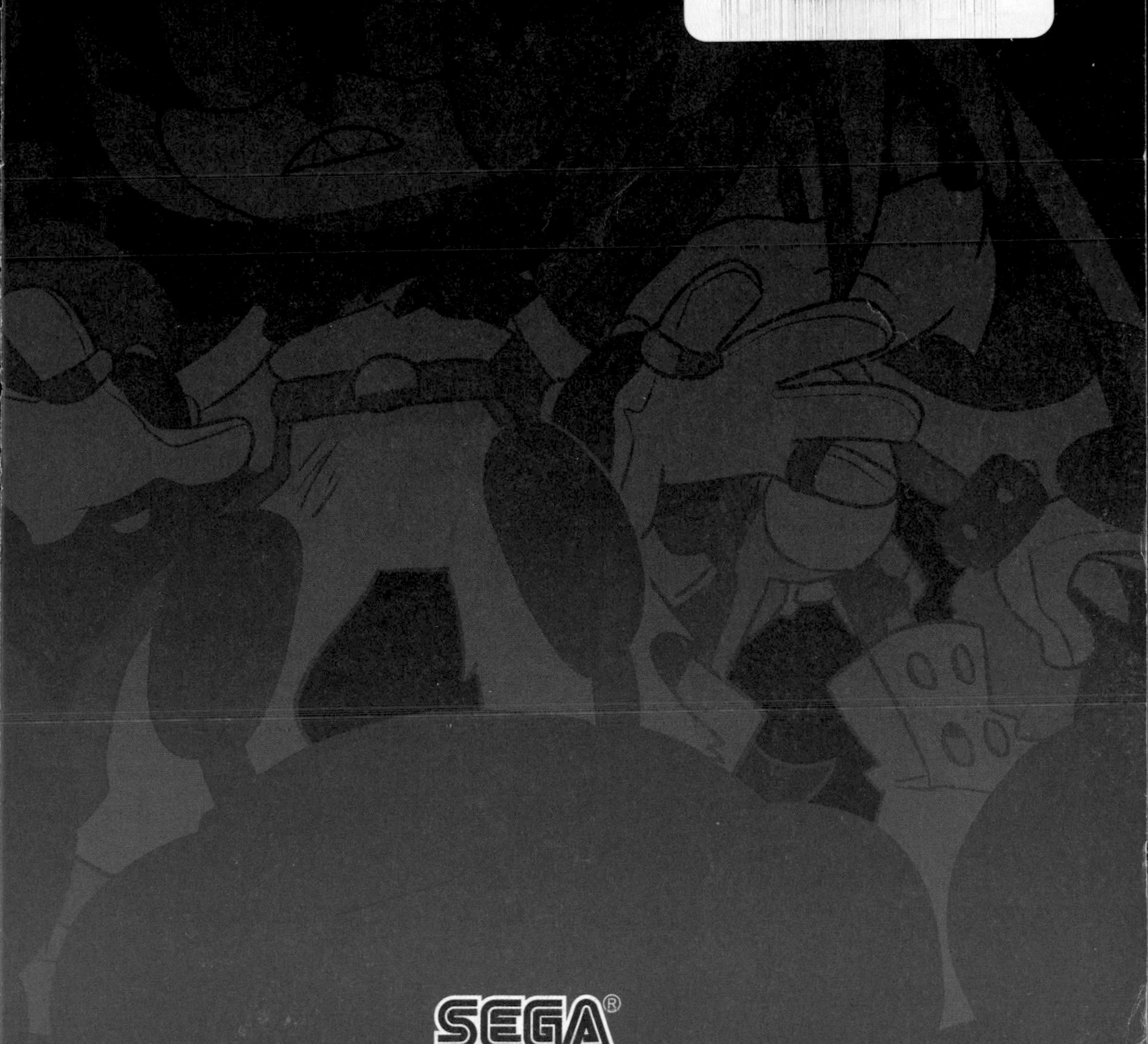

SEGA®

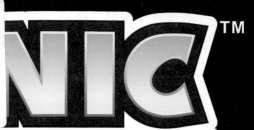

@IDWpublishing
IDWpublishing.com

COVER ARTIST:
Ben Bates & **Mari Takeyama**

SERIES EDITORS:
David Mariotte & **Riley Farmer**

COLLECTION EDITORS:
Alonzo Simon and **Zac Boone**

978-1-68405-900-3   25 24 23 22   1 2 3 4

Originally published as SONIC THE HEDGEHOG: IMPOSTER SYNDROME issues #1-4.

Nachie Marsham, Publisher
Blake Kobashigawa, SVP Sales, Marketing & Strategy
Mark Doyle, VP Creative & Editorial Strategy
Tara McCrillis, VP Publishing Operations
Anna Morrow, VP Marketing & Publicity
Alex Hargett, VP Sales
Jamie S. Rich, Executive Editorial Director
Scott Dunbier, Director, Special Projects
Greg Gustin, Sr. Director, Content Strategy
Kevin Schwoer, Sr. Director of Talent Relations
Lauren LePera, Sr. Managing Editor
Keith Davidsen, Director, Marketing & PR
Topher Alford, Sr. Digital Marketing Manager
Patrick O'Connell, Sr. Manager, Direct Market Sales
Shauna Monteforte, Sr. Director of Manufacturing Operations
Greg Foreman, Director DTC Sales & Operations
Nathan Widick, Director of Design
Neil Uyetake, Sr. Art Director, Design & Production
Shawn Lee, Art Director, Design & Production
Jack Rivera, Art Director, Marketing

Ted Adams and Robbie Robbins, IDW Founders

For international rights, contact licensing@idwpublishing.com.

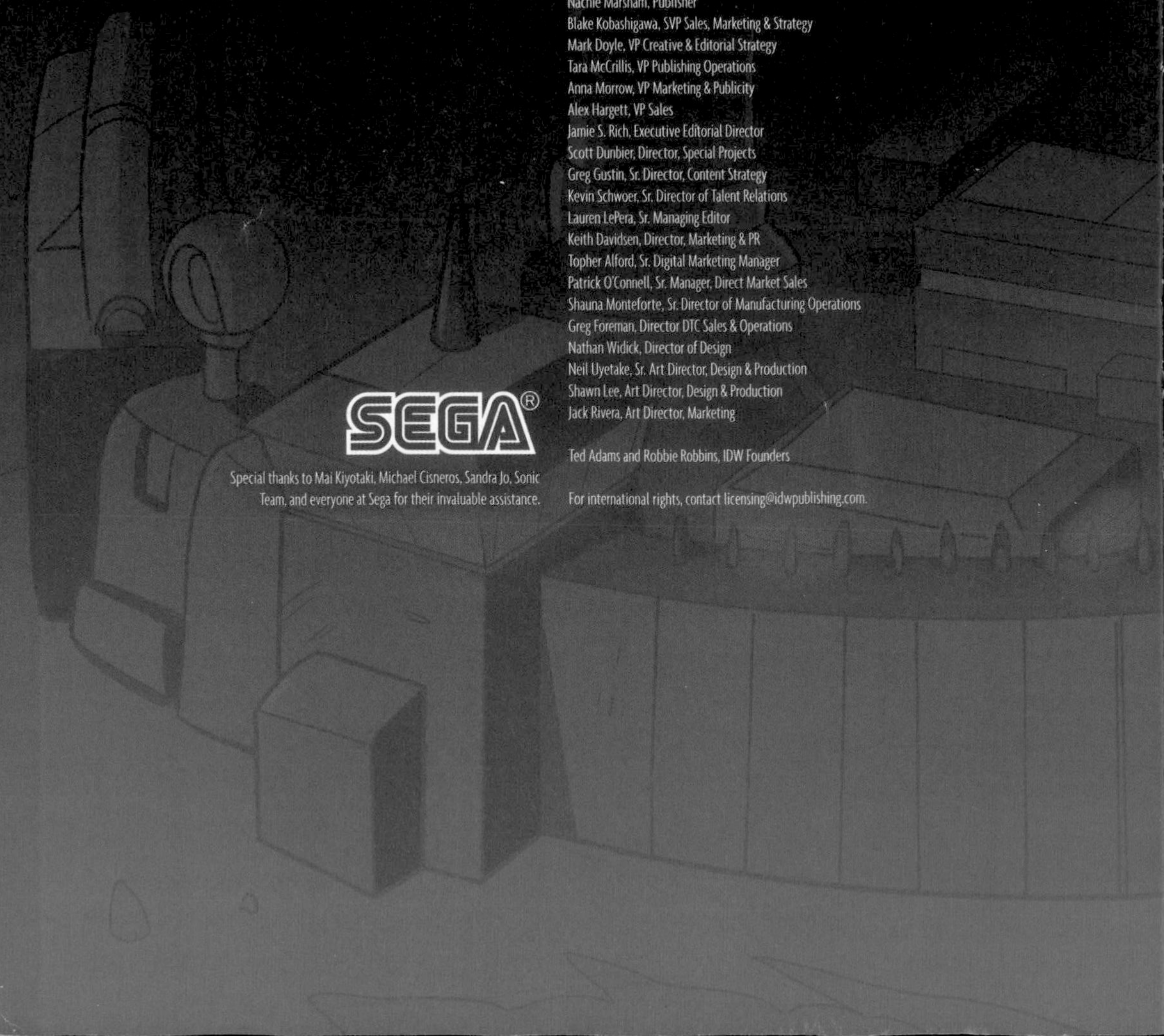

Special thanks to Mai Kiyotaki, Michael Cisneros, Sandra Jo, Sonic Team, and everyone at Sega for their invaluable assistance.

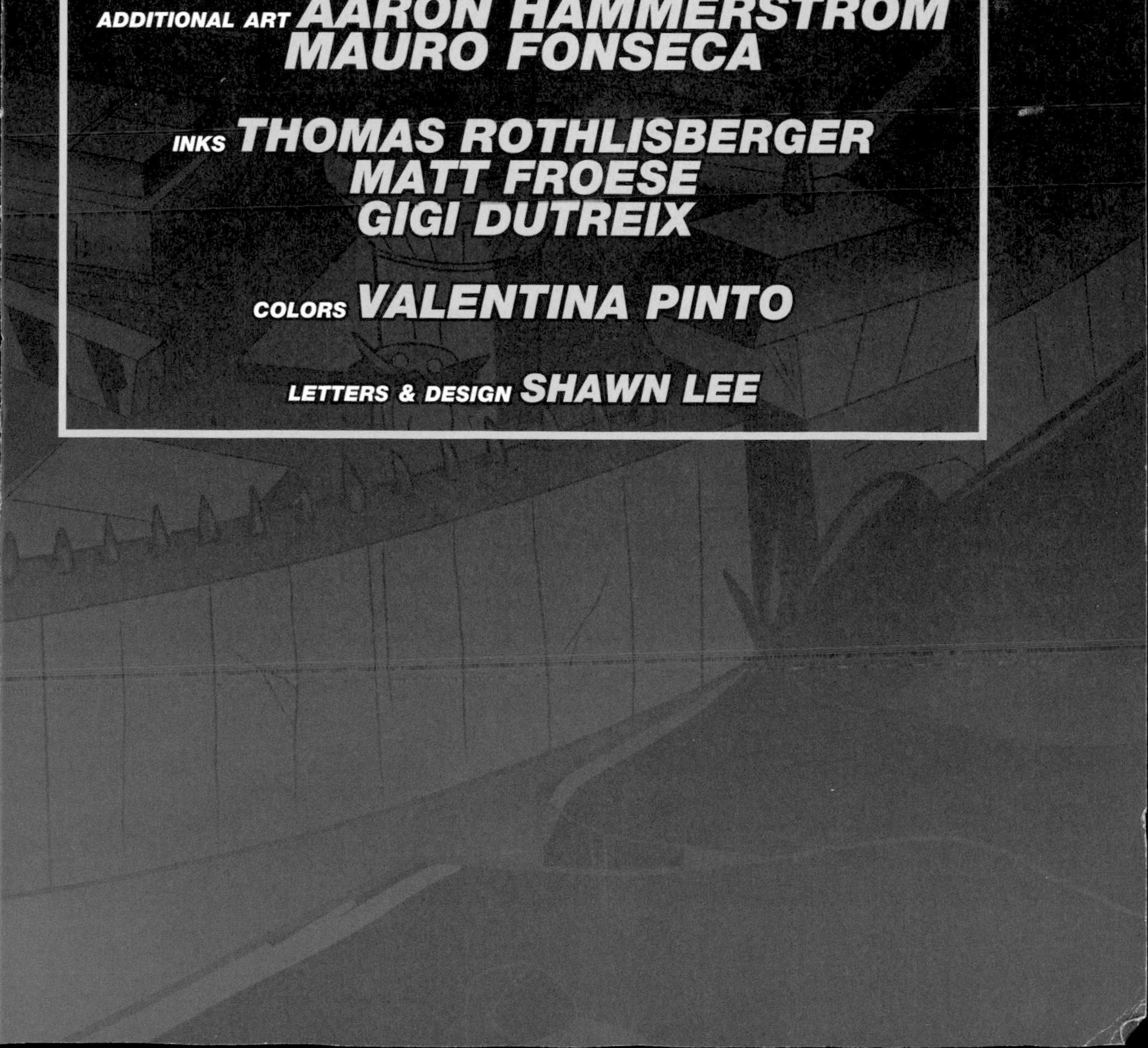

STORY **IAN FLYNN**

ART **THOMAS ROTHLISBERGER**

ADDITIONAL ART **AARON HAMMERSTROM**
MAURO FONSECA

INKS **THOMAS ROTHLISBERGER**
MATT FROESE
GIGI DUTREIX

COLORS **VALENTINA PINTO**

LETTERS & DESIGN **SHAWN LEE**

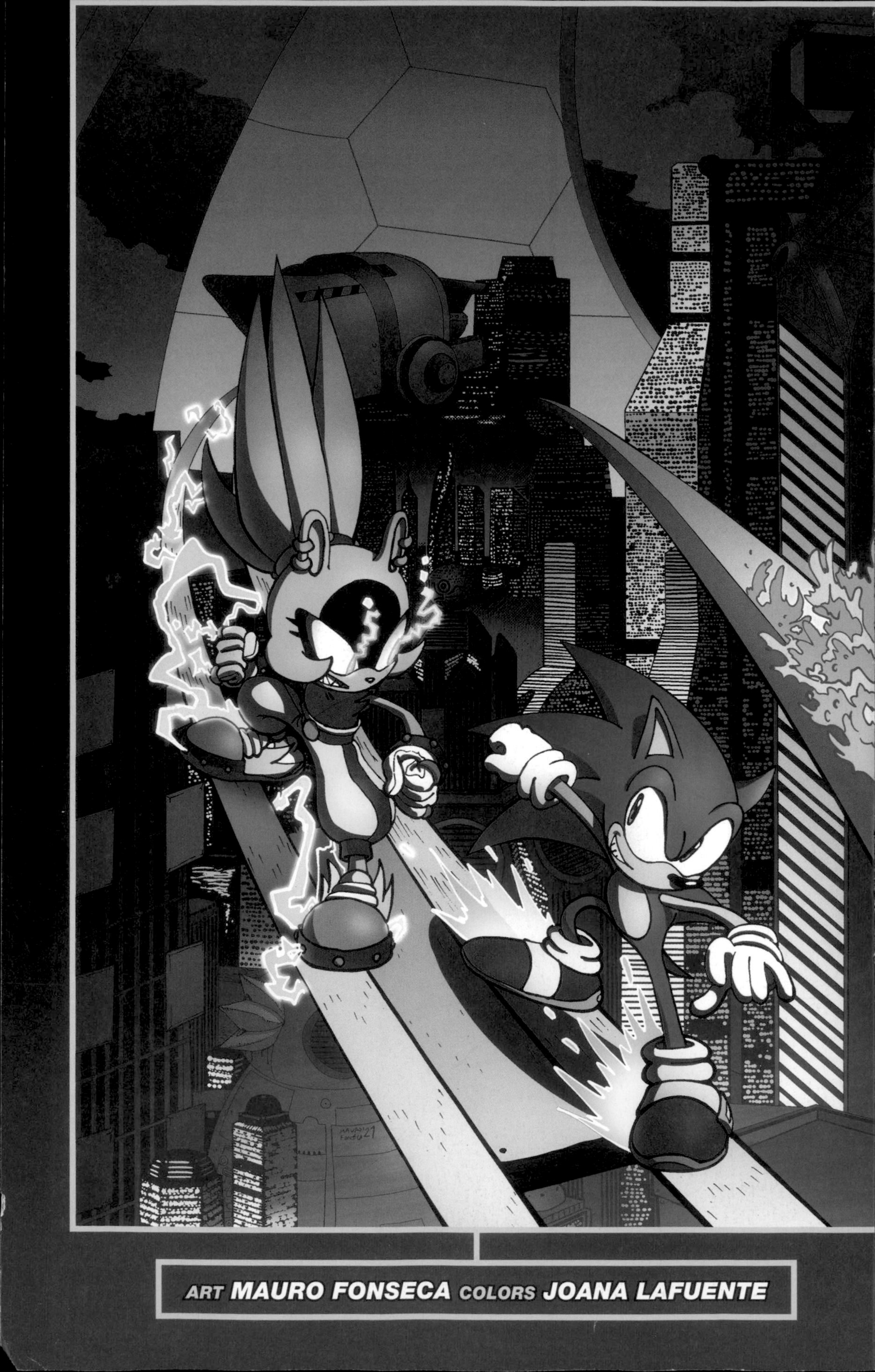

ART MAURO FONSECA COLORS JOANA LAFUENTE

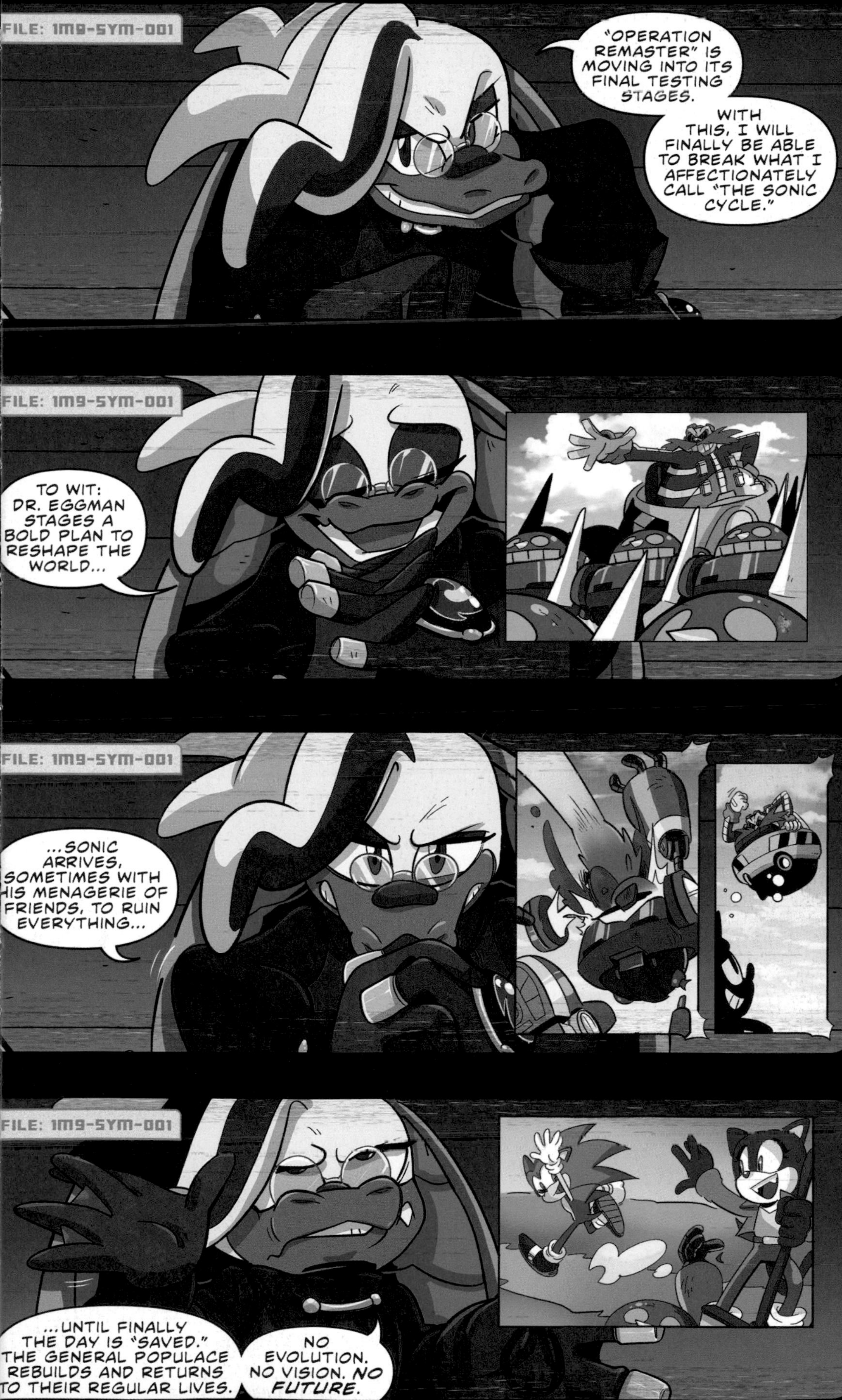
FILE: 1M9-SYM-001
"OPERATION REMASTER" IS MOVING INTO ITS FINAL TESTING STAGES.
WITH THIS, I WILL FINALLY BE ABLE TO BREAK WHAT I AFFECTIONATELY CALL "THE SONIC CYCLE."
FILE: 1M9-SYM-001
TO WIT: DR. EGGMAN STAGES A BOLD PLAN TO RESHAPE THE WORLD...
FILE: 1M9-SYM-001
...SONIC ARRIVES, SOMETIMES WITH HIS MENAGERIE OF FRIENDS, TO RUIN EVERYTHING...
FILE: 1M9-SYM-001
...UNTIL FINALLY THE DAY IS "SAVED." THE GENERAL POPULACE REBUILDS AND RETURNS TO THEIR REGULAR LIVES.
NO EVOLUTION. NO VISION. *NO FUTURE*.

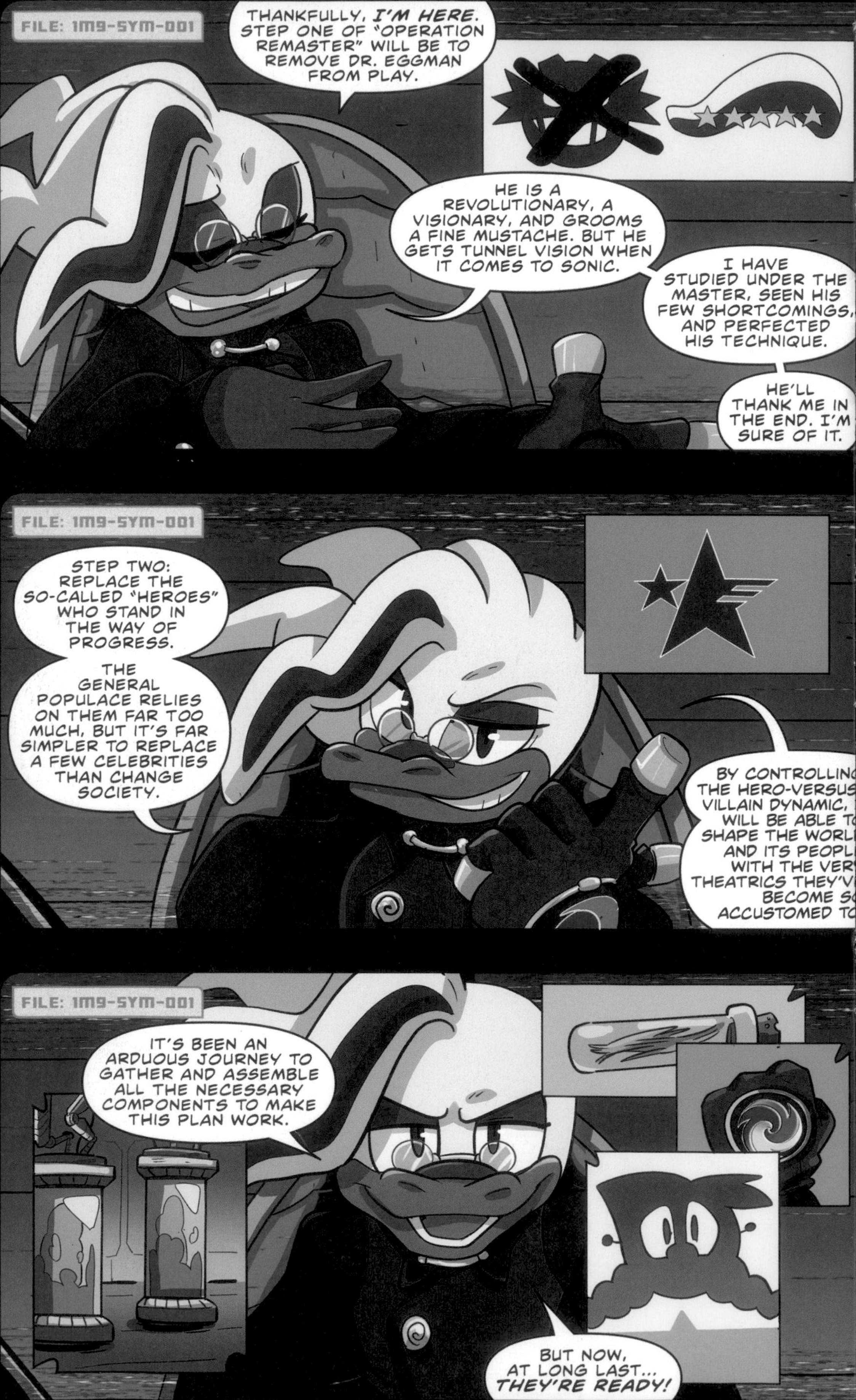
FILE: 1M9-SYM-001
THANKFULLY, *I'M HERE.* STEP ONE OF "OPERATION REMASTER" WILL BE TO REMOVE DR. EGGMAN FROM PLAY.
HE IS A REVOLUTIONARY, A VISIONARY, AND GROOMS A FINE MUSTACHE. BUT HE GETS TUNNEL VISION WHEN IT COMES TO SONIC.
I HAVE STUDIED UNDER THE MASTER, SEEN HIS FEW SHORTCOMINGS, AND PERFECTED HIS TECHNIQUE.
HE'LL THANK ME IN THE END. I'M SURE OF IT.
FILE: 1M9-SYM-001
STEP TWO: REPLACE THE SO-CALLED "HEROES" WHO STAND IN THE WAY OF PROGRESS.
THE GENERAL POPULACE RELIES ON THEM FAR TOO MUCH, BUT IT'S FAR SIMPLER TO REPLACE A FEW CELEBRITIES THAN CHANGE SOCIETY.
BY CONTROLLIN THE HERO-VERSUS VILLAIN DYNAMIC, WILL BE ABLE T SHAPE THE WORL AND ITS PEOPL WITH THE VER THEATRICS THEY'V BECOME S ACCUSTOMED T
FILE: 1M9-SYM-001
IT'S BEEN AN ARDUOUS JOURNEY TO GATHER AND ASSEMBLE ALL THE NECESSARY COMPONENTS TO MAKE THIS PLAN WORK.
BUT NOW, AT LONG LAST... *THEY'RE READY!*

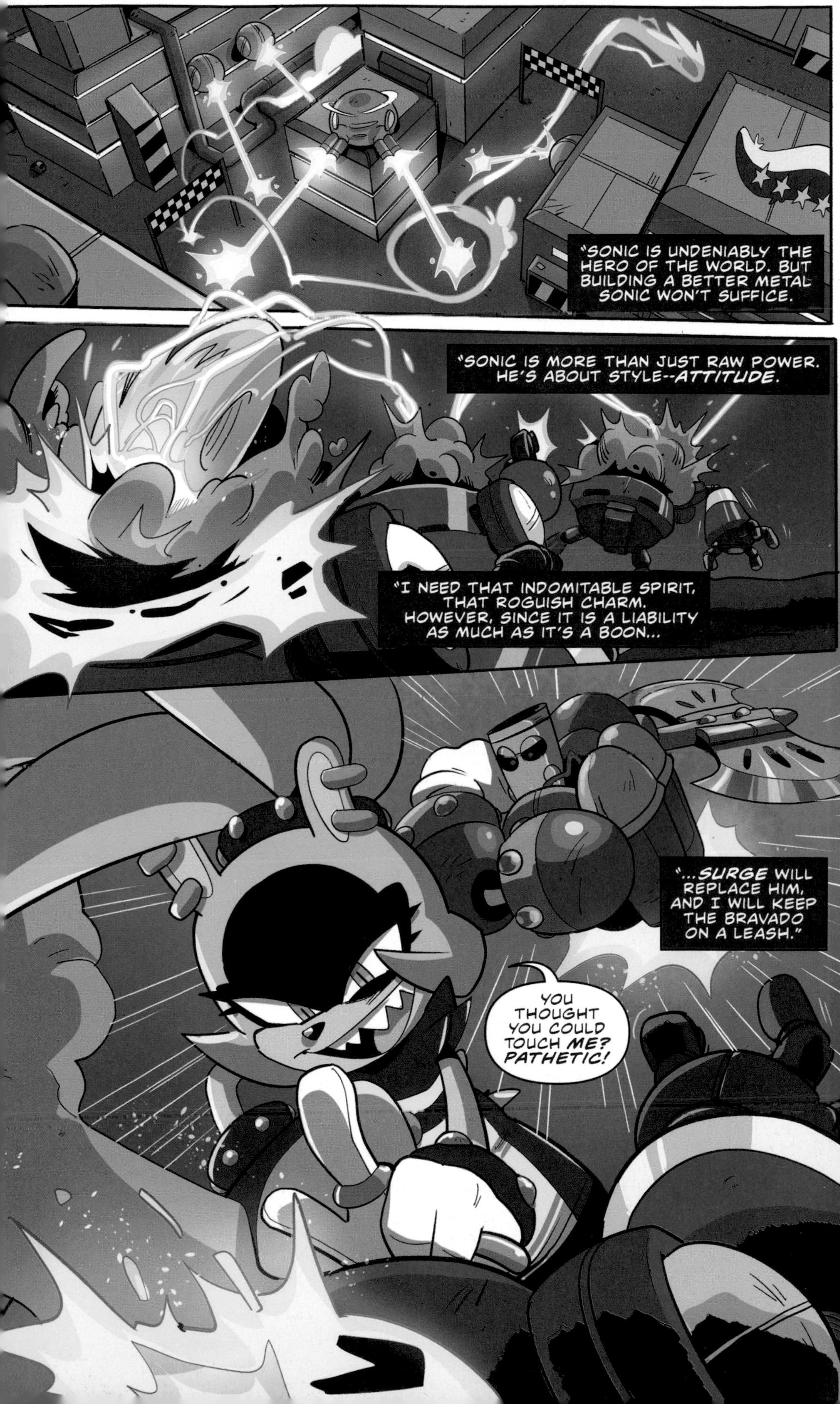
"SONIC IS UNDENIABLY THE HERO OF THE WORLD. BUT BUILDING A BETTER METAL SONIC WON'T SUFFICE.
"SONIC IS MORE THAN JUST RAW POWER. HE'S ABOUT STYLE--ATTITUDE.
"I NEED THAT INDOMITABLE SPIRIT, THAT ROGUISH CHARM. HOWEVER, SINCE IT IS A LIABILITY AS MUCH AS IT'S A BOON...
"...SURGE WILL REPLACE HIM, AND I WILL KEEP THE BRAVADO ON A LEASH."
YOU THOUGHT YOU COULD TOUCH ME? PATHETIC!

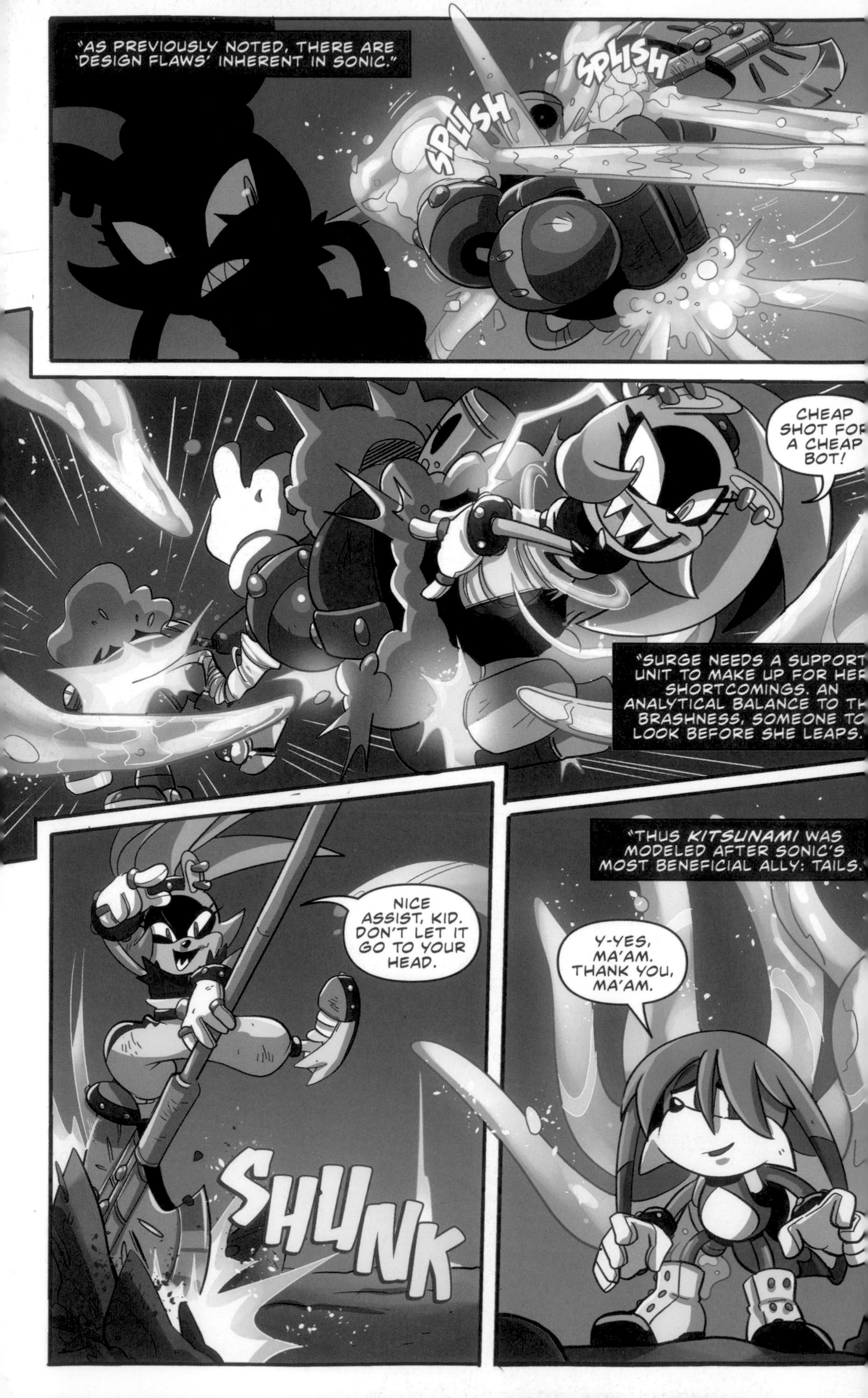
"AS PREVIOUSLY NOTED, THERE ARE 'DESIGN FLAWS' INHERENT IN SONIC."
SPLISH
SPLISH
CHEAP SHOT FOR A CHEAP BOT!
"SURGE NEEDS A SUPPORT UNIT TO MAKE UP FOR HER SHORTCOMINGS. AN ANALYTICAL BALANCE TO TH BRASHNESS, SOMEONE TO LOOK BEFORE SHE LEAPS.
NICE ASSIST, KID. DON'T LET IT GO TO YOUR HEAD.
SHUNK
"THUS KITSUNAMI WAS MODELED AFTER SONIC'S MOST BENEFICIAL ALLY: TAILS.
Y-YES, MA'AM. THANK YOU, MA'AM.

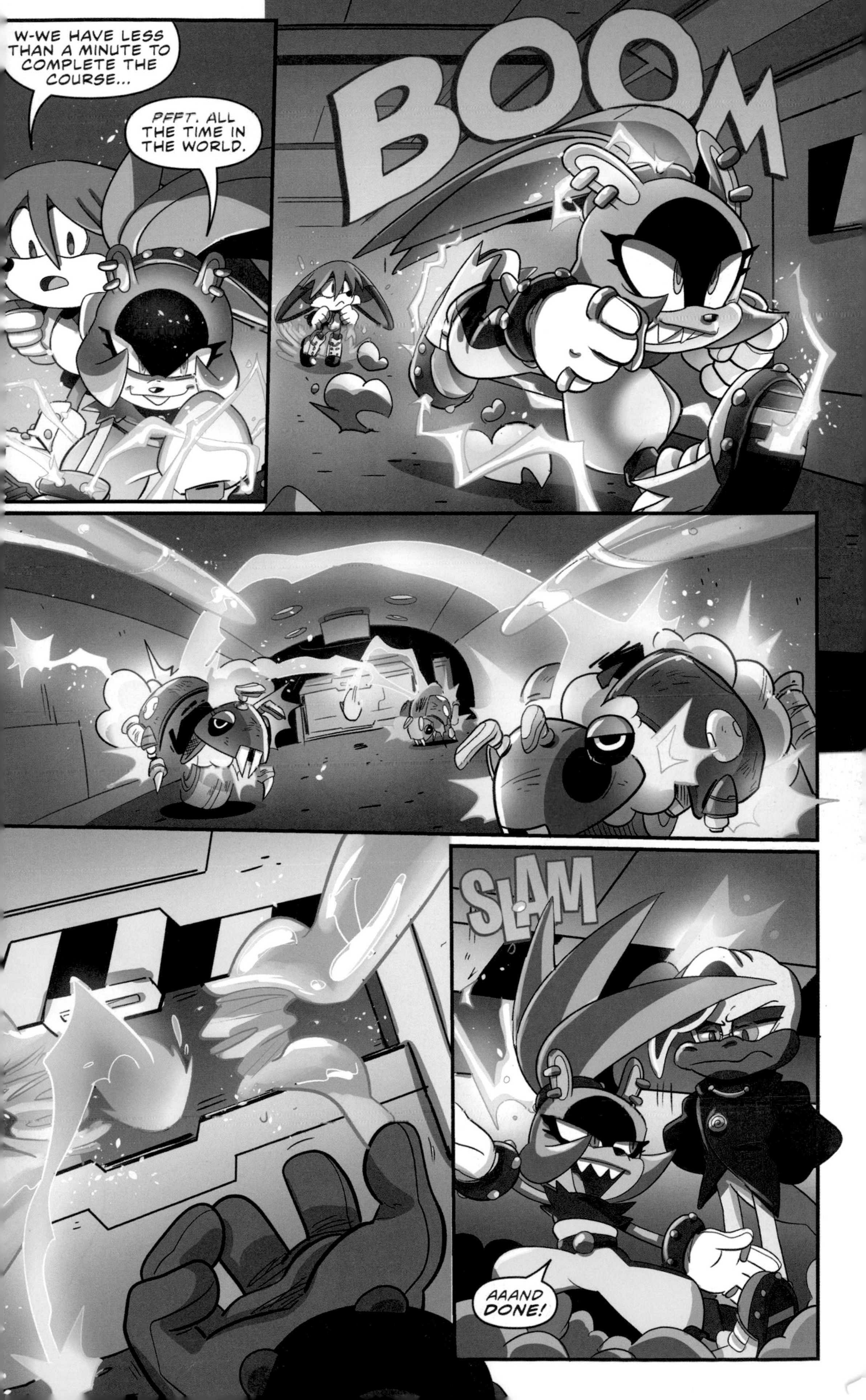
W-WE HAVE LESS THAN A MINUTE TO COMPLETE THE COURSE...
PFFT. ALL THE TIME IN THE WORLD.
BOOM
SLAM
AAAND DONE!

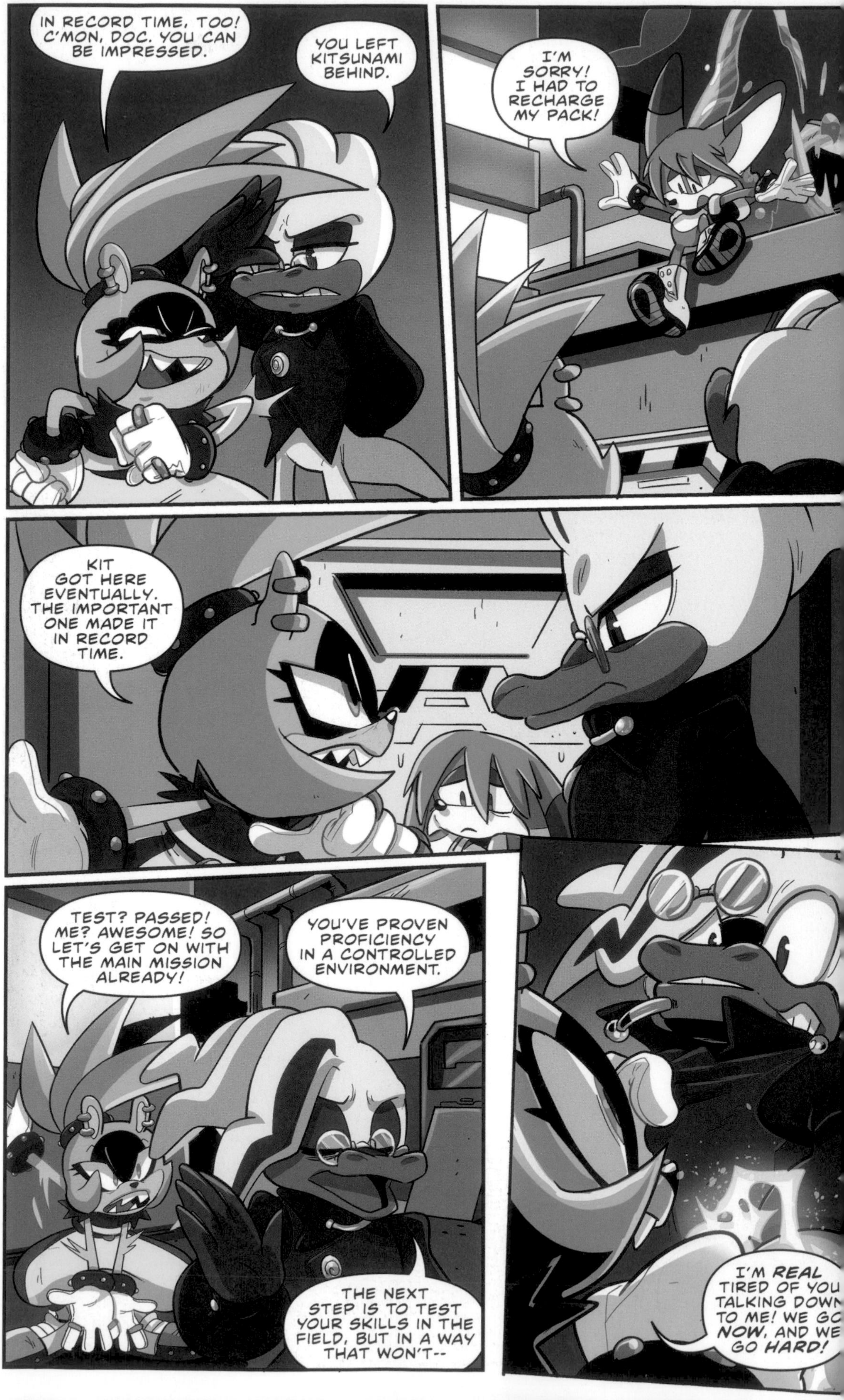
IN RECORD TIME, TOO! C'MON, DOC. YOU CAN BE IMPRESSED.
YOU LEFT KITSUNAMI BEHIND.
I'M SORRY! I HAD TO RECHARGE MY PACK!
KIT GOT HERE EVENTUALLY. THE IMPORTANT ONE MADE IT IN RECORD TIME.
TEST? PASSED! ME? AWESOME! SO LET'S GET ON WITH THE MAIN MISSION ALREADY!
YOU'VE PROVEN PROFICIENCY IN A CONTROLLED ENVIRONMENT.
THE NEXT STEP IS TO TEST YOUR SKILLS IN THE FIELD, BUT IN A WAY THAT WON'T--
I'M *REAL* TIRED OF YOU TALKING DOWN TO ME! WE GO *NOW*, AND WE GO *HARD*!

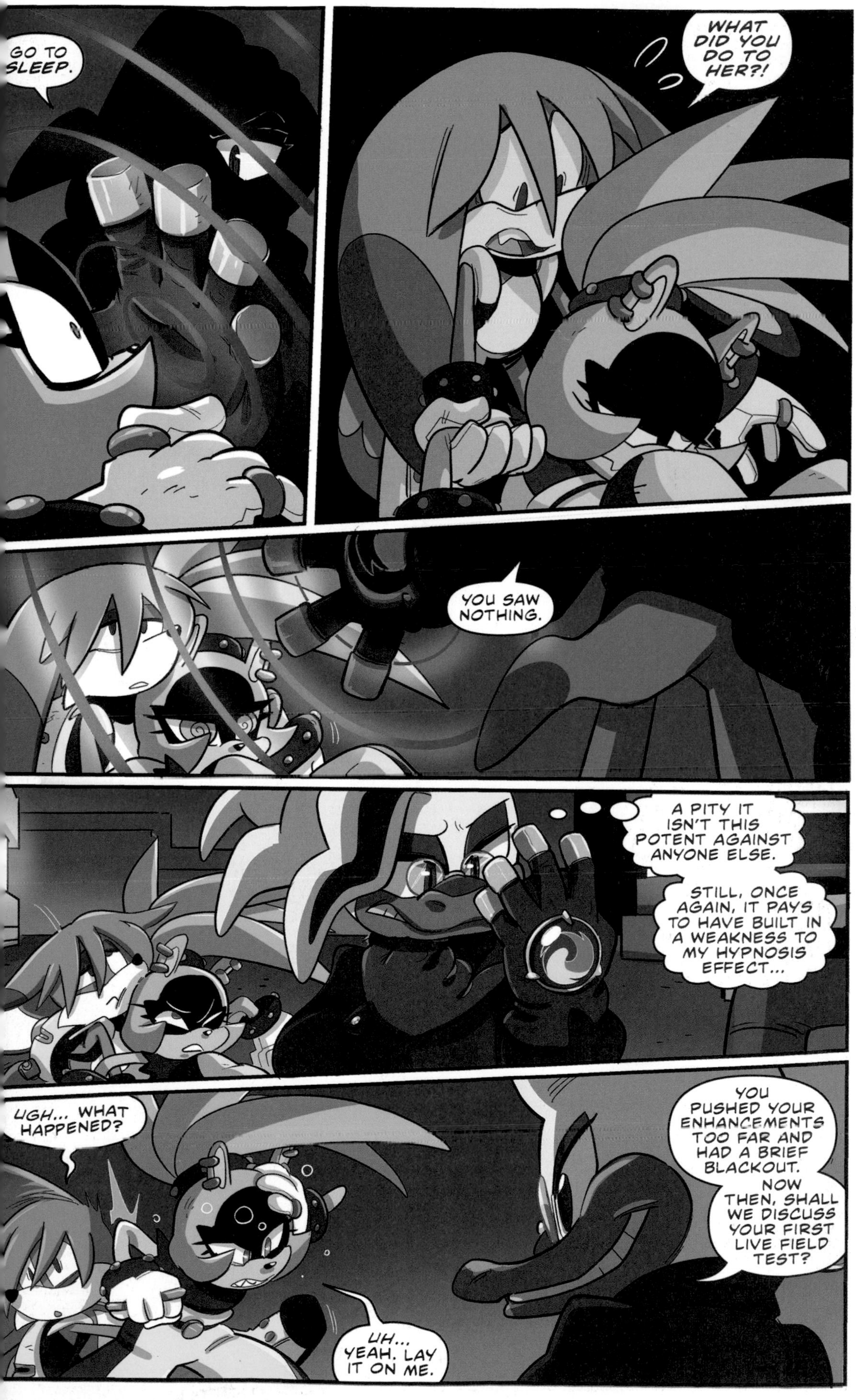
GO TO SLEEP.
WHAT DID YOU DO TO HER?!
YOU SAW NOTHING.
A PITY IT ISN'T THIS POTENT AGAINST ANYONE ELSE.
STILL, ONCE AGAIN, IT PAYS TO HAVE BUILT IN A WEAKNESS TO MY HYPNOSIS EFFECT...
UGH... WHAT HAPPENED?
YOU PUSHED YOUR ENHANCEMENTS TOO FAR AND HAD A BRIEF BLACKOUT.
NOW THEN, SHALL WE DISCUSS YOUR FIRST LIVE FIELD TEST?
UH... YEAH. LAY IT ON ME.

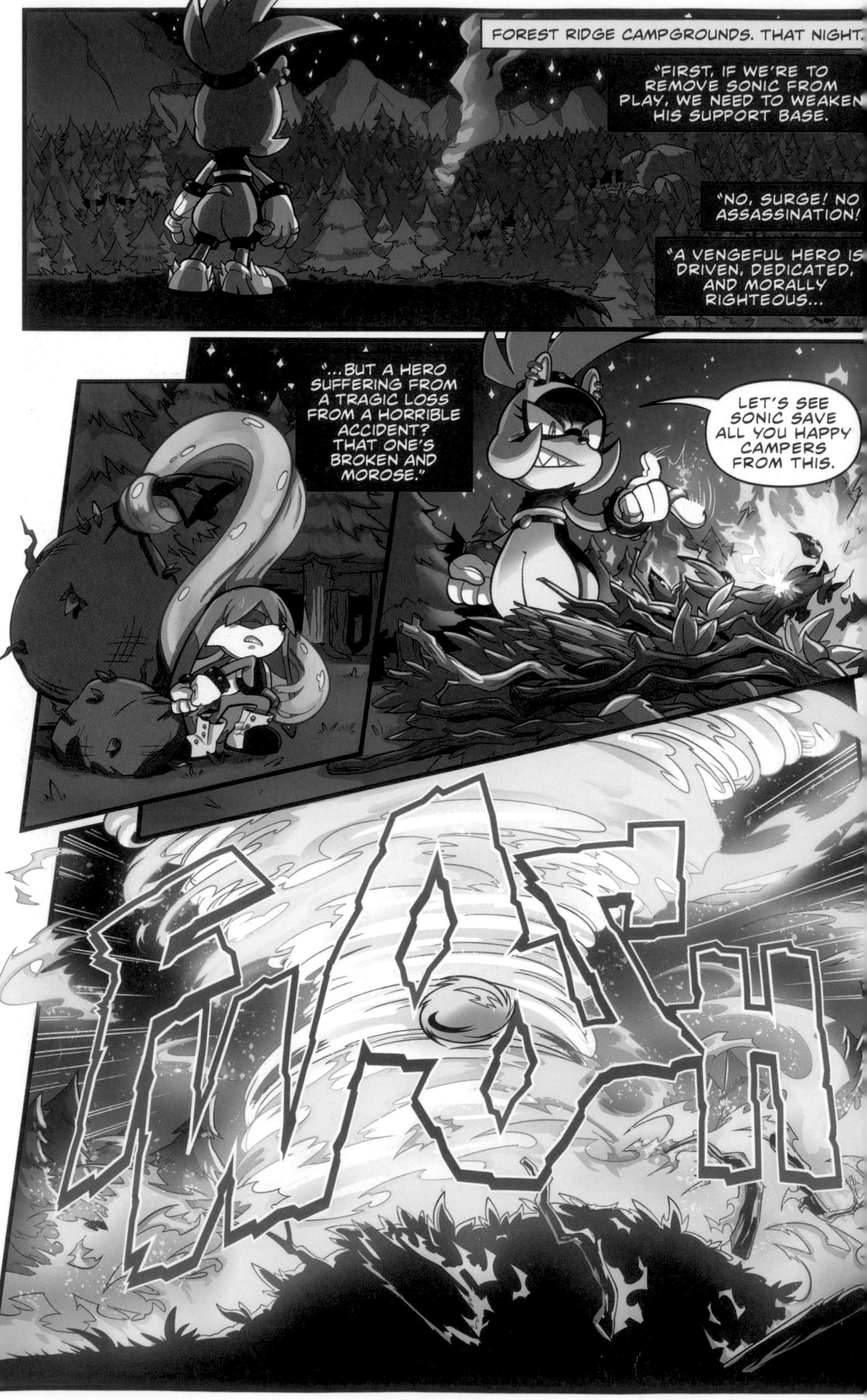
FOREST RIDGE CAMPGROUNDS. THAT NIGHT.
"FIRST, IF WE'RE TO REMOVE SONIC FROM PLAY, WE NEED TO WEAKEN HIS SUPPORT BASE.
"NO, SURGE! NO ASSASSINATION!
"A VENGEFUL HERO IS DRIVEN, DEDICATED, AND MORALLY RIGHTEOUS...
"...BUT A HERO SUFFERING FROM A TRAGIC LOSS FROM A HORRIBLE ACCIDENT? THAT ONE'S BROKEN AND MOROSE."
LET'S SEE SONIC SAVE ALL YOU HAPPY CAMPERS FROM THIS.
WOOSH

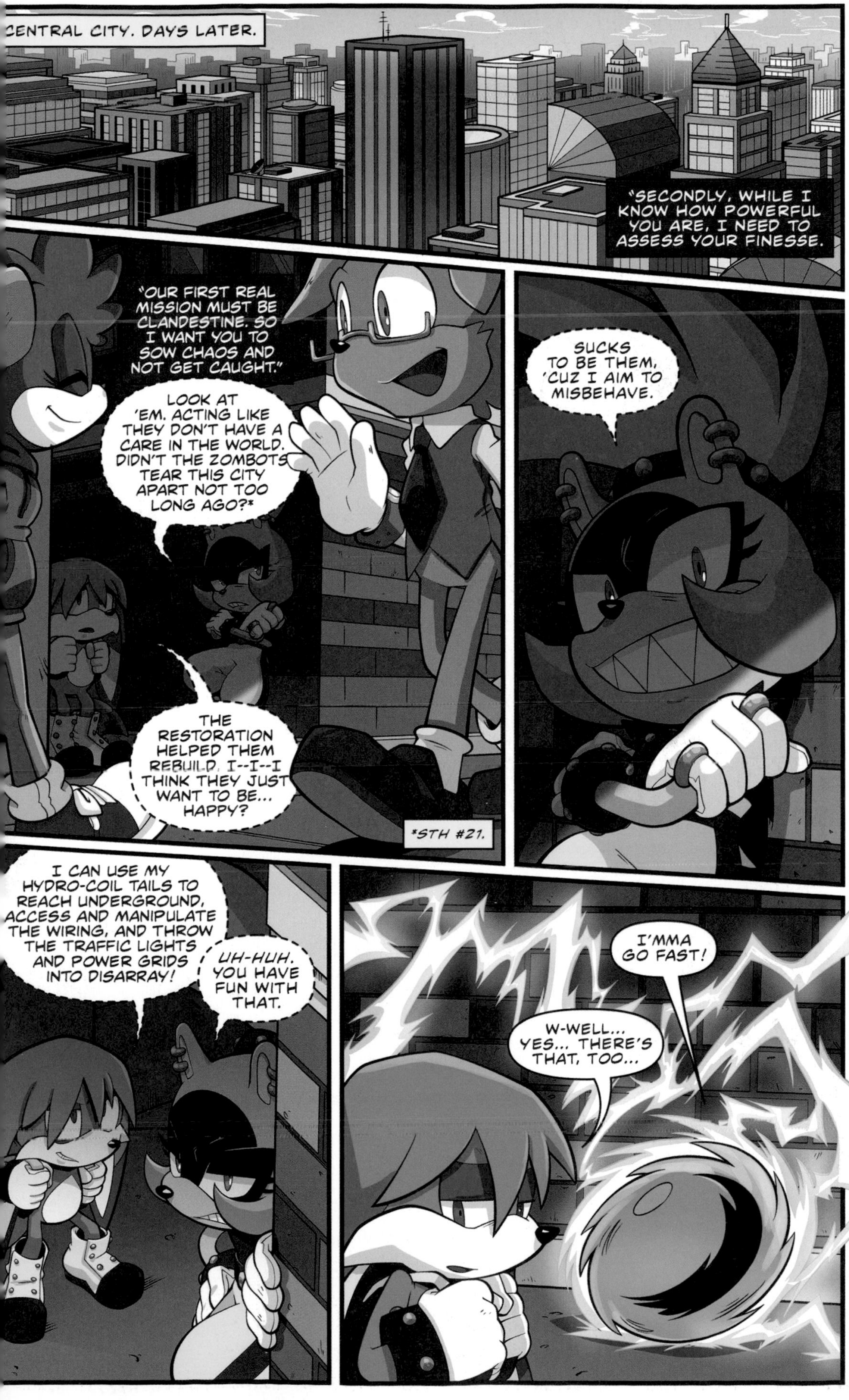

CENTRAL CITY. DAYS LATER.
"SECONDLY, WHILE I KNOW HOW POWERFUL YOU ARE, I NEED TO ASSESS YOUR FINESSE.
"OUR FIRST REAL MISSION MUST BE CLANDESTINE. SO I WANT YOU TO SOW CHAOS AND NOT GET CAUGHT."
LOOK AT 'EM. ACTING LIKE THEY DON'T HAVE A CARE IN THE WORLD. DIDN'T THE ZOMBOTS TEAR THIS CITY APART NOT TOO LONG AGO?*
THE RESTORATION HELPED THEM REBUILD. I--I--I THINK THEY JUST WANT TO BE... HAPPY?
*STH #21.
SUCKS TO BE THEM, 'CUZ I AIM TO MISBEHAVE.
I CAN USE MY HYDRO-COIL TAILS TO REACH UNDERGROUND, ACCESS AND MANIPULATE THE WIRING, AND THROW THE TRAFFIC LIGHTS AND POWER GRIDS INTO DISARRAY!
UH-HUH. YOU HAVE FUN WITH THAT.
I'MMA GO FAST!
W-WELL... YES... THERE'S THAT, TOO...

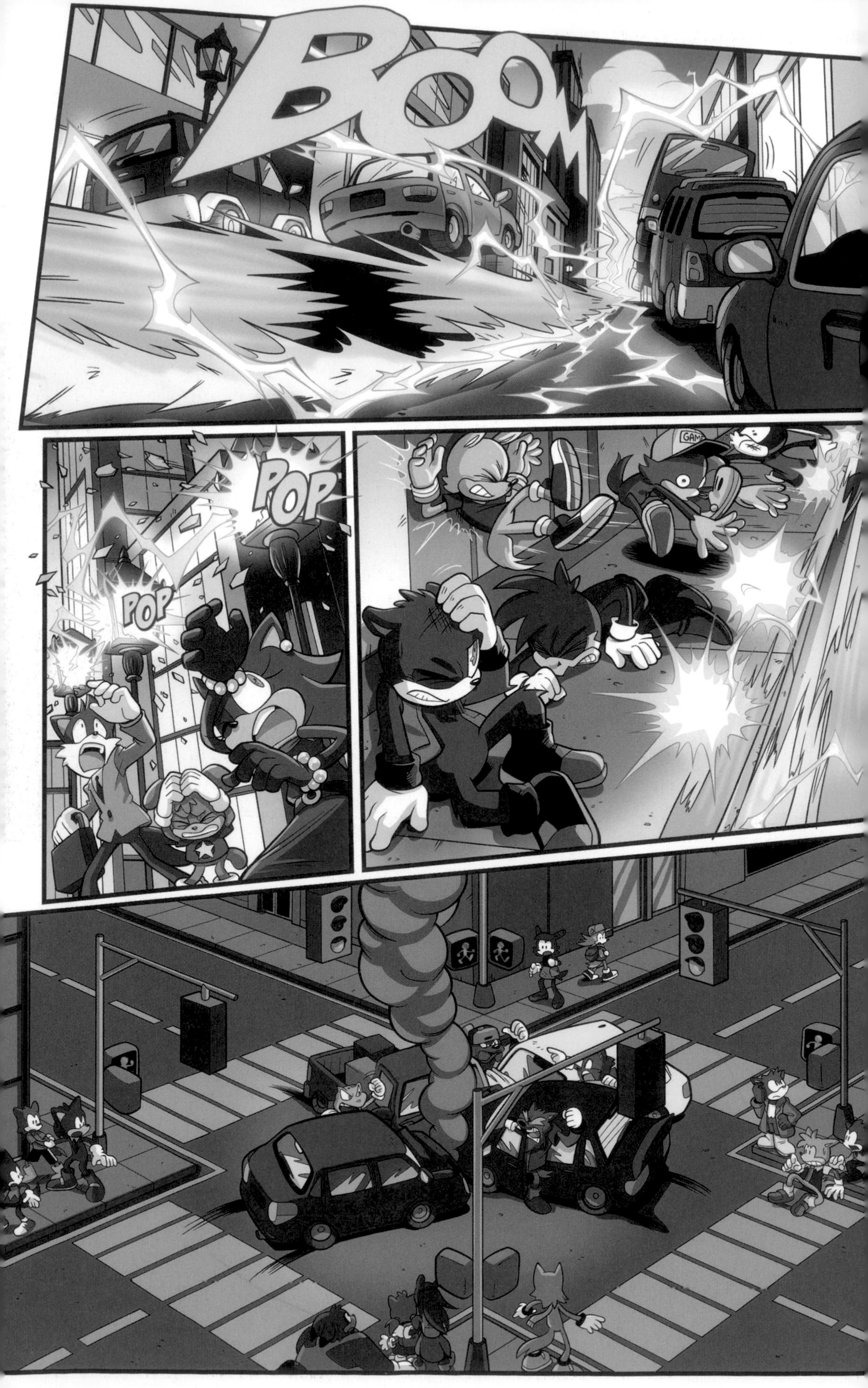
BOOM
POP
POP

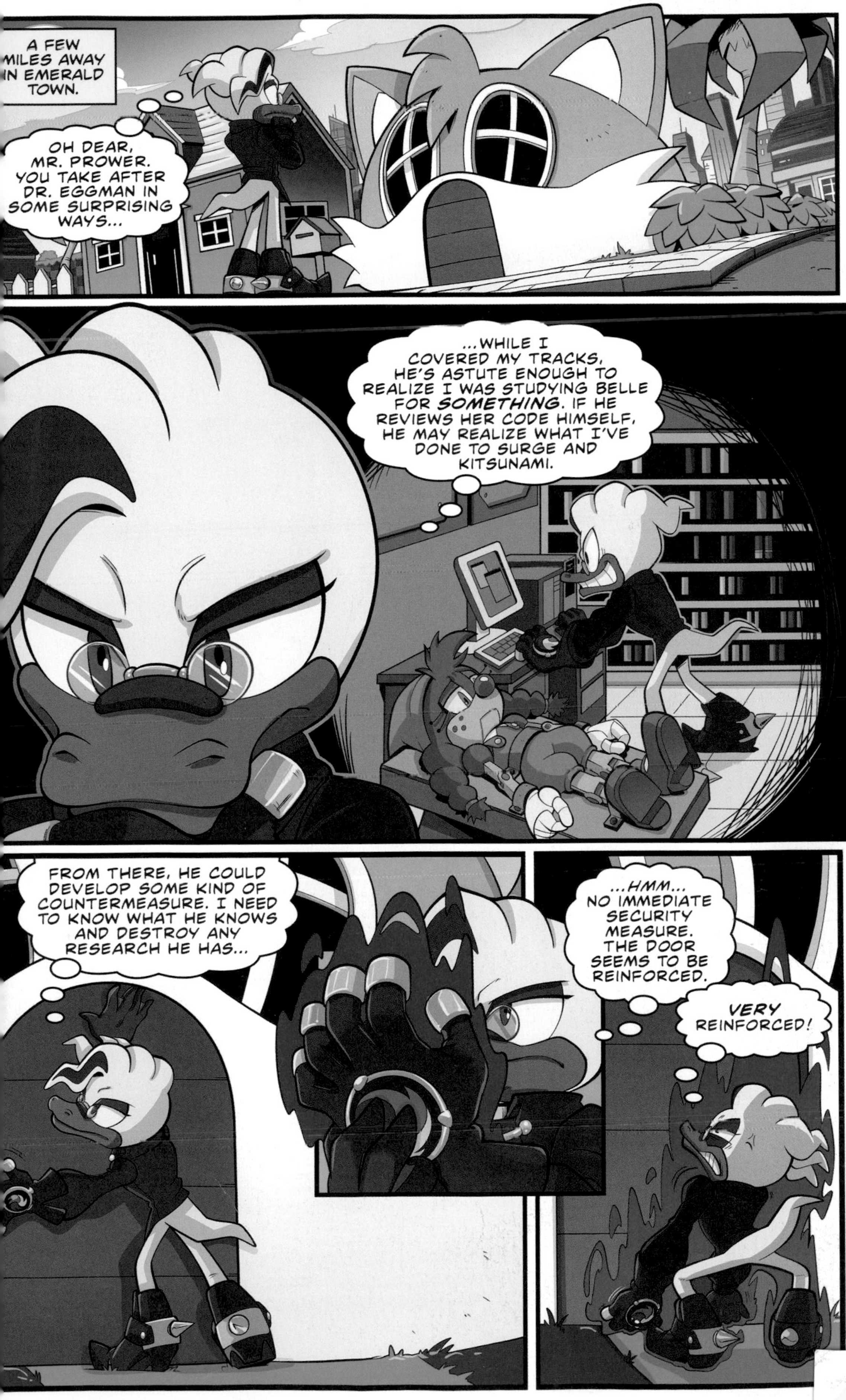
A FEW MILES AWAY IN EMERALD TOWN.
OH DEAR, MR. PROWER. YOU TAKE AFTER DR. EGGMAN IN SOME SURPRISING WAYS...
...WHILE I COVERED MY TRACKS, HE'S ASTUTE ENOUGH TO REALIZE I WAS STUDYING BELLE FOR SOMETHING. IF HE REVIEWS HER CODE HIMSELF, HE MAY REALIZE WHAT I'VE DONE TO SURGE AND KITSUNAMI.
FROM THERE, HE COULD DEVELOP SOME KIND OF COUNTERMEASURE. I NEED TO KNOW WHAT HE KNOWS AND DESTROY ANY RESEARCH HE HAS...
...HMM... NO IMMEDIATE SECURITY MEASURE. THE DOOR SEEMS TO BE REINFORCED.
VERY REINFORCED!

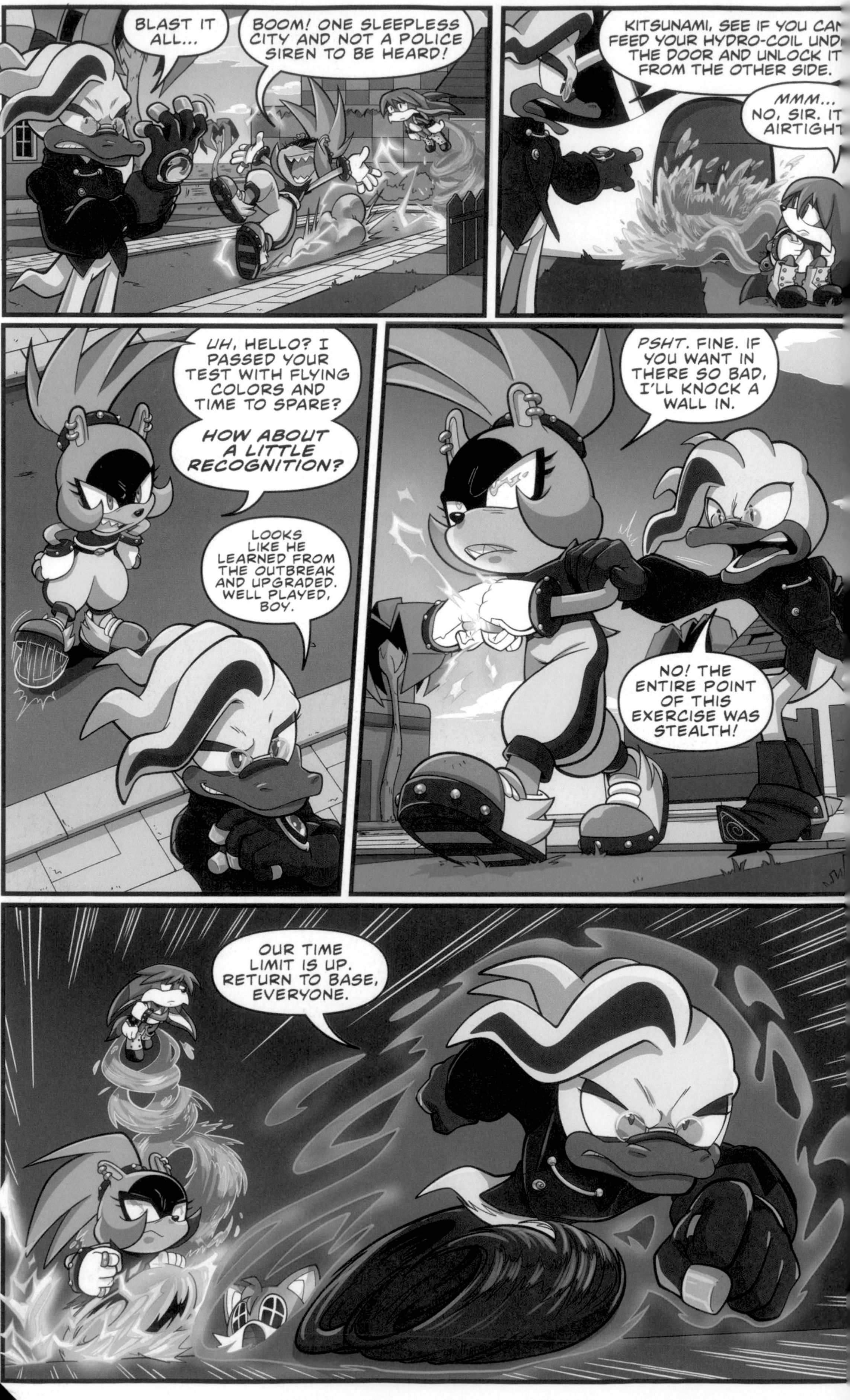
BLAST IT ALL...
BOOM! ONE SLEEPLESS CITY AND NOT A POLICE SIREN TO BE HEARD!
KITSUNAMI, SEE IF YOU CAN FEED YOUR HYDRO-COIL UND THE DOOR AND UNLOCK IT FROM THE OTHER SIDE.
MMM... NO, SIR. IT AIRTIGHT
UH, HELLO? I PASSED YOUR TEST WITH FLYING COLORS AND TIME TO SPARE?
HOW ABOUT A LITTLE RECOGNITION?
LOOKS LIKE HE LEARNED FROM THE OUTBREAK AND UPGRADED. WELL PLAYED, BOY.
PSHT. FINE. IF YOU WANT IN THERE SO BAD, I'LL KNOCK A WALL IN.
NO! THE ENTIRE POINT OF THIS EXERCISE WAS STEALTH!
OUR TIME LIMIT IS UP. RETURN TO BASE, EVERYONE.

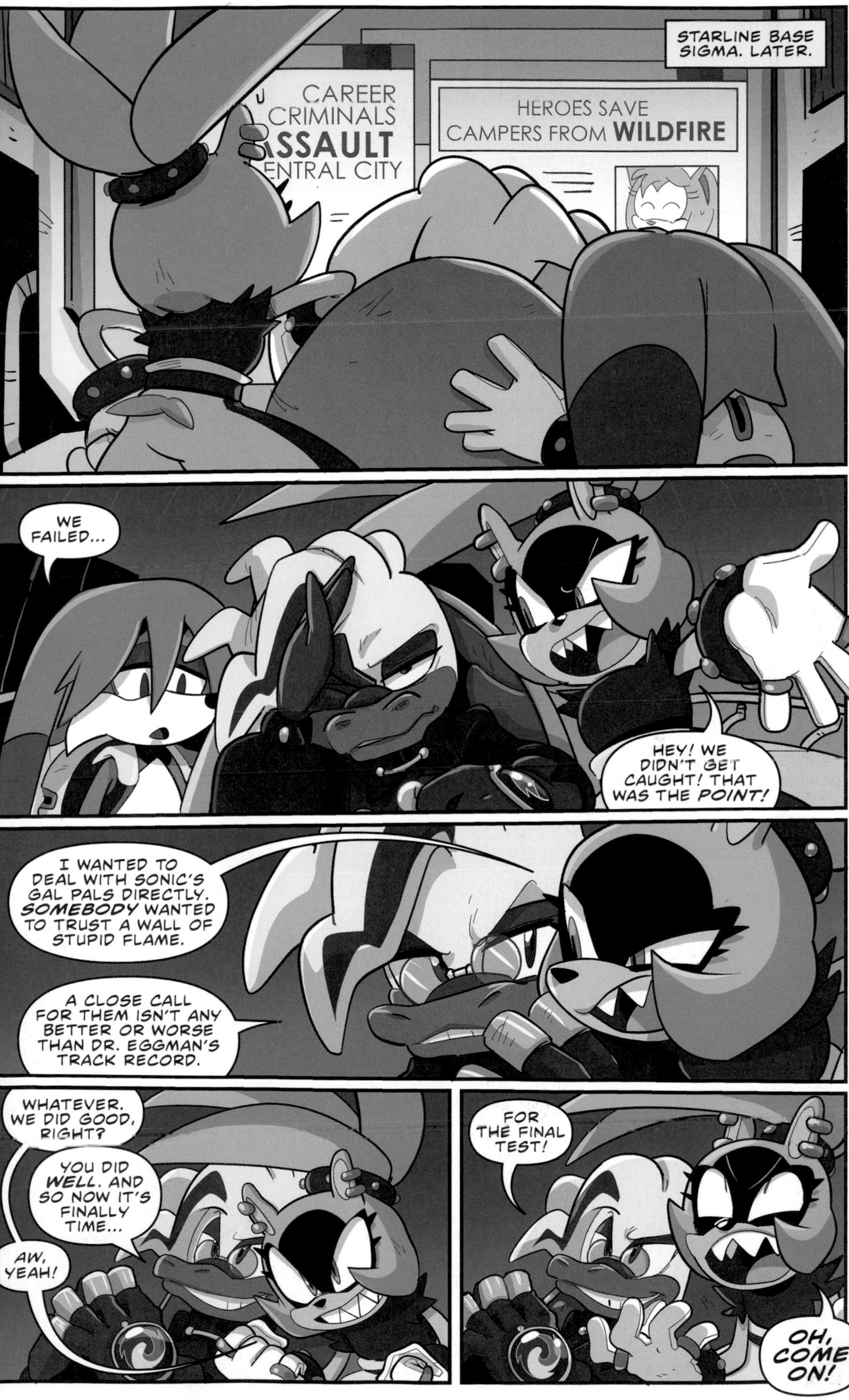
STARLINE BASE SIGMA. LATER.
CAREER CRIMINALS ASSAULT ENTRAL CITY
HEROES SAVE CAMPERS FROM WILDFIRE
WE FAILED...
HEY! WE DIDN'T GET CAUGHT! THAT WAS THE POINT!
I WANTED TO DEAL WITH SONIC'S GAL PALS DIRECTLY. SOMEBODY WANTED TO TRUST A WALL OF STUPID FLAME.
A CLOSE CALL FOR THEM ISN'T ANY BETTER OR WORSE THAN DR. EGGMAN'S TRACK RECORD.
WHATEVER. WE DID GOOD, RIGHT?
YOU DID WELL. AND SO NOW IT'S FINALLY TIME...
AW, YEAH!
FOR THE FINAL TEST!
OH, COME ON!

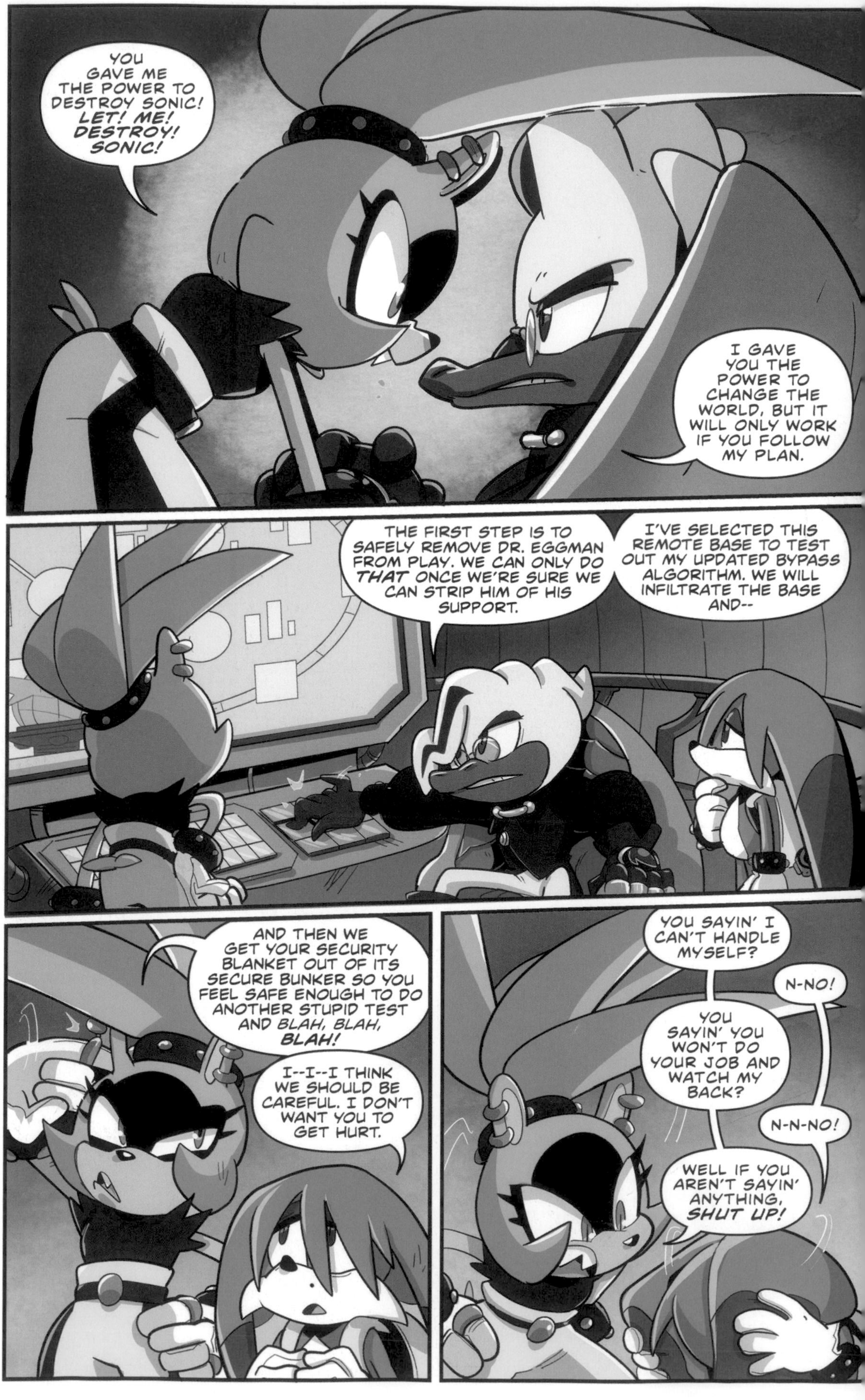
YOU GAVE ME THE POWER TO DESTROY SONIC! LET! ME! DESTROY! SONIC!
I GAVE YOU THE POWER TO CHANGE THE WORLD, BUT IT WILL ONLY WORK IF YOU FOLLOW MY PLAN.
THE FIRST STEP IS TO SAFELY REMOVE DR. EGGMAN FROM PLAY. WE CAN ONLY DO THAT ONCE WE'RE SURE WE CAN STRIP HIM OF HIS SUPPORT.
I'VE SELECTED THIS REMOTE BASE TO TEST OUT MY UPDATED BYPASS ALGORITHM. WE WILL INFILTRATE THE BASE AND--
AND THEN WE GET YOUR SECURITY BLANKET OUT OF ITS SECURE BUNKER SO YOU FEEL SAFE ENOUGH TO DO ANOTHER STUPID TEST AND BLAH, BLAH, BLAH!
I--I--I THINK WE SHOULD BE CAREFUL. I DON'T WANT YOU TO GET HURT.
YOU SAYIN' I CAN'T HANDLE MYSELF?
N-NO!
YOU SAYIN' YOU WON'T DO YOUR JOB AND WATCH MY BACK?
N-N-NO!
WELL IF YOU AREN'T SAYIN' ANYTHING, SHUT UP!

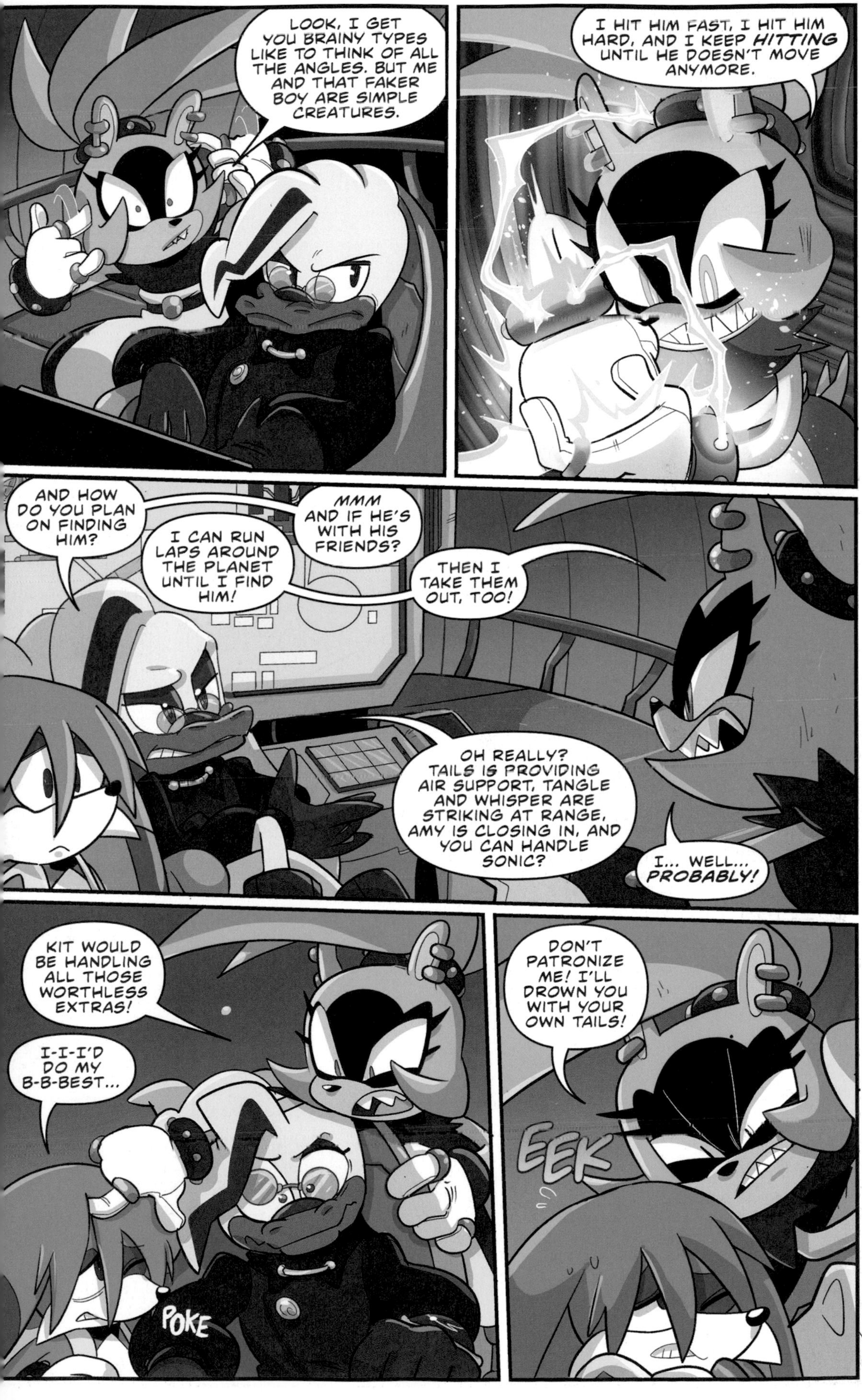
LOOK, I GET YOU BRAINY TYPES LIKE TO THINK OF ALL THE ANGLES. BUT ME AND THAT FAKER BOY ARE SIMPLE CREATURES.
I HIT HIM FAST, I HIT HIM HARD, AND I KEEP HITTING UNTIL HE DOESN'T MOVE ANYMORE.
AND HOW DO YOU PLAN ON FINDING HIM?
I CAN RUN LAPS AROUND THE PLANET UNTIL I FIND HIM!
MMM AND IF HE'S WITH HIS FRIENDS?
THEN I TAKE THEM OUT, TOO!
OH REALLY? TAILS IS PROVIDING AIR SUPPORT, TANGLE AND WHISPER ARE STRIKING AT RANGE, AMY IS CLOSING IN, AND YOU CAN HANDLE SONIC?
I... WELL... PROBABLY!
KIT WOULD BE HANDLING ALL THOSE WORTHLESS EXTRAS!
I-I-I'D DO MY B-B-BEST...
POKE
DON'T PATRONIZE ME! I'LL DROWN YOU WITH YOUR OWN TAILS!
EEK

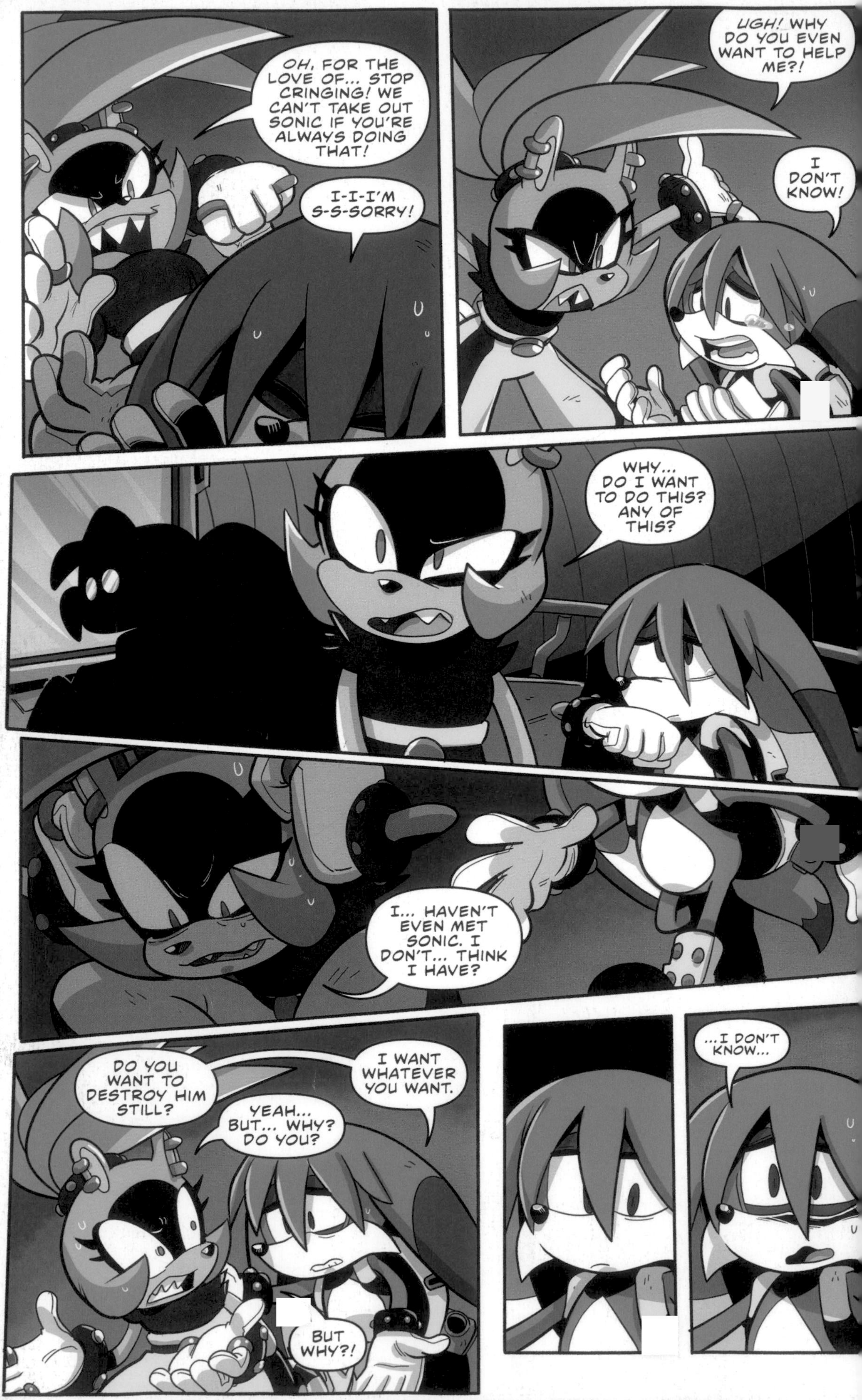
OH, FOR THE LOVE OF... STOP CRINGING! WE CAN'T TAKE OUT SONIC IF YOU'RE ALWAYS DOING THAT!
I-I-I'M S-S-SORRY!
UGH! WHY DO YOU EVEN WANT TO HELP ME?!
I DON'T KNOW!
WHY... DO I WANT TO DO THIS? ANY OF THIS?
I... HAVEN'T EVEN MET SONIC. I DON'T... THINK I HAVE?
DO YOU WANT TO DESTROY HIM STILL?
YEAH... BUT... WHY? DO YOU?
I WANT WHATEVER YOU WANT.
BUT WHY?!
...I DON'T KNOW...

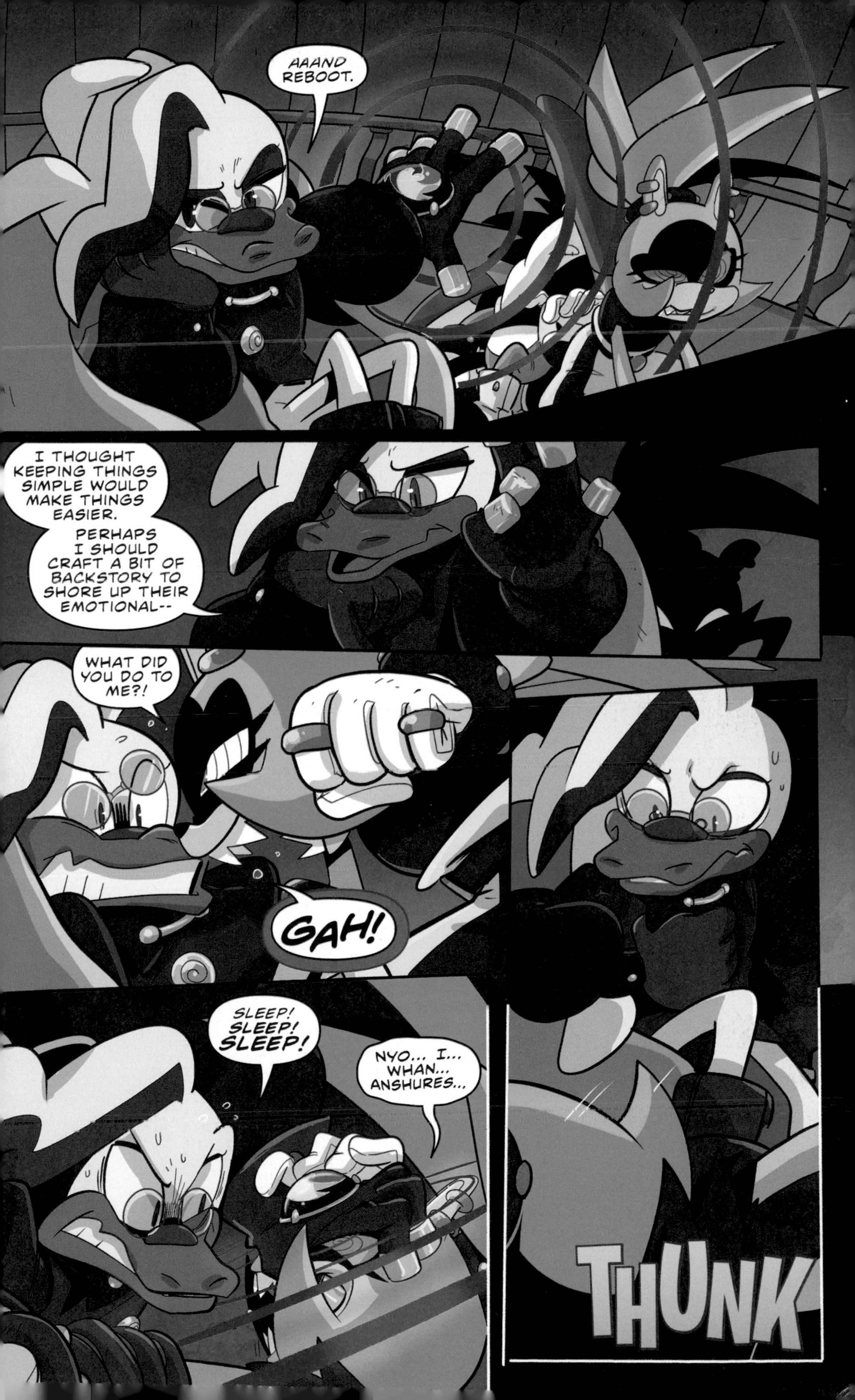
AAAND REBOOT.
I THOUGHT KEEPING THINGS SIMPLE WOULD MAKE THINGS EASIER.
PERHAPS I SHOULD CRAFT A BIT OF BACKSTORY TO SHORE UP THEIR EMOTIONAL--
WHAT DID YOU DO TO ME?!
GAH!
SLEEP! SLEEP! SLEEP!
NYO... I... WHAN... ANSHURES...
THUNK

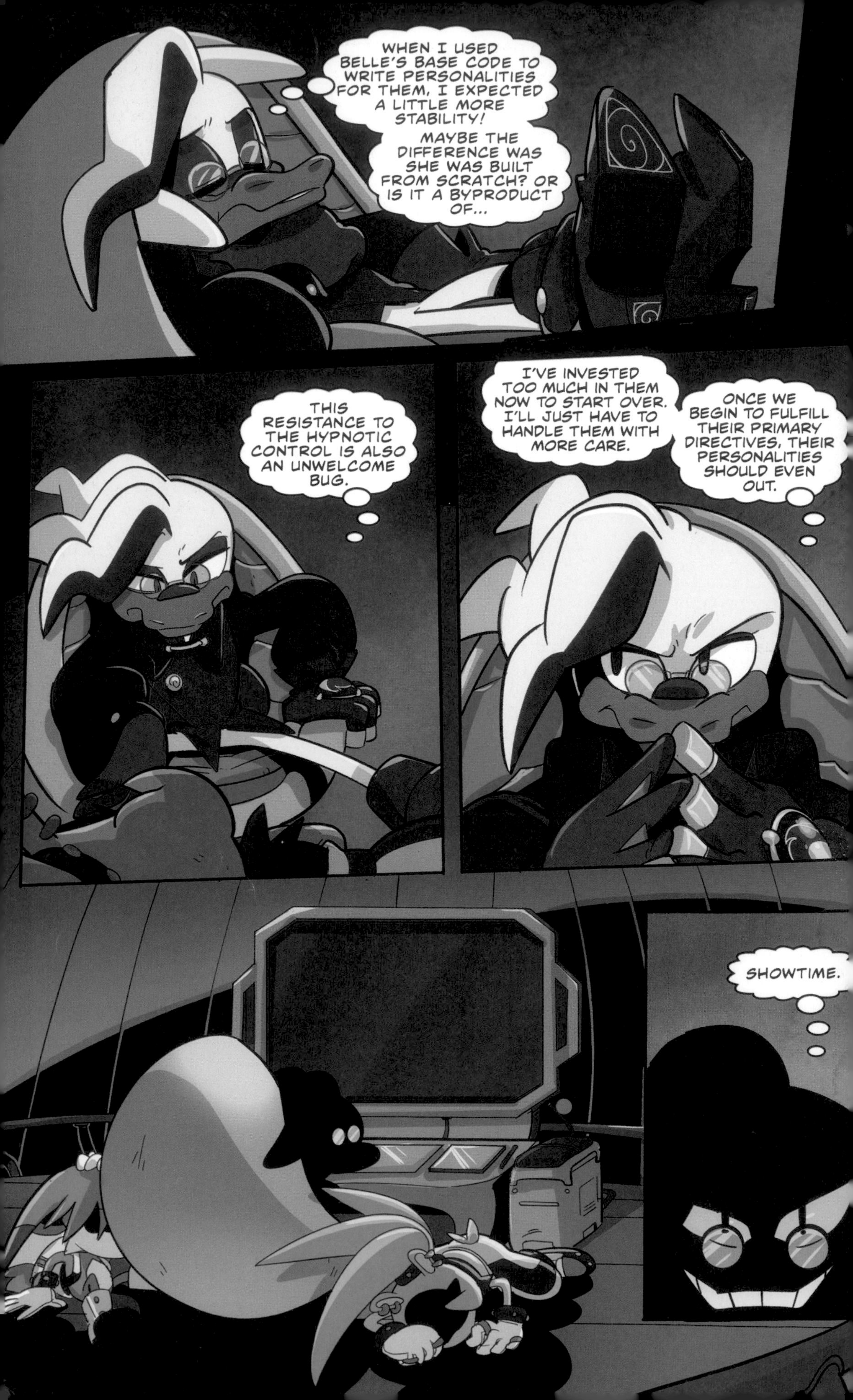
WHEN I USED BELLE'S BASE CODE TO WRITE PERSONALITIES FOR THEM, I EXPECTED A LITTLE MORE STABILITY!
MAYBE THE DIFFERENCE WAS SHE WAS BUILT FROM SCRATCH? OR IS IT A BYPRODUCT OF...
THIS RESISTANCE TO THE HYPNOTIC CONTROL IS ALSO AN UNWELCOME BUG.
I'VE INVESTED TOO MUCH IN THEM NOW TO START OVER. I'LL JUST HAVE TO HANDLE THEM WITH MORE CARE.
ONCE WE BEGIN TO FULFILL THEIR PRIMARY DIRECTIVES, THEIR PERSONALITIES SHOULD EVEN OUT.
SHOWTIME.

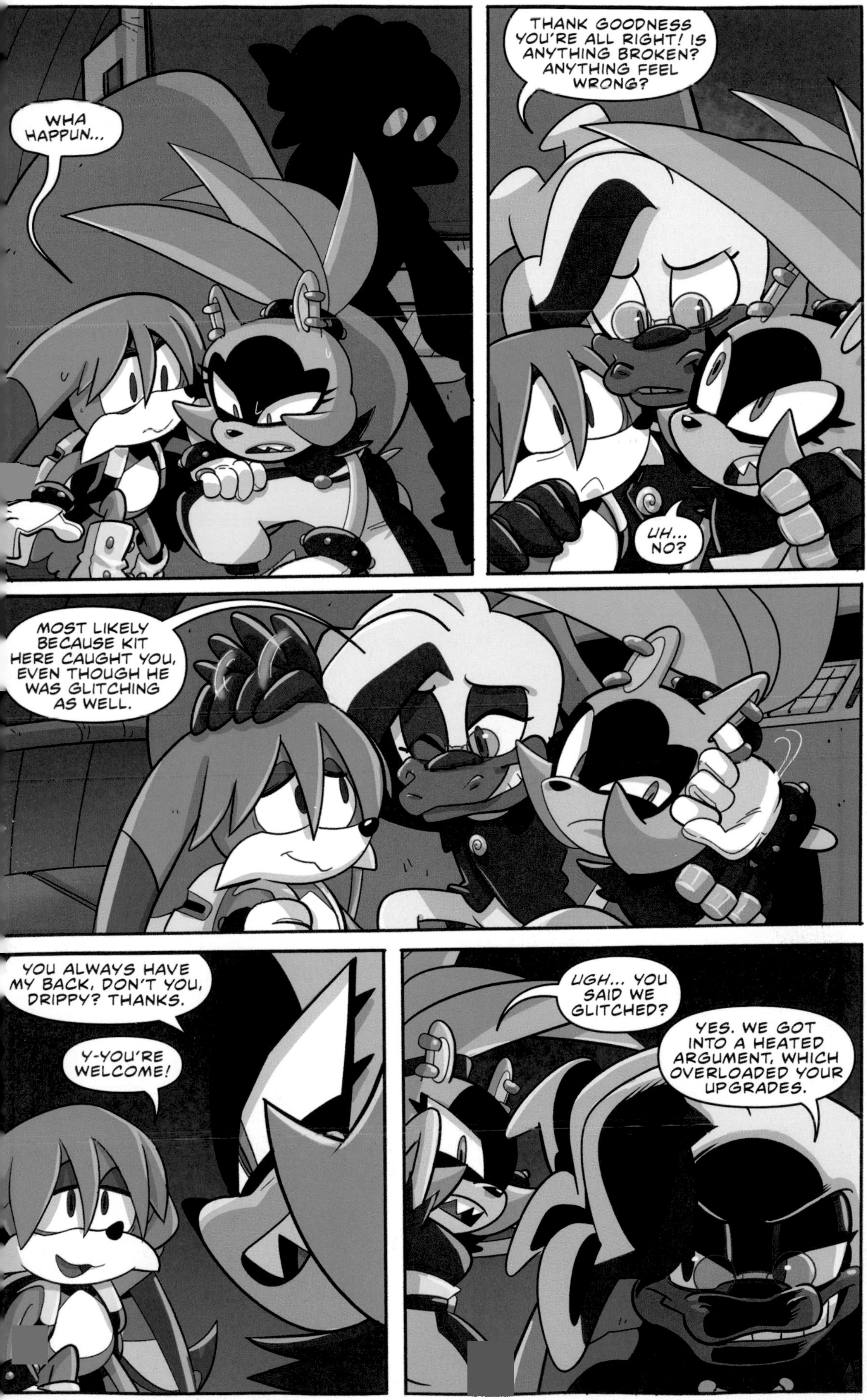
WHA HAPPUN...
THANK GOODNESS YOU'RE ALL RIGHT! IS ANYTHING BROKEN? ANYTHING FEEL WRONG?
UH... NO?
MOST LIKELY BECAUSE KIT HERE CAUGHT YOU, EVEN THOUGH HE WAS GLITCHING AS WELL.
YOU ALWAYS HAVE MY BACK, DON'T YOU, DRIPPY? THANKS.
Y-YOU'RE WELCOME!
UGH... YOU SAID WE GLITCHED?
YES. WE GOT INTO A HEATED ARGUMENT, WHICH OVERLOADED YOUR UPGRADES.

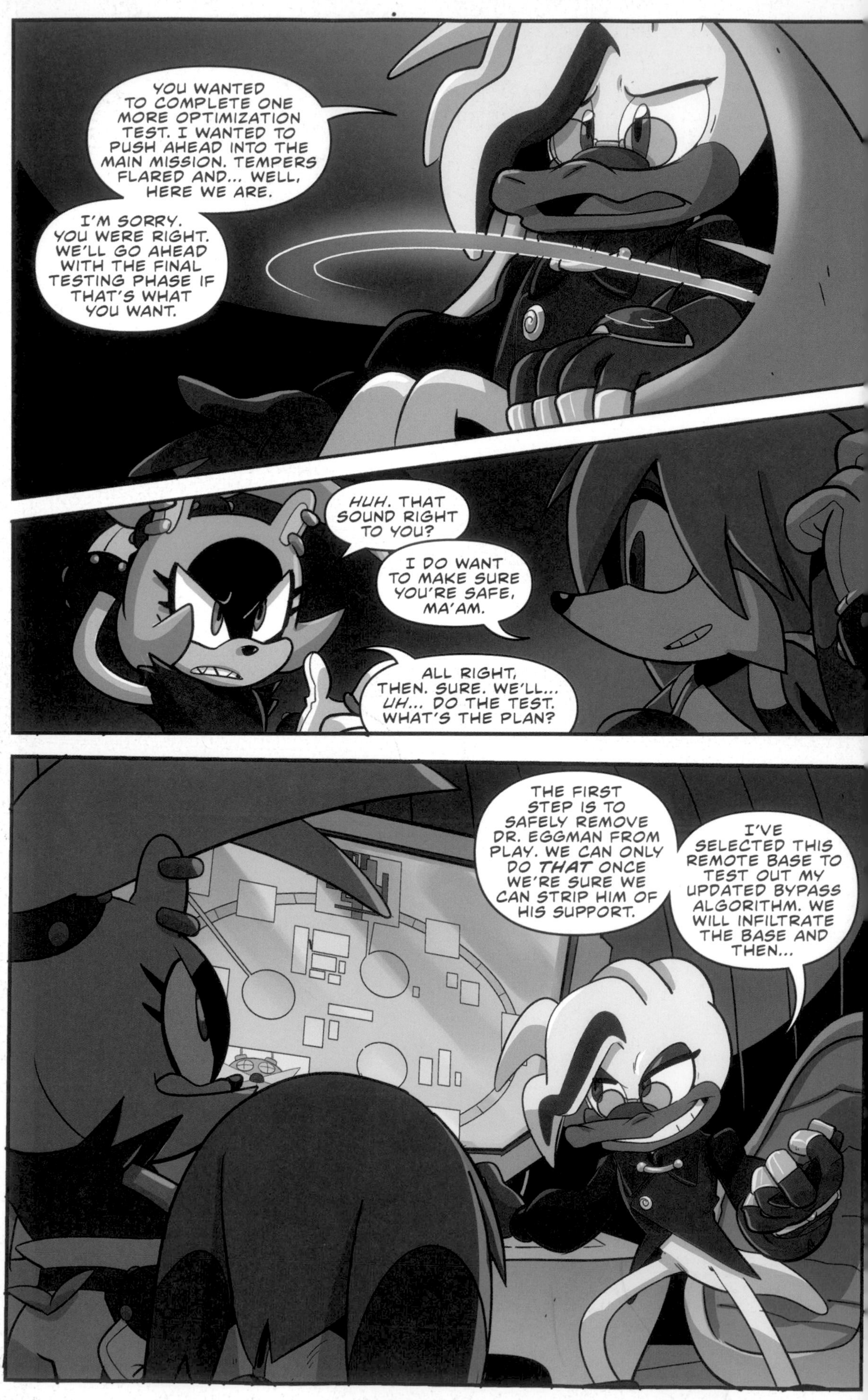

YOU WANTED TO COMPLETE ONE MORE OPTIMIZATION TEST. I WANTED TO PUSH AHEAD INTO THE MAIN MISSION. TEMPERS FLARED AND... WELL, HERE WE ARE.
I'M SORRY. YOU WERE RIGHT. WE'LL GO AHEAD WITH THE FINAL TESTING PHASE IF THAT'S WHAT YOU WANT.
HUH. THAT SOUND RIGHT TO YOU?
I DO WANT TO MAKE SURE YOU'RE SAFE, MA'AM.
ALL RIGHT, THEN. SURE. WE'LL... *UH*... DO THE TEST. WHAT'S THE PLAN?
THE FIRST STEP IS TO SAFELY REMOVE DR. EGGMAN FROM PLAY. WE CAN ONLY DO *THAT* ONCE WE'RE SURE WE CAN STRIP HIM OF HIS SUPPORT.
I'VE SELECTED THIS REMOTE BASE TO TEST OUT MY UPDATED BYPASS ALGORITHM. WE WILL INFILTRATE THE BASE AND THEN...

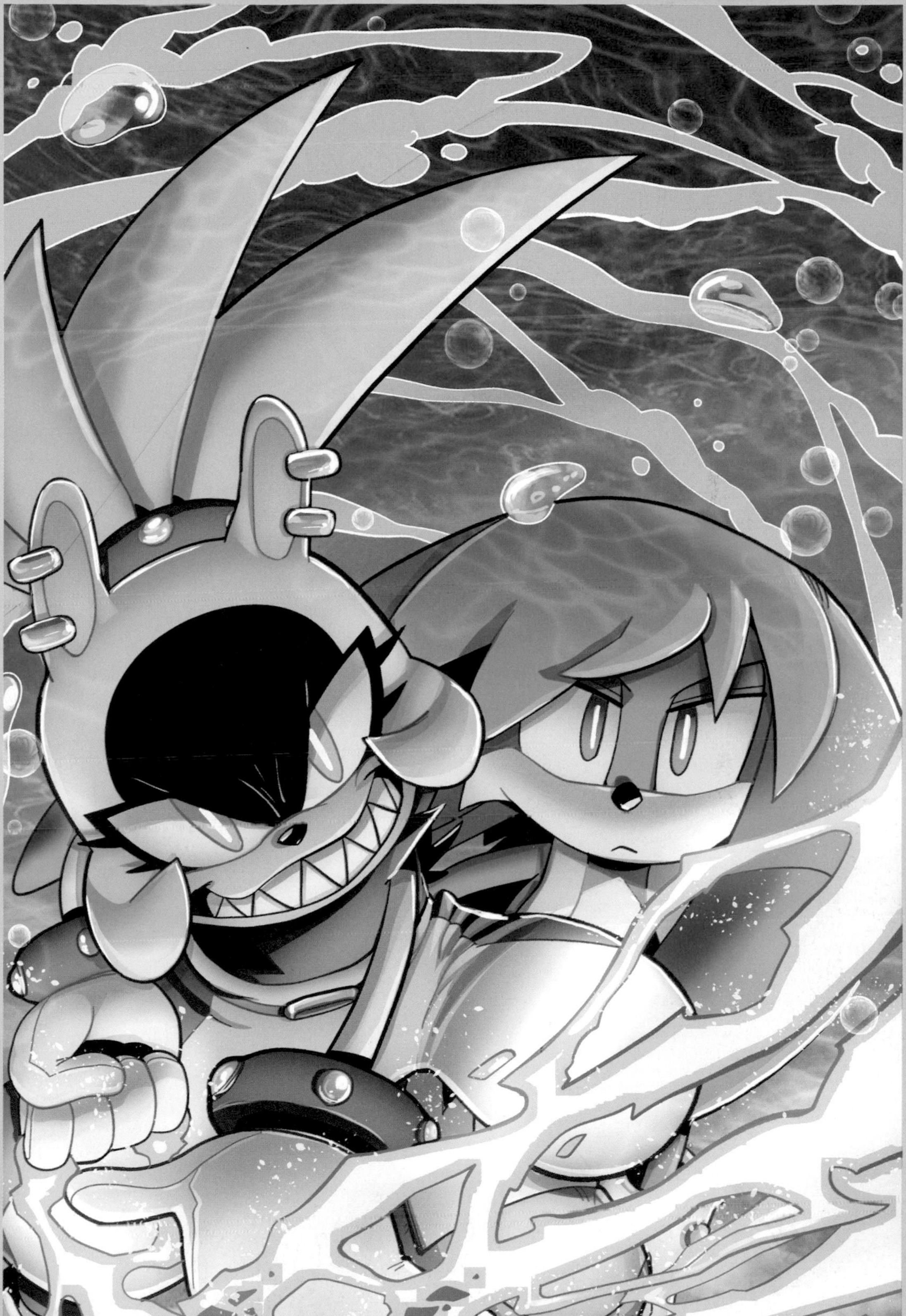

ART THOMAS ROTHLISBERGER COLORS VALENTINA PINTO

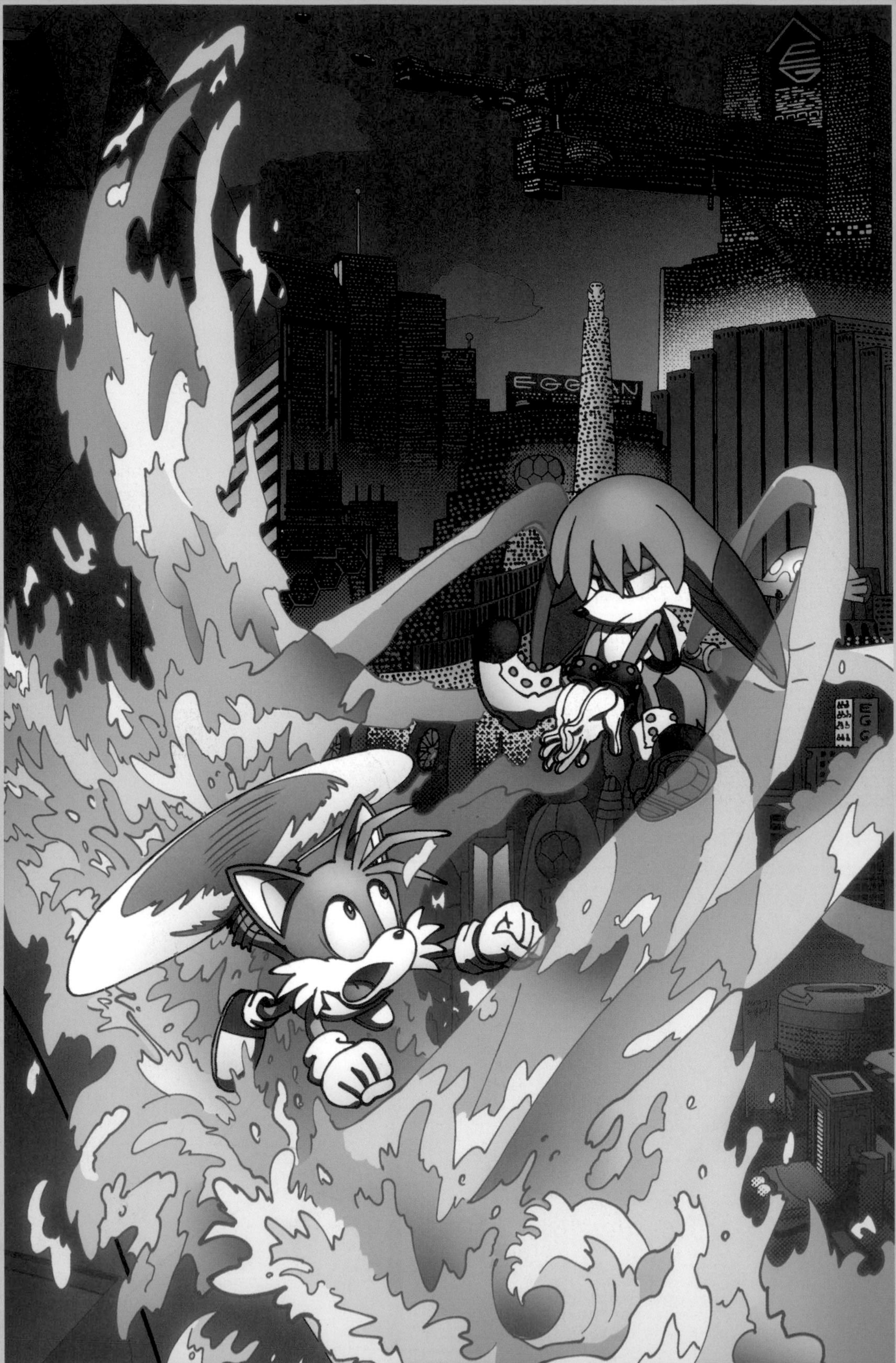
EGG

ART MAURO FONSECA COLORS JOANA LAFUENTE

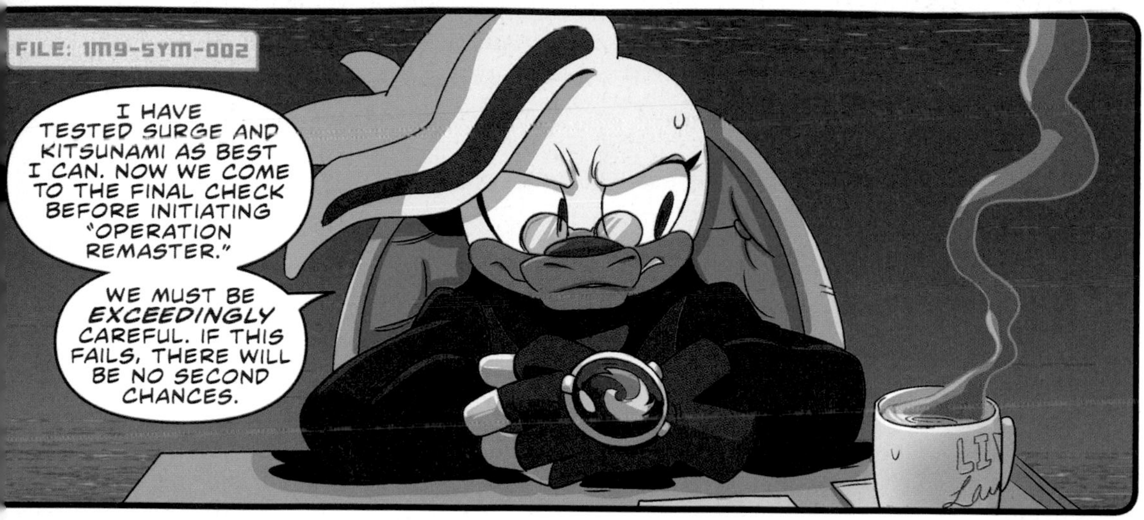
FILE: 1M9-SYM-002
I HAVE TESTED SURGE AND KITSUNAMI AS BEST I CAN. NOW WE COME TO THE FINAL CHECK BEFORE INITIATING "OPERATION REMASTER."
WE MUST BE *EXCEEDINGLY* CAREFUL. IF THIS FAILS, THERE WILL BE NO SECOND CHANCES.

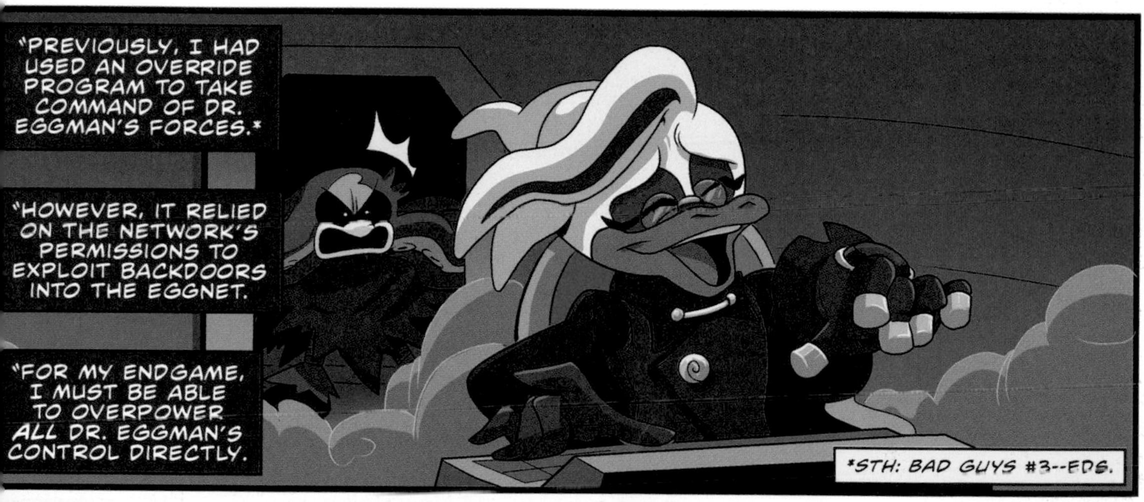
"PREVIOUSLY, I HAD USED AN OVERRIDE PROGRAM TO TAKE COMMAND OF DR. EGGMAN'S FORCES.*
"HOWEVER, IT RELIED ON THE NETWORK'S PERMISSIONS TO EXPLOIT BACKDOORS INTO THE EGGNET.
"FOR MY ENDGAME, I MUST BE ABLE TO OVERPOWER *ALL* DR. EGGMAN'S CONTROL DIRECTLY.
*STH: BAD GUYS #3--EDS.

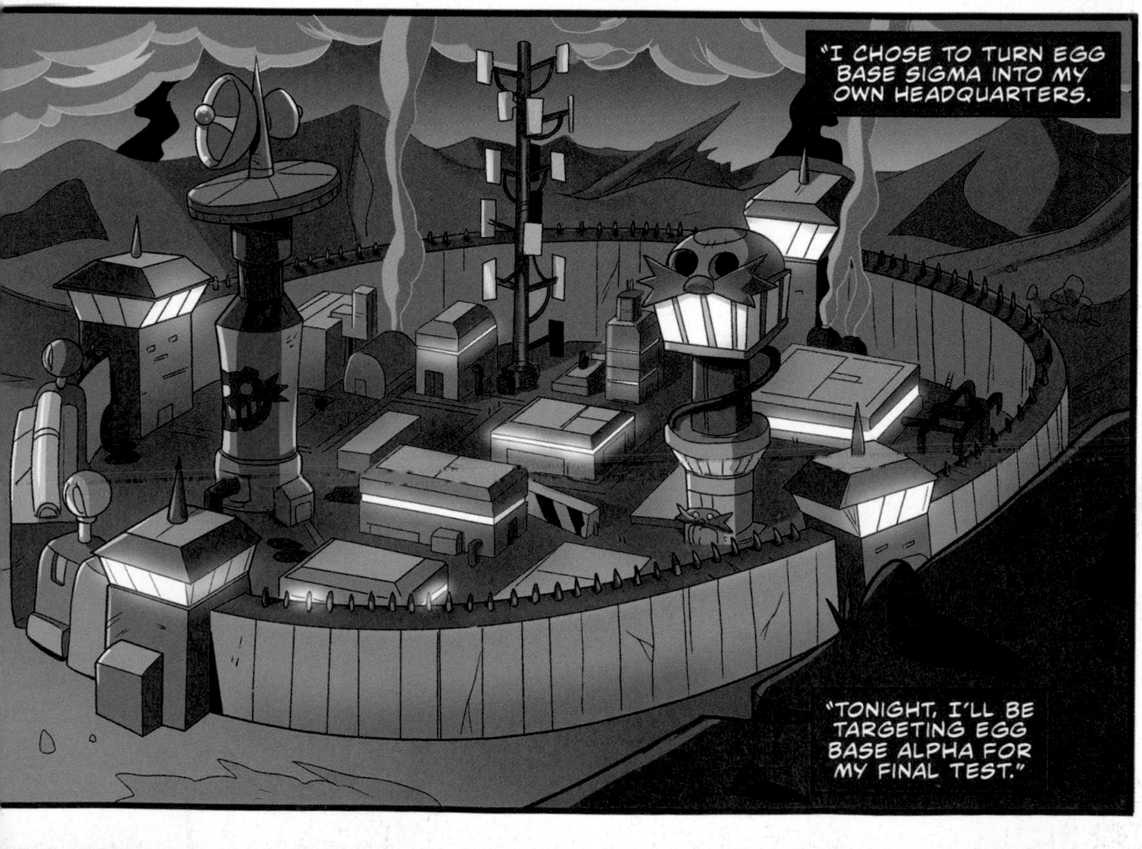
"I CHOSE TO TURN EGG BASE SIGMA INTO MY OWN HEADQUARTERS.
"TONIGHT, I'LL BE TARGETING EGG BASE ALPHA FOR MY FINAL TEST."

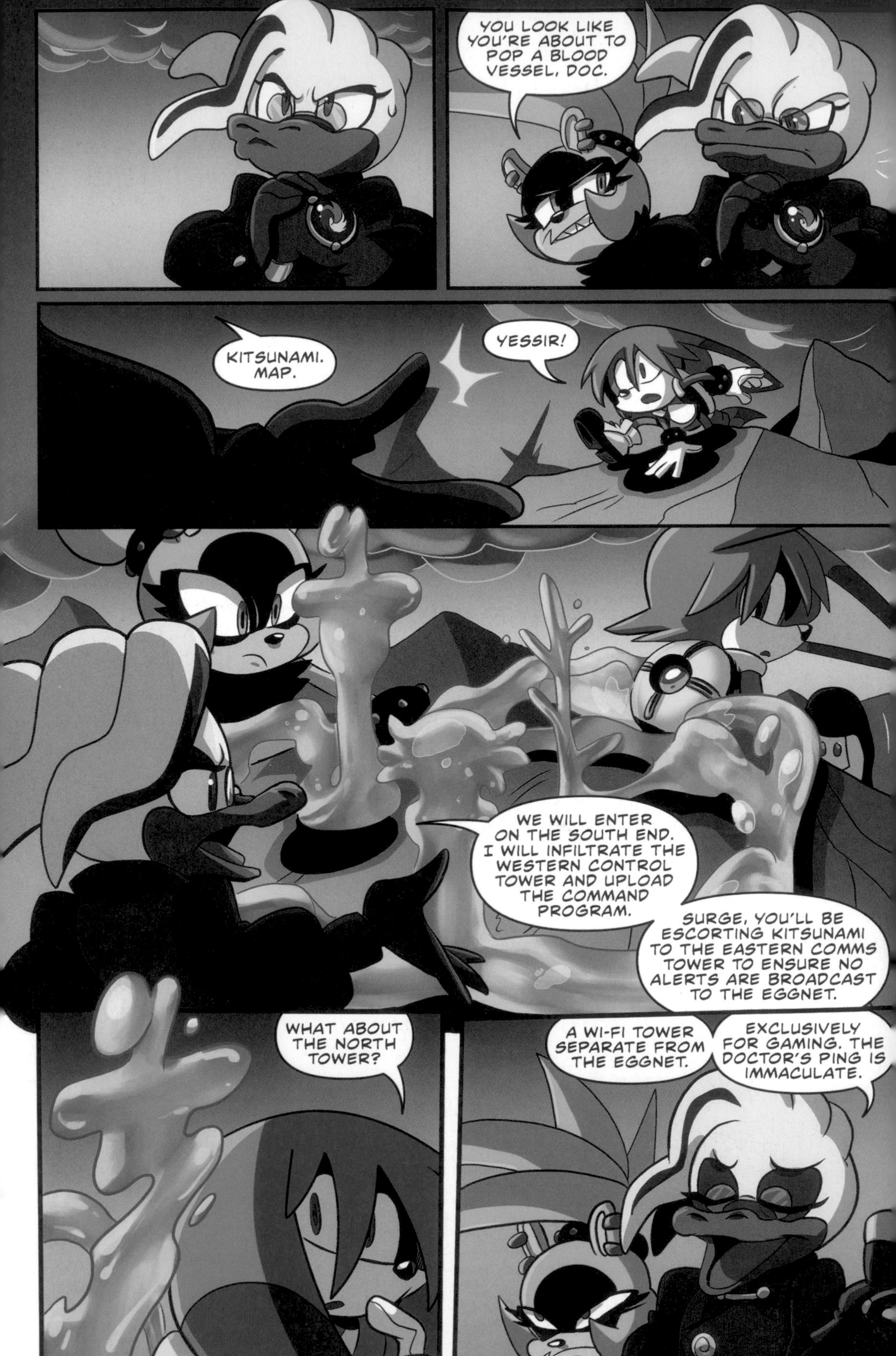
YOU LOOK LIKE YOU'RE ABOUT TO POP A BLOOD VESSEL, DOC.
KITSUNAMI. MAP.
YESSIR!
WE WILL ENTER ON THE SOUTH END. I WILL INFILTRATE THE WESTERN CONTROL TOWER AND UPLOAD THE COMMAND PROGRAM.
SURGE, YOU'LL BE ESCORTING KITSUNAMI TO THE EASTERN COMMS TOWER TO ENSURE NO ALERTS ARE BROADCAST TO THE EGGNET.
WHAT ABOUT THE NORTH TOWER?
A WI-FI TOWER SEPARATE FROM THE EGGNET.
EXCLUSIVELY FOR GAMING. THE DOCTOR'S PING IS IMMACULATE.

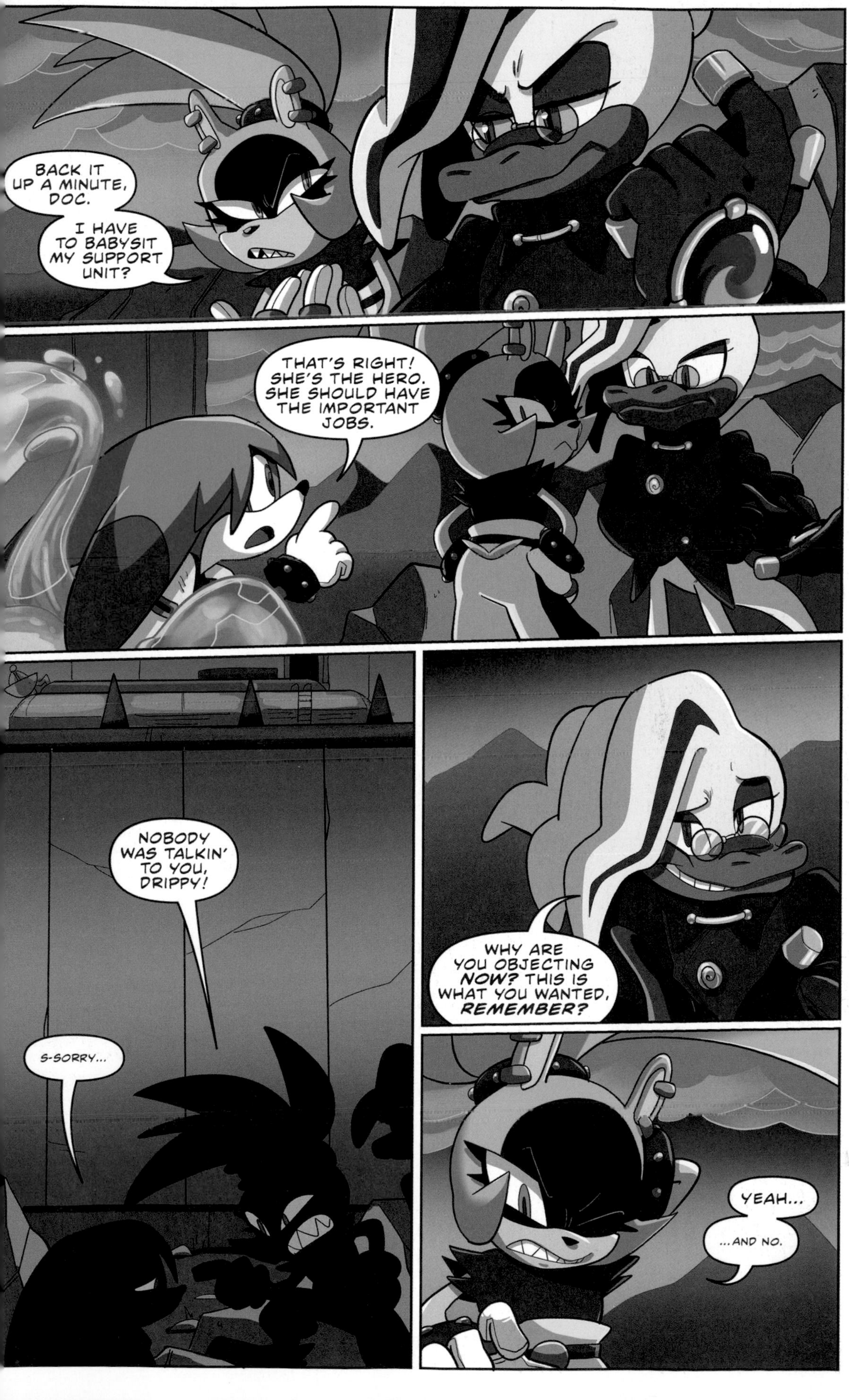
BACK IT UP A MINUTE, DOC.
I HAVE TO BABYSIT MY SUPPORT UNIT?
THAT'S RIGHT! SHE'S THE HERO. SHE SHOULD HAVE THE IMPORTANT JOBS.
NOBODY WAS TALKIN' TO YOU, DRIPPY!
S-SORRY...
WHY ARE YOU OBJECTING NOW? THIS IS WHAT YOU WANTED, REMEMBER?
YEAH...
...AND NO.

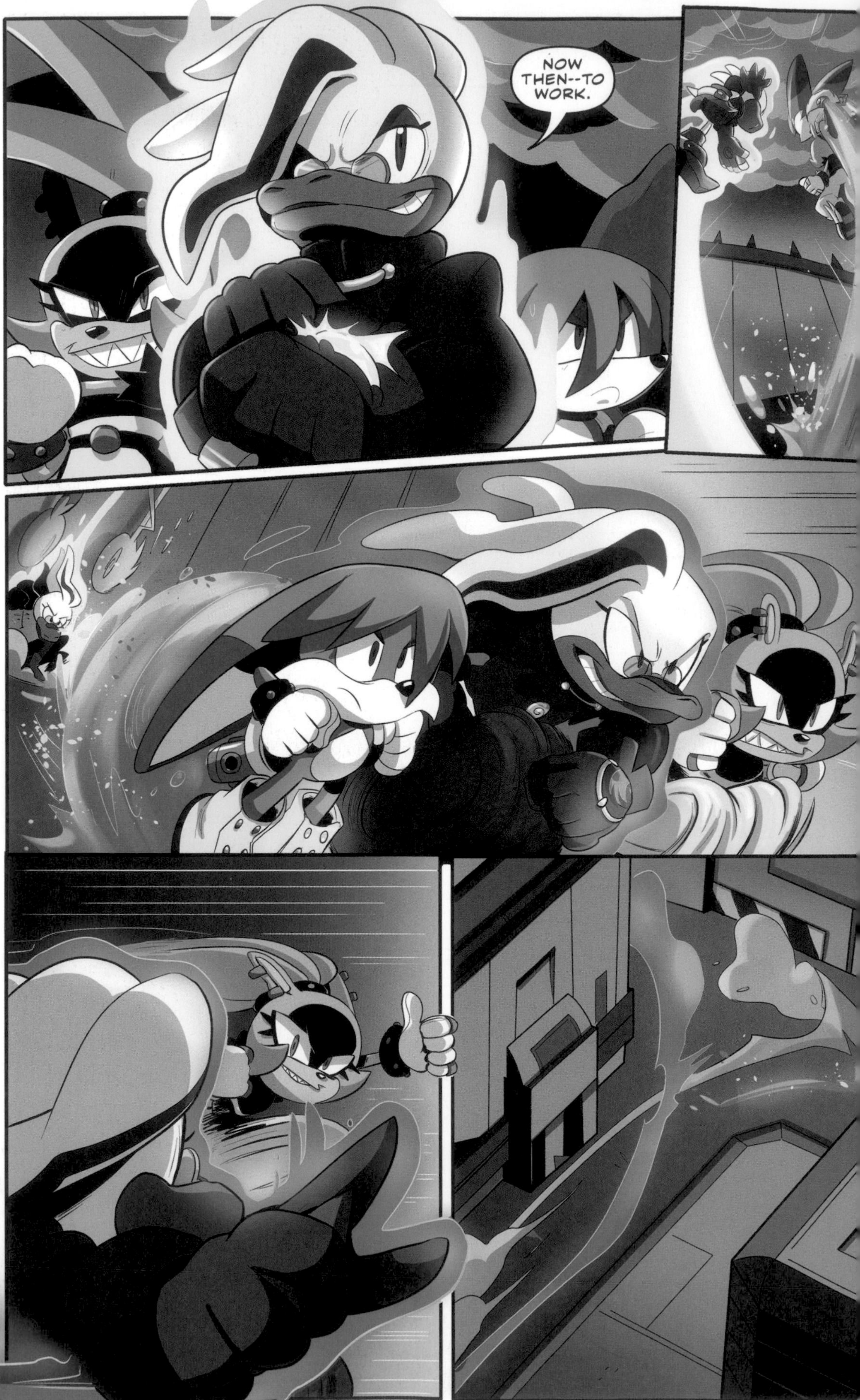
NOW THEN--TO WORK.

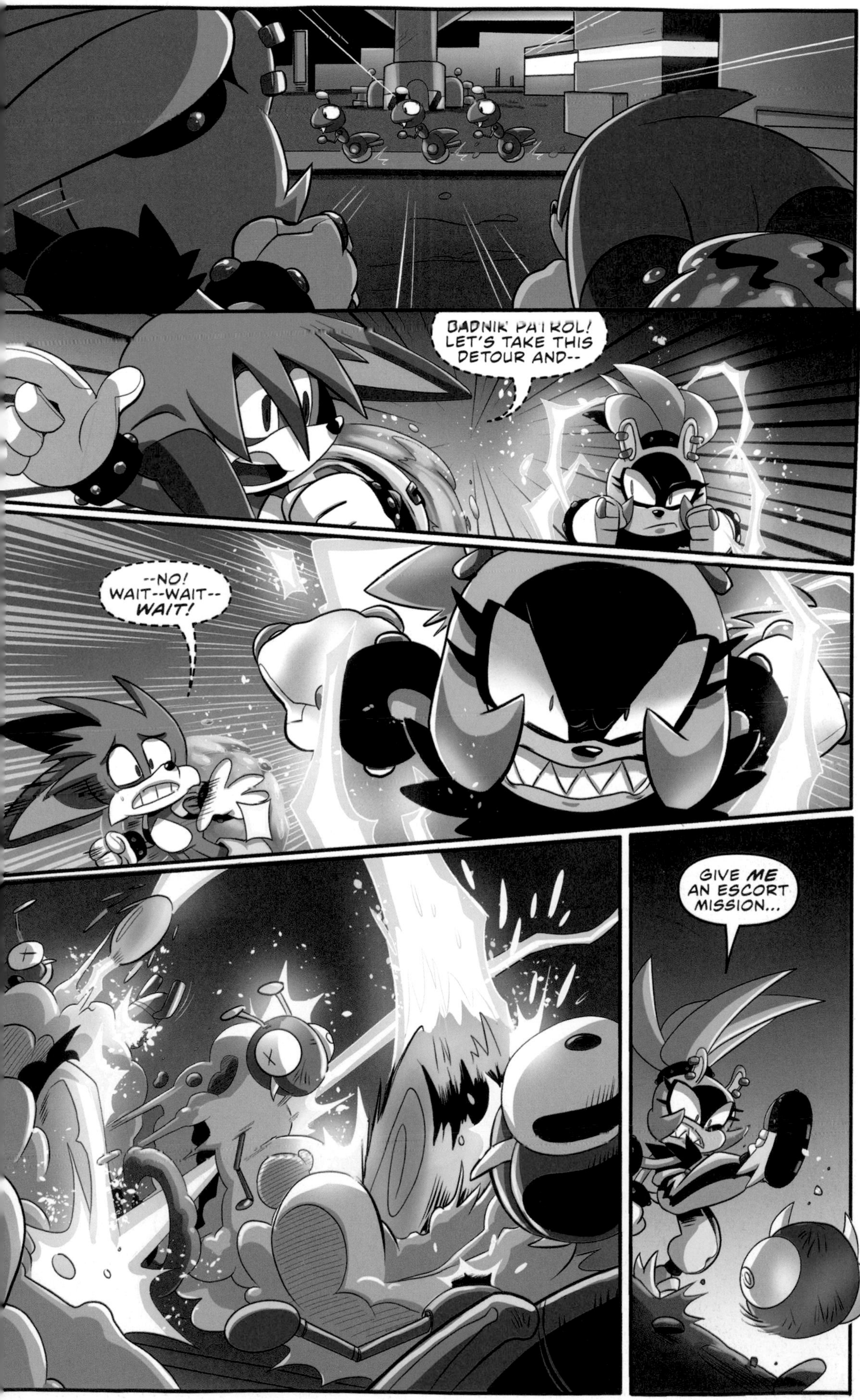
BADNIK PATROL! LET'S TAKE THIS DETOUR AND--
--NO! WAIT--WAIT--WAIT!
GIVE ME AN ESCORT MISSION...

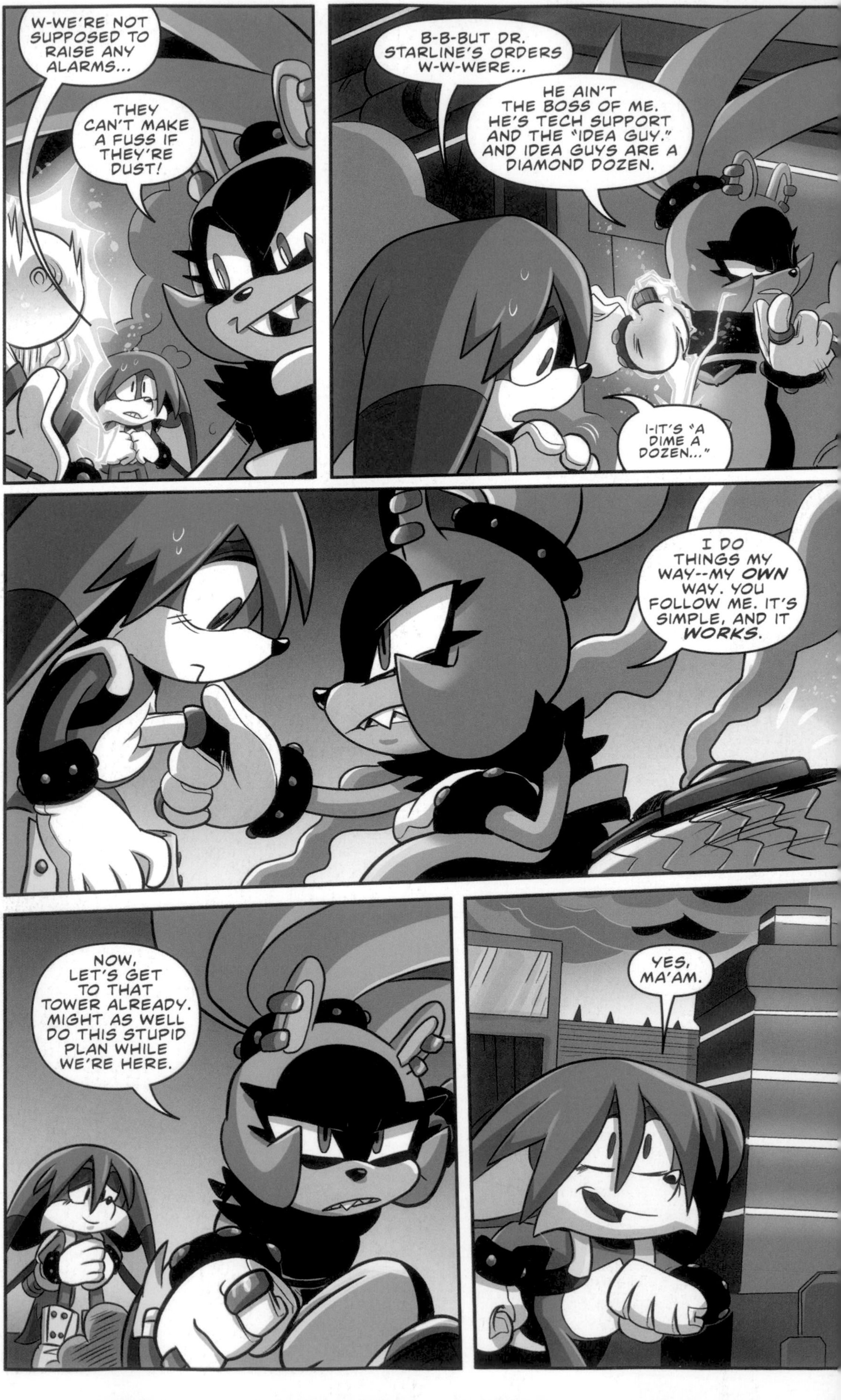
W-WE'RE NOT SUPPOSED TO RAISE ANY ALARMS...
THEY CAN'T MAKE A FUSS IF THEY'RE DUST!
B-B-BUT DR. STARLINE'S ORDERS W-W-WERE...
HE AIN'T THE BOSS OF ME. HE'S TECH SUPPORT AND THE "IDEA GUY." AND IDEA GUYS ARE A DIAMOND DOZEN.
I-IT'S "A DIME A DOZEN..."
I DO THINGS MY WAY--MY OWN WAY. YOU FOLLOW ME. IT'S SIMPLE, AND IT WORKS.
NOW, LET'S GET TO THAT TOWER ALREADY. MIGHT AS WELL DO THIS STUPID PLAN WHILE WE'RE HERE.
YES, MA'AM.

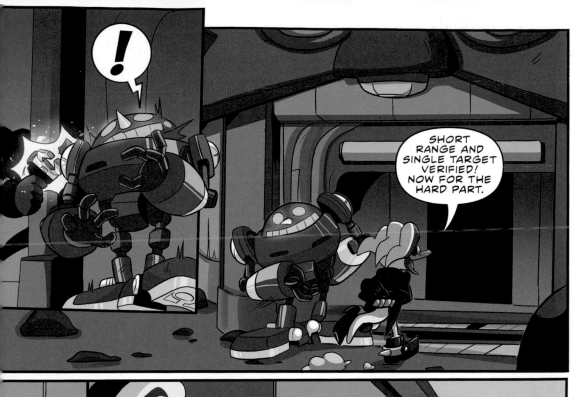

SHORT RANGE AND SINGLE TARGET VERIFIED! NOW FOR THE HARD PART.

EGG CAVE

I'M AHEAD OF SCHEDULE. I CAN AFFORD A SMALL DETOUR.

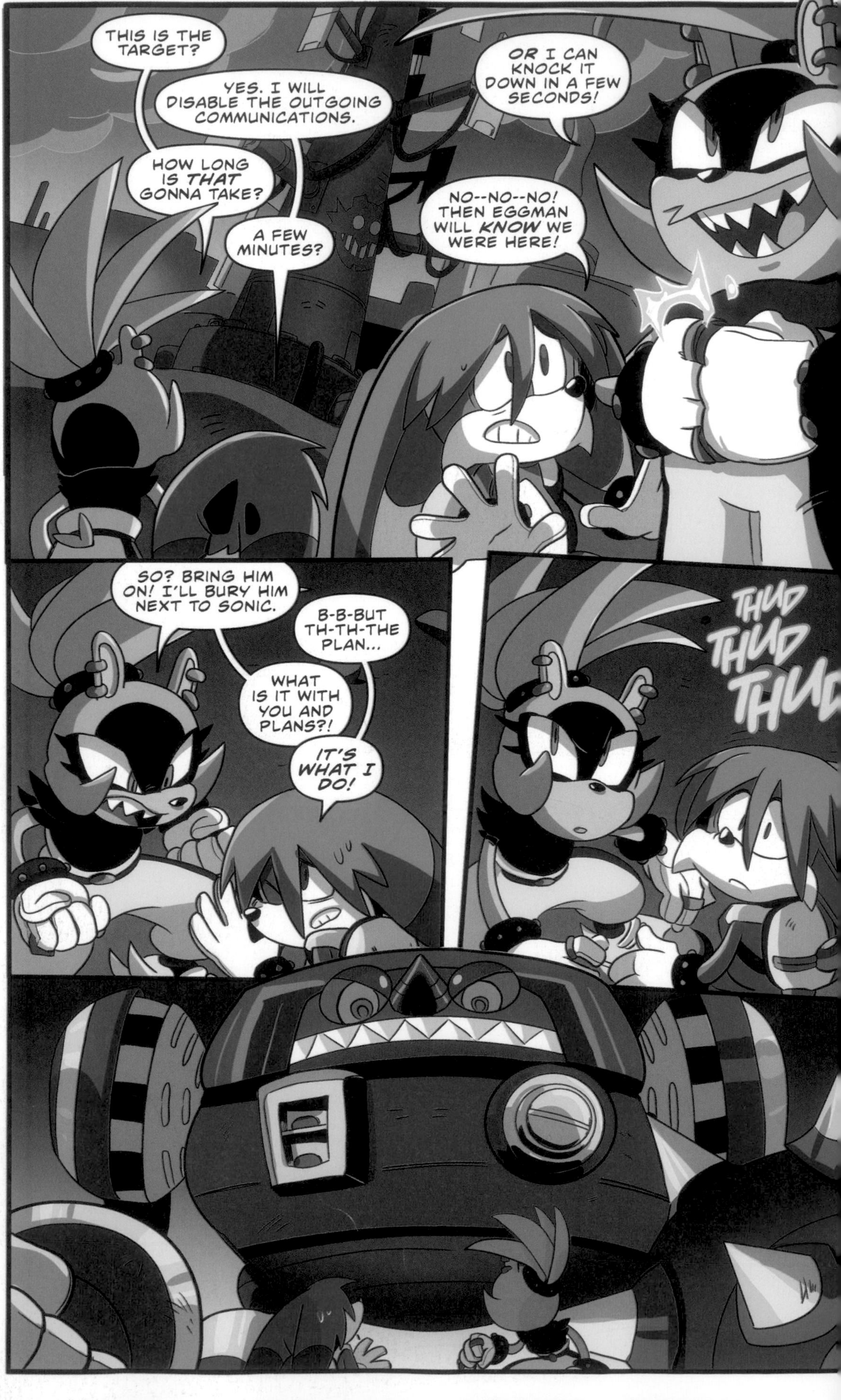
THIS IS THE TARGET?
YES. I WILL DISABLE THE OUTGOING COMMUNICATIONS.
HOW LONG IS *THAT* GONNA TAKE?
A FEW MINUTES?
OR I CAN KNOCK IT DOWN IN A FEW SECONDS!
NO--NO--NO! THEN EGGMAN WILL *KNOW* WE WERE HERE!
SO? BRING HIM ON! I'LL BURY HIM NEXT TO SONIC.
B-B-BUT TH-TH-THE PLAN...
WHAT IS IT WITH YOU AND PLANS?!
IT'S WHAT I DO!
THUD
THUD
THUD

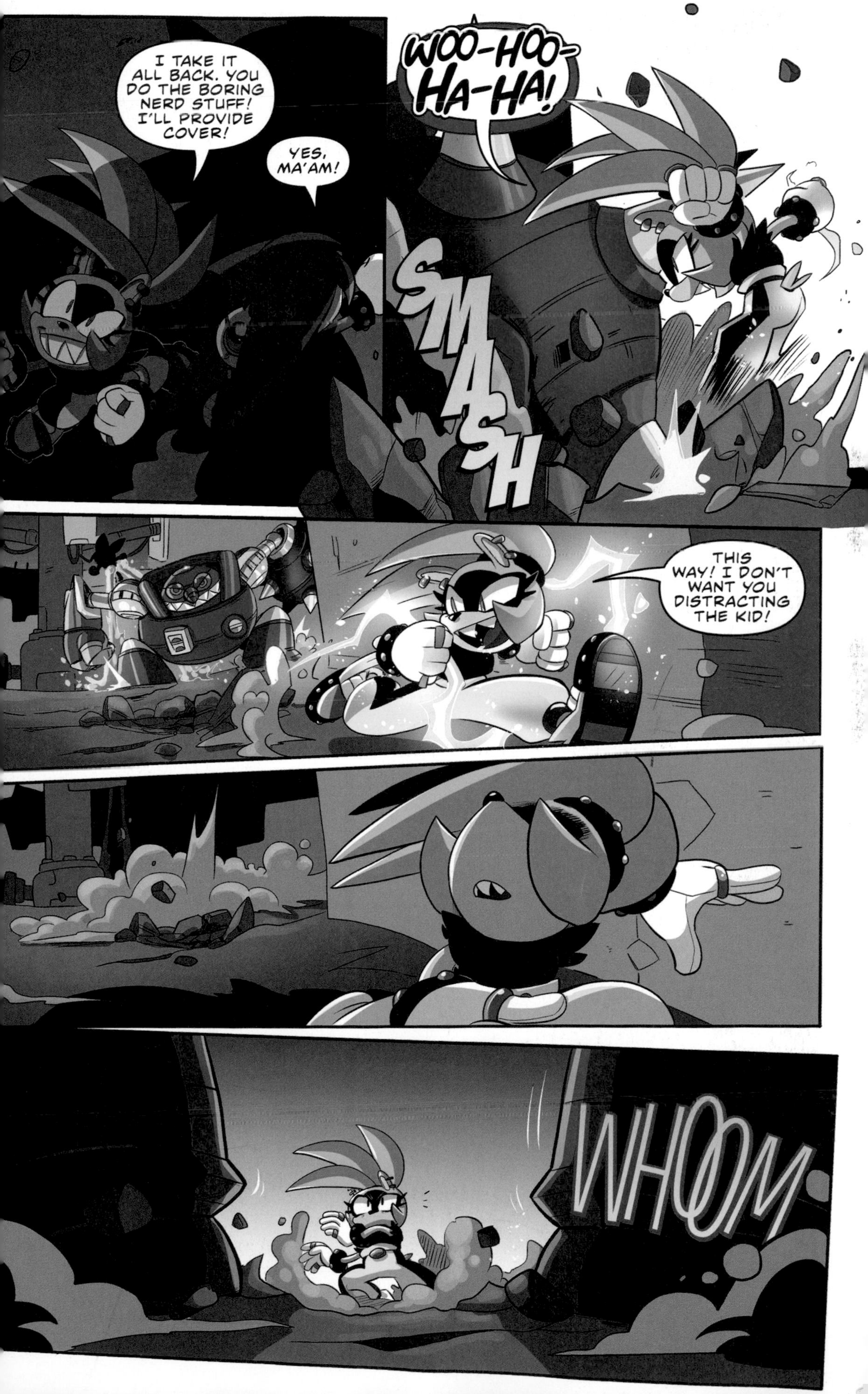
I TAKE IT ALL BACK. YOU DO THE BORING NERD STUFF! I'LL PROVIDE COVER!
YES, MA'AM!
WOO-HOO-HA-HA!
SMASH
THIS WAY! I DON'T WANT YOU DISTRACTING THE KID!
WHOOM

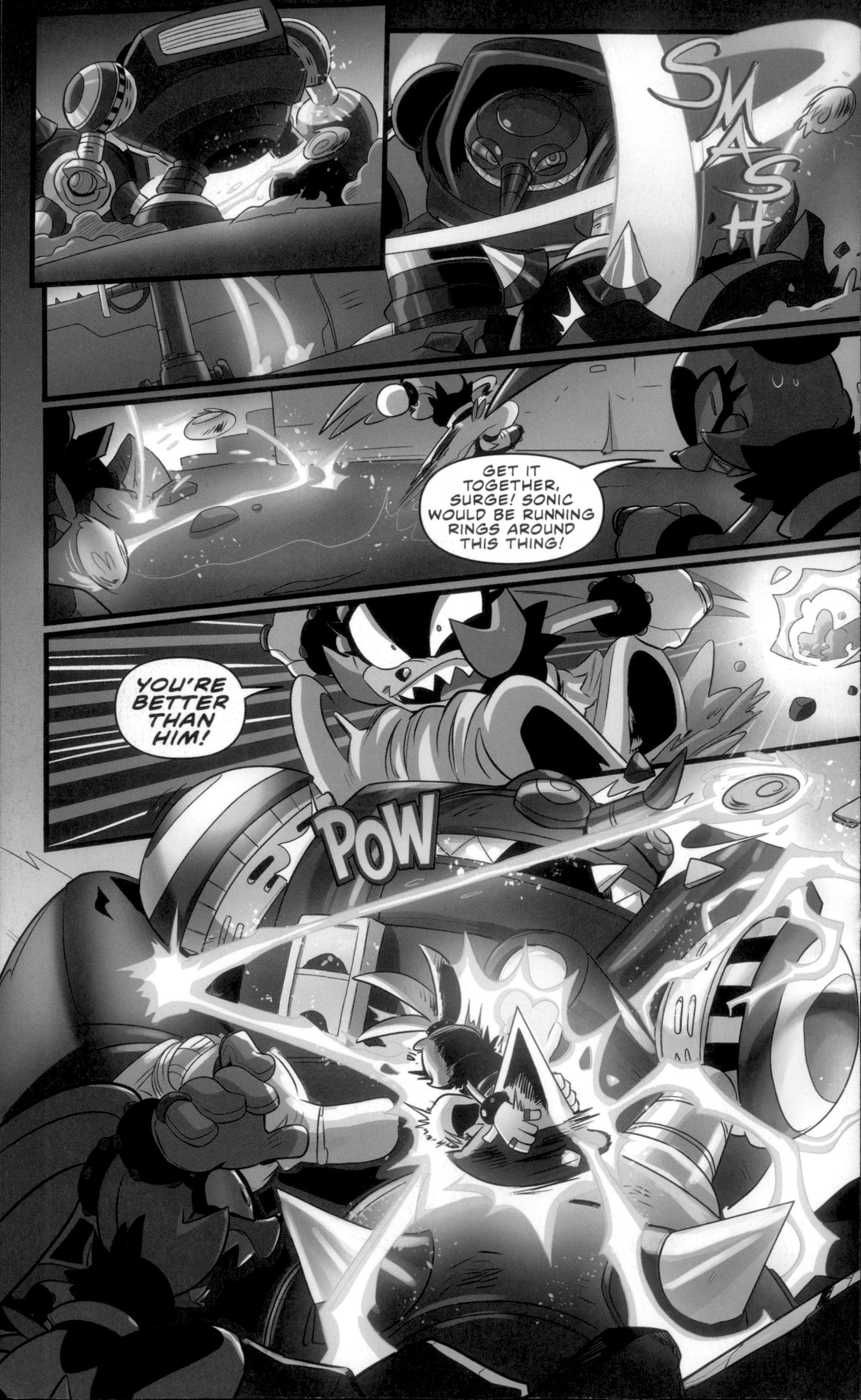
SMASH
GET IT TOGETHER, SURGE! SONIC WOULD BE RUNNING RINGS AROUND THIS THING!
YOU'RE BETTER THAN HIM!
POW

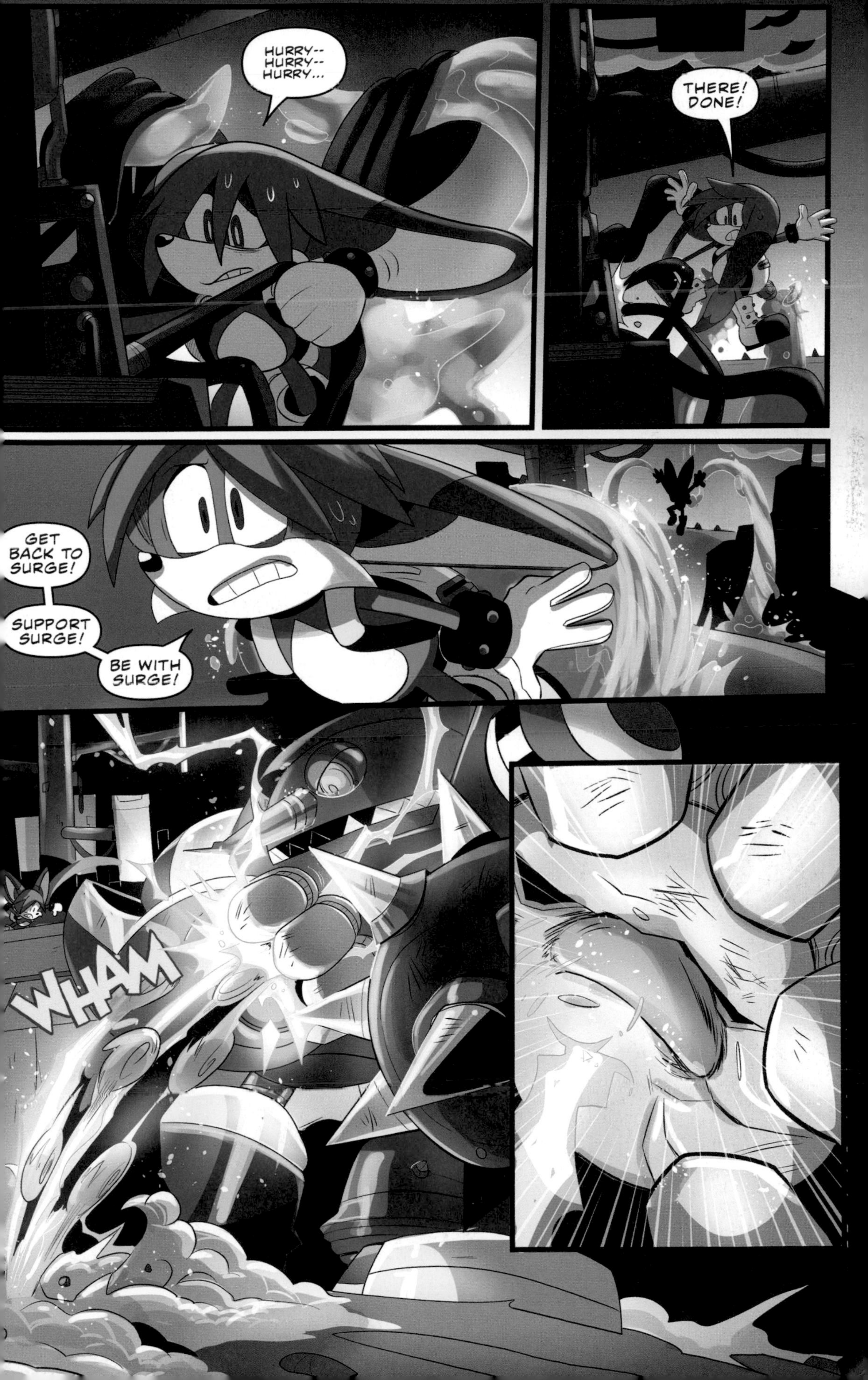
HURRY-- HURRY-- HURRY...
THERE! DONE!
GET BACK TO SURGE!
SUPPORT SURGE!
BE WITH SURGE!
WHAM

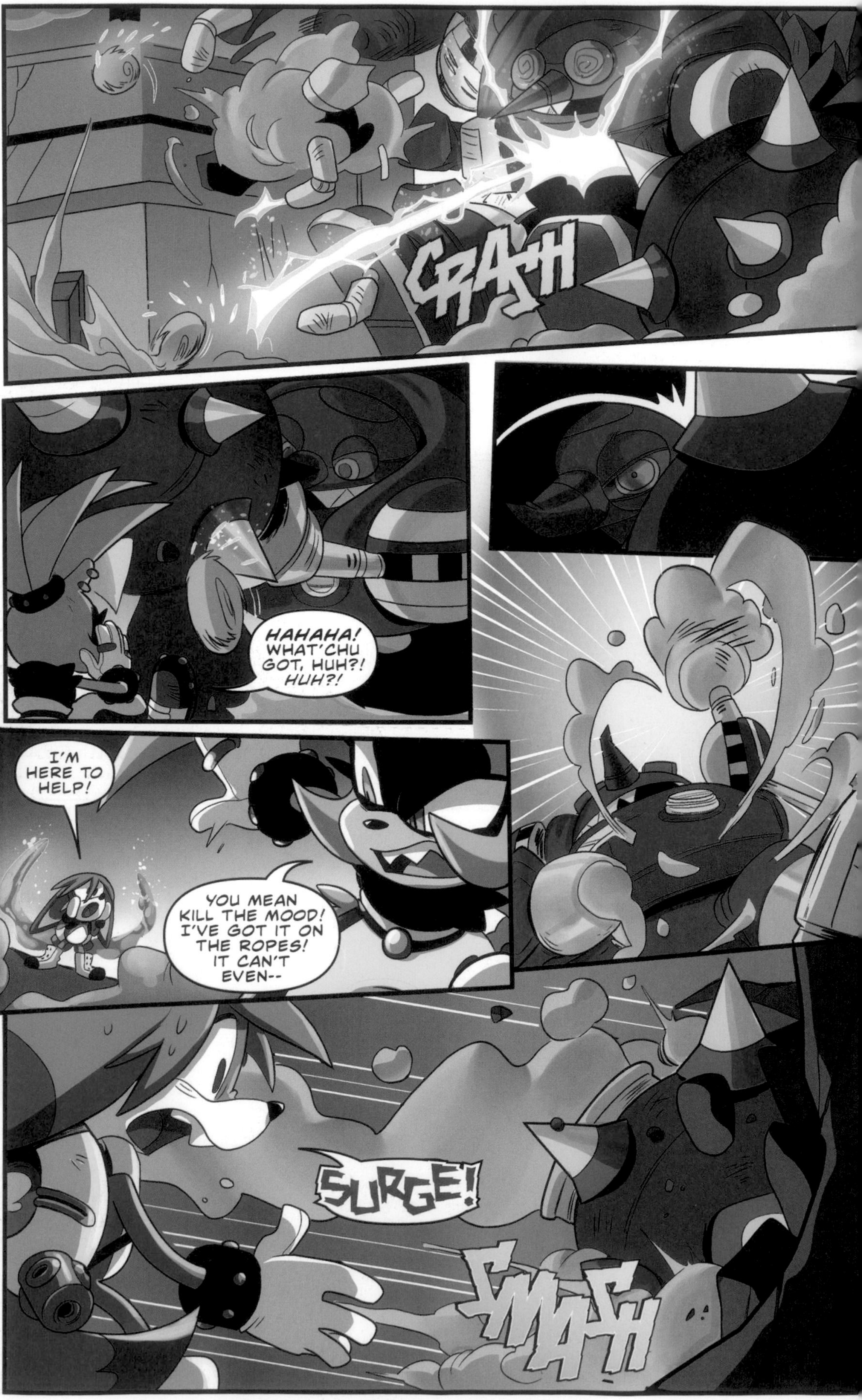
CRASH
HAHAHA! WHAT'CHU GOT, HUH?! HUH?!
I'M HERE TO HELP!
YOU MEAN KILL THE MOOD! I'VE GOT IT ON THE ROPES! IT CAN'T EVEN--
SURGE!
SMASH

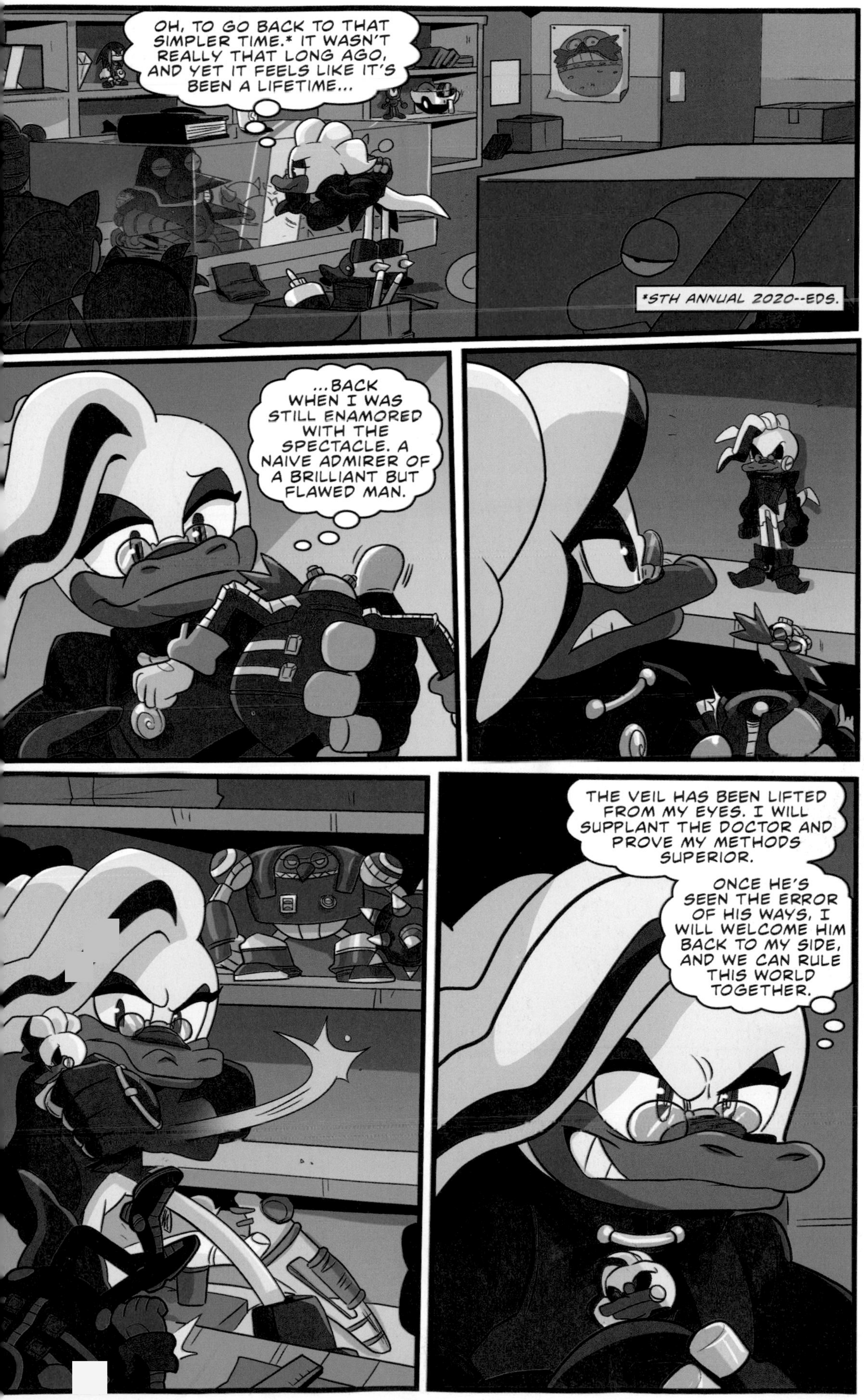
OH, TO GO BACK TO THAT SIMPLER TIME.* IT WASN'T REALLY THAT LONG AGO, AND YET IT FEELS LIKE IT'S BEEN A LIFETIME...
*5TH ANNUAL 2020--EDS.
...BACK WHEN I WAS STILL ENAMORED WITH THE SPECTACLE. A NAIVE ADMIRER OF A BRILLIANT BUT FLAWED MAN.
THE VEIL HAS BEEN LIFTED FROM MY EYES. I WILL SUPPLANT THE DOCTOR AND PROVE MY METHODS SUPERIOR.
ONCE HE'S SEEN THE ERROR OF HIS WAYS, I WILL WELCOME HIM BACK TO MY SIDE, AND WE CAN RULE THIS WORLD TOGETHER.

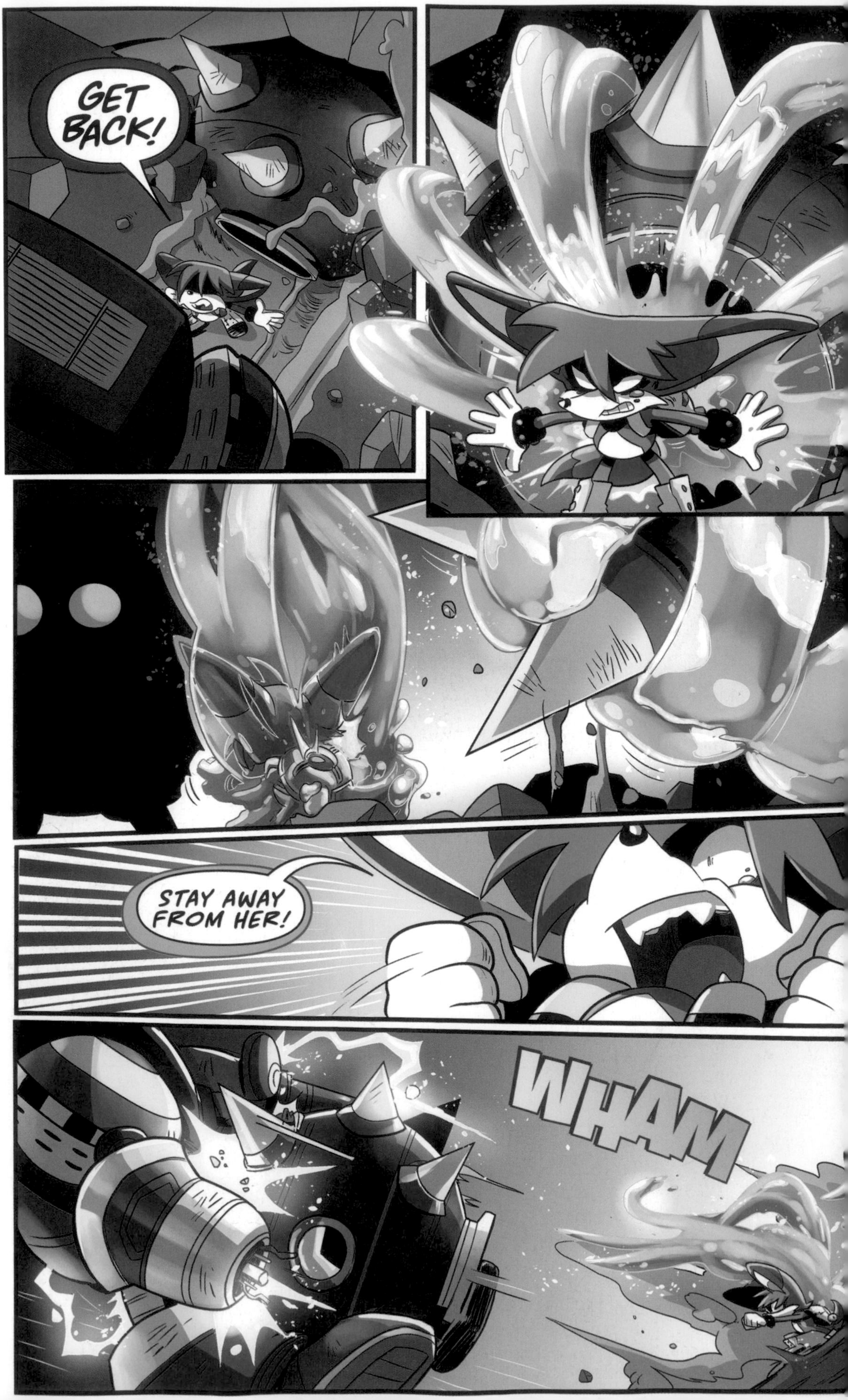
GET BACK!
STAY AWAY FROM HER!
WHAM

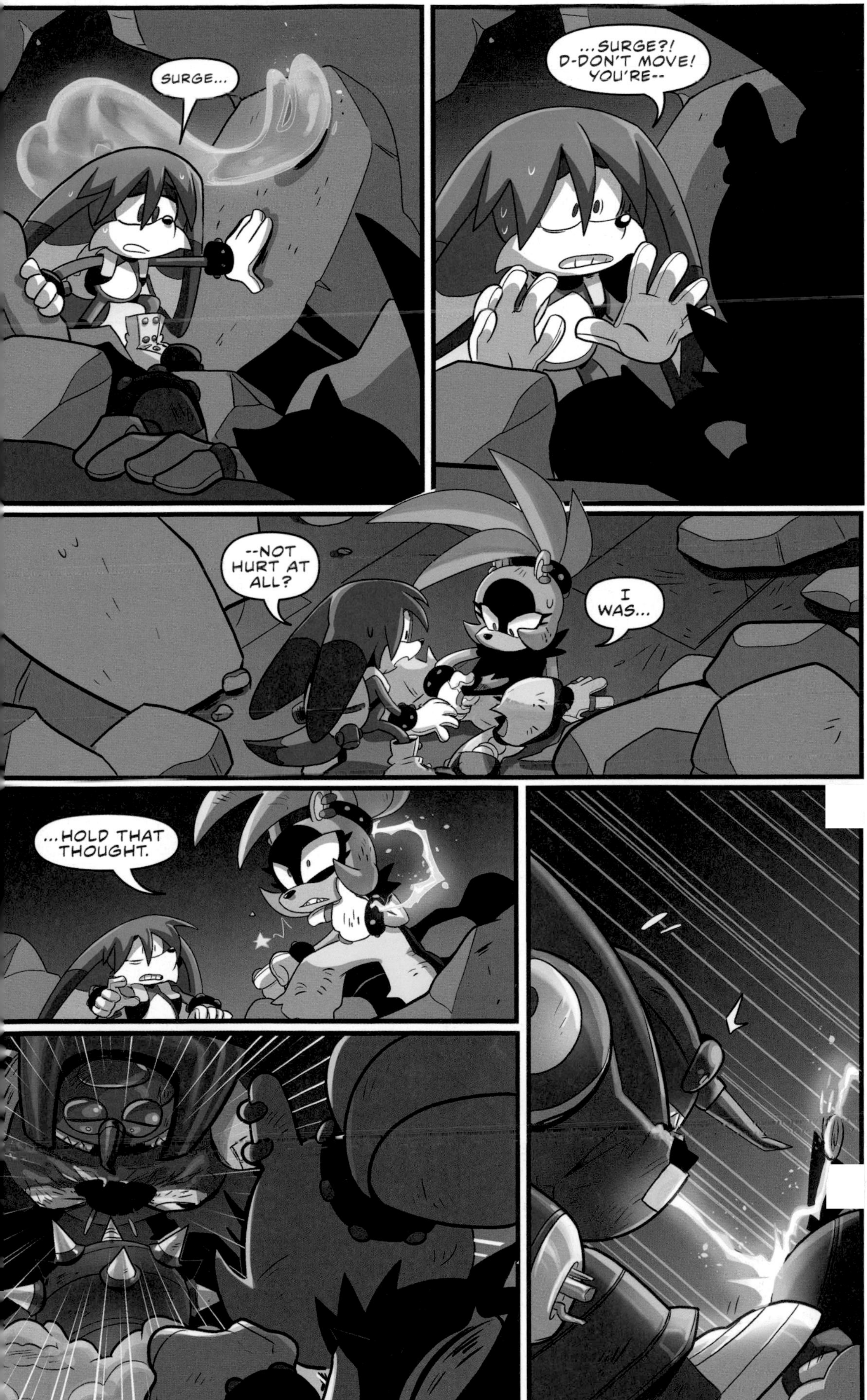
SURGE...
...SURGE?! D-DON'T MOVE! YOU'RE--
--NOT HURT AT ALL?
I WAS...
...HOLD THAT THOUGHT.

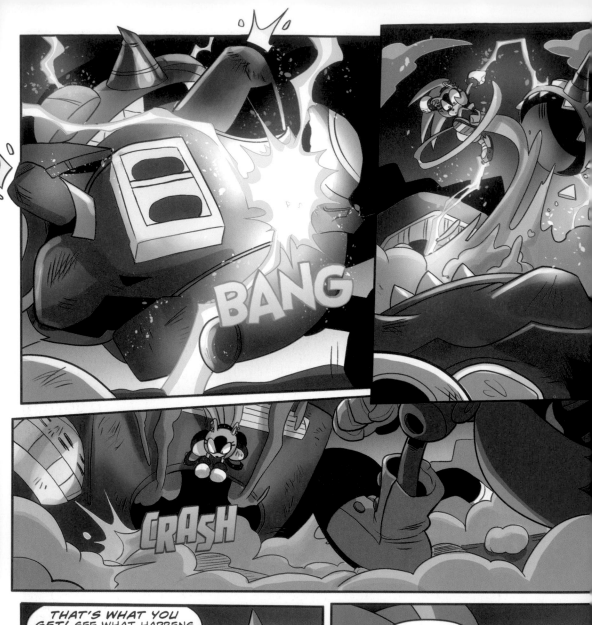

BANG

CRASH

THAT'S WHAT YOU GET! SEE WHAT HAPPENS WHEN YOU MESS WITH THE BEST?! HUH?! HUH?!

M-MA'AM?

WHAT?!

TH-THE FIGHT ALERTED THE OTHERS...

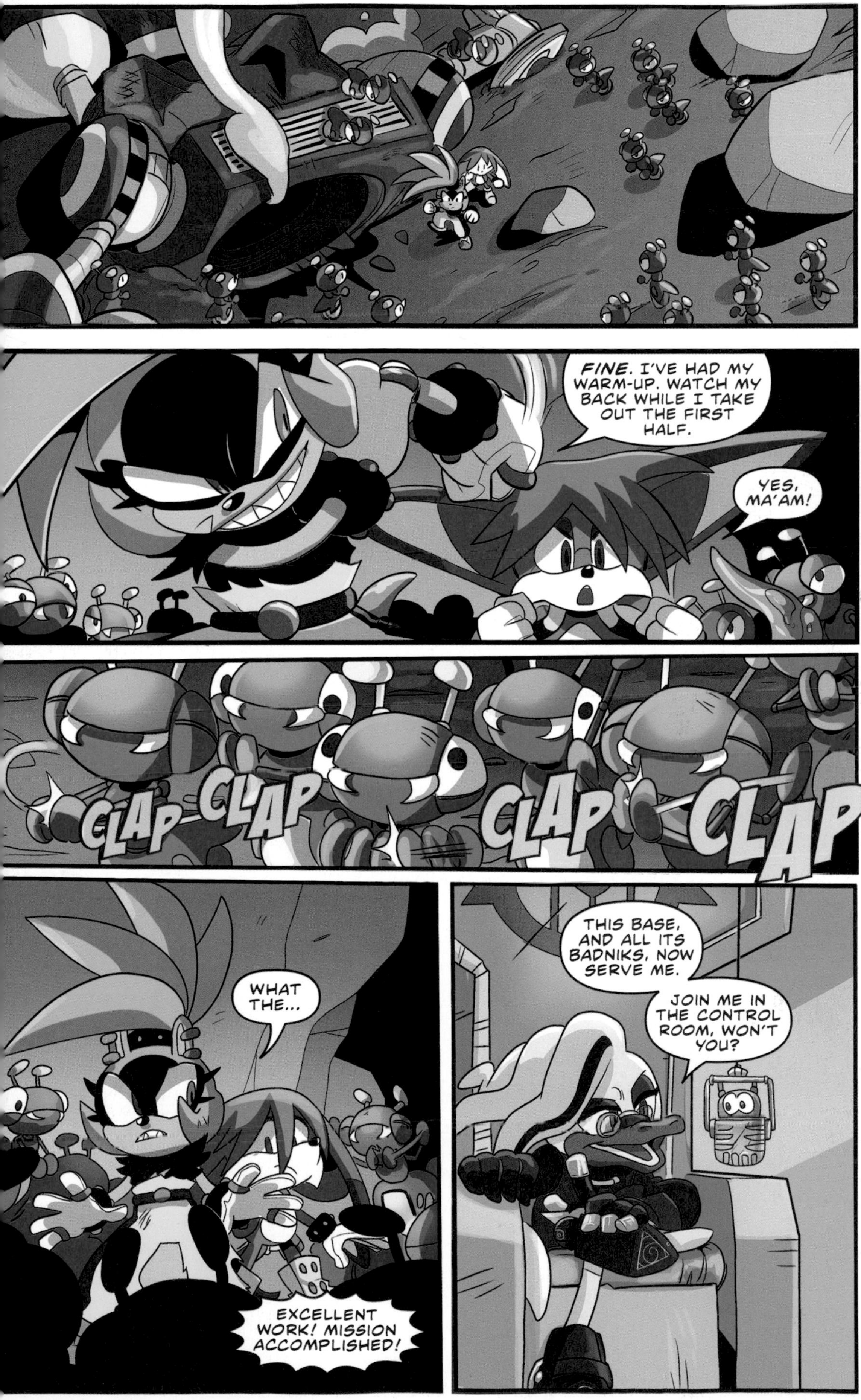
FINE. I'VE HAD MY WARM-UP. WATCH MY BACK WHILE I TAKE OUT THE FIRST HALF.
YES, MA'AM!
CLAP CLAP CLAP CLAP
WHAT THE...
EXCELLENT WORK! MISSION ACCOMPLISHED!
THIS BASE, AND ALL ITS BADNIKS, NOW SERVE ME.
JOIN ME IN THE CONTROL ROOM, WON'T YOU?

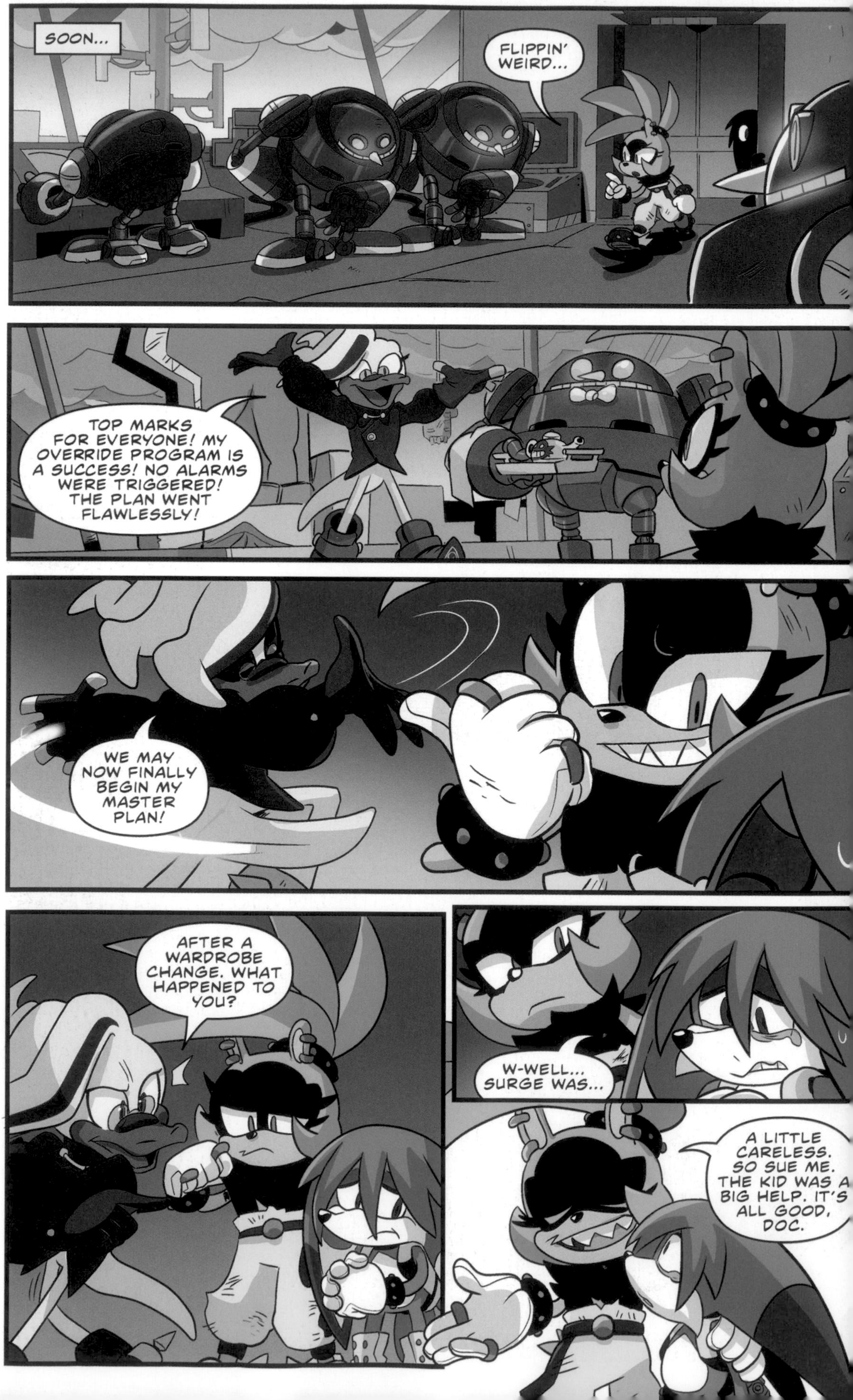
SOON...
FLIPPIN' WEIRD...
TOP MARKS FOR EVERYONE! MY OVERRIDE PROGRAM IS A SUCCESS! NO ALARMS WERE TRIGGERED! THE PLAN WENT FLAWLESSLY!
WE MAY NOW FINALLY BEGIN MY MASTER PLAN!
AFTER A WARDROBE CHANGE. WHAT HAPPENED TO YOU?
W-WELL... SURGE WAS...
A LITTLE CARELESS. SO SUE ME. THE KID WAS A BIG HELP. IT'S ALL GOOD, DOC.

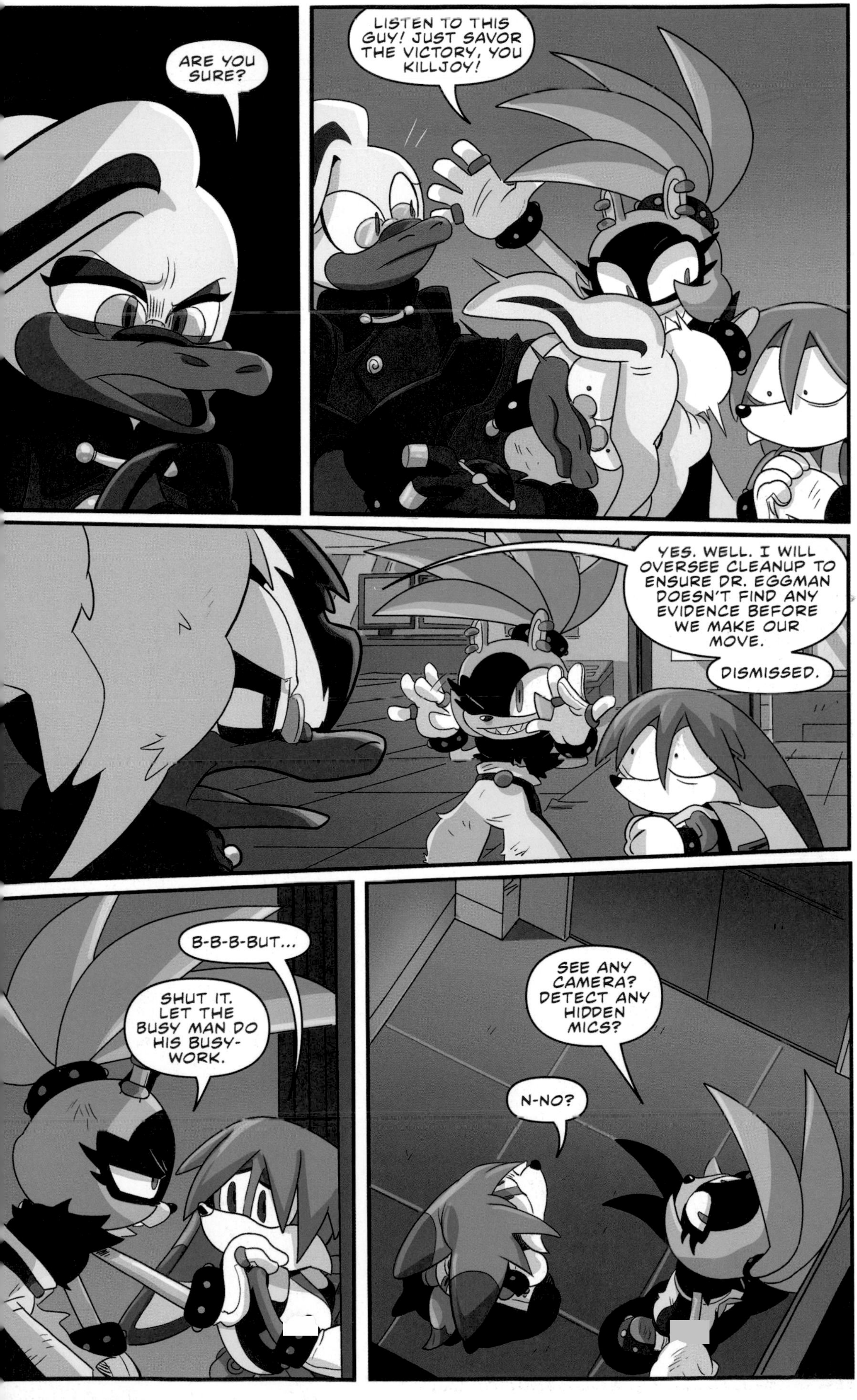
ARE YOU SURE?
LISTEN TO THIS GUY! JUST SAVOR THE VICTORY, YOU KILLJOY!
YES. WELL. I WILL OVERSEE CLEANUP TO ENSURE DR. EGGMAN DOESN'T FIND ANY EVIDENCE BEFORE WE MAKE OUR MOVE.
DISMISSED.
B-B-B-BUT...
SHUT IT. LET THE BUSY MAN DO HIS BUSY-WORK.
SEE ANY CAMERA? DETECT ANY HIDDEN MICS?
N-NO?

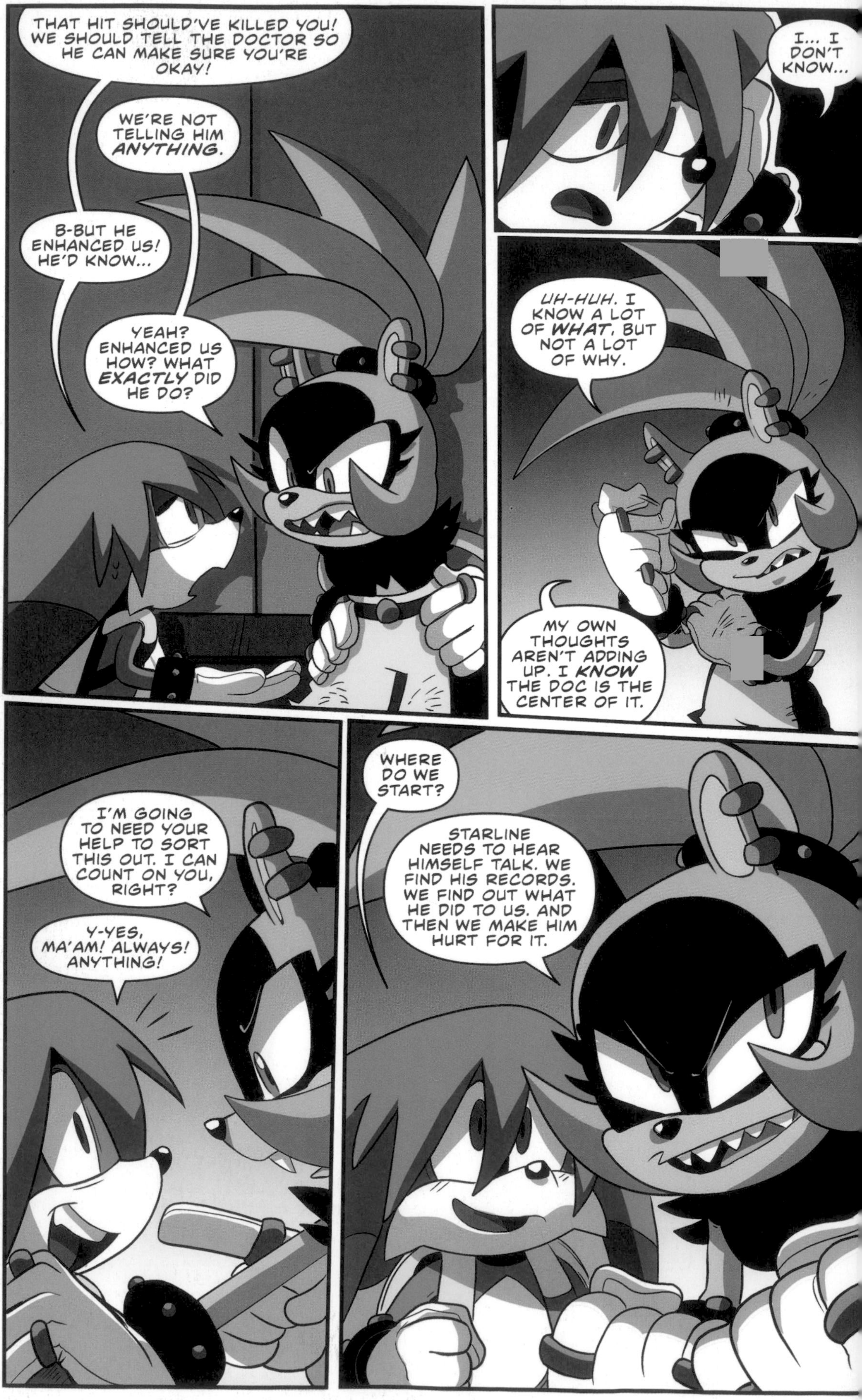
THAT HIT SHOULD'VE KILLED YOU! WE SHOULD TELL THE DOCTOR SO HE CAN MAKE SURE YOU'RE OKAY!
WE'RE NOT TELLING HIM *ANYTHING*.
B-BUT HE ENHANCED US! HE'D KNOW...
YEAH? ENHANCED US HOW? WHAT *EXACTLY* DID HE DO?
I... I DON'T KNOW...
UH-HUH. I KNOW A LOT OF *WHAT*, BUT NOT A LOT OF WHY.
MY OWN THOUGHTS AREN'T ADDING UP. I *KNOW* THE DOC IS THE CENTER OF IT.
I'M GOING TO NEED YOUR HELP TO SORT THIS OUT. I CAN COUNT ON YOU, RIGHT?
Y-YES, MA'AM! ALWAYS! ANYTHING!
WHERE DO WE START?
STARLINE NEEDS TO HEAR HIMSELF TALK. WE FIND HIS RECORDS. WE FIND OUT WHAT HE DID TO US. AND THEN WE MAKE HIM HURT FOR IT.

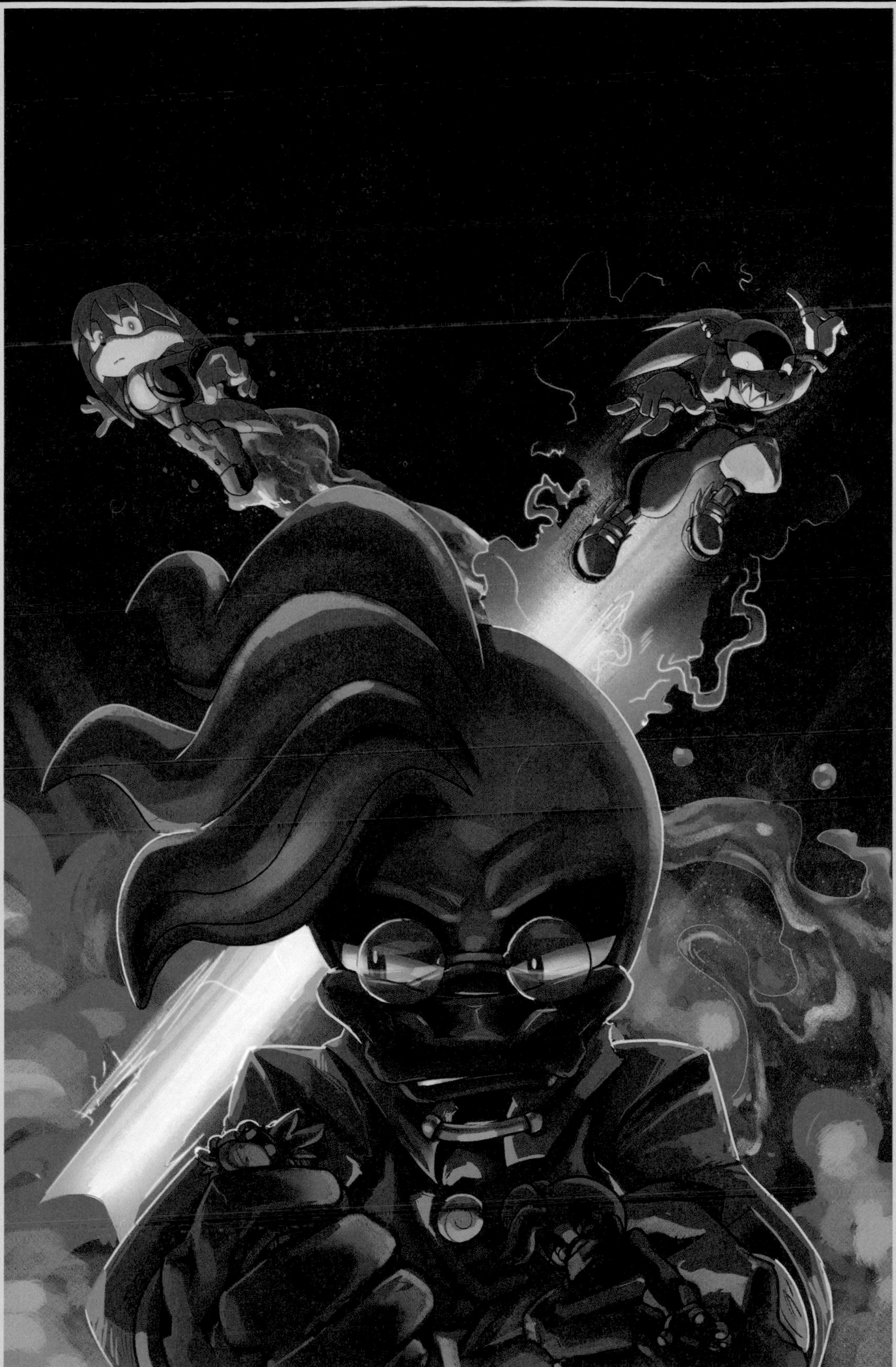

ART GIGI DUTREIX

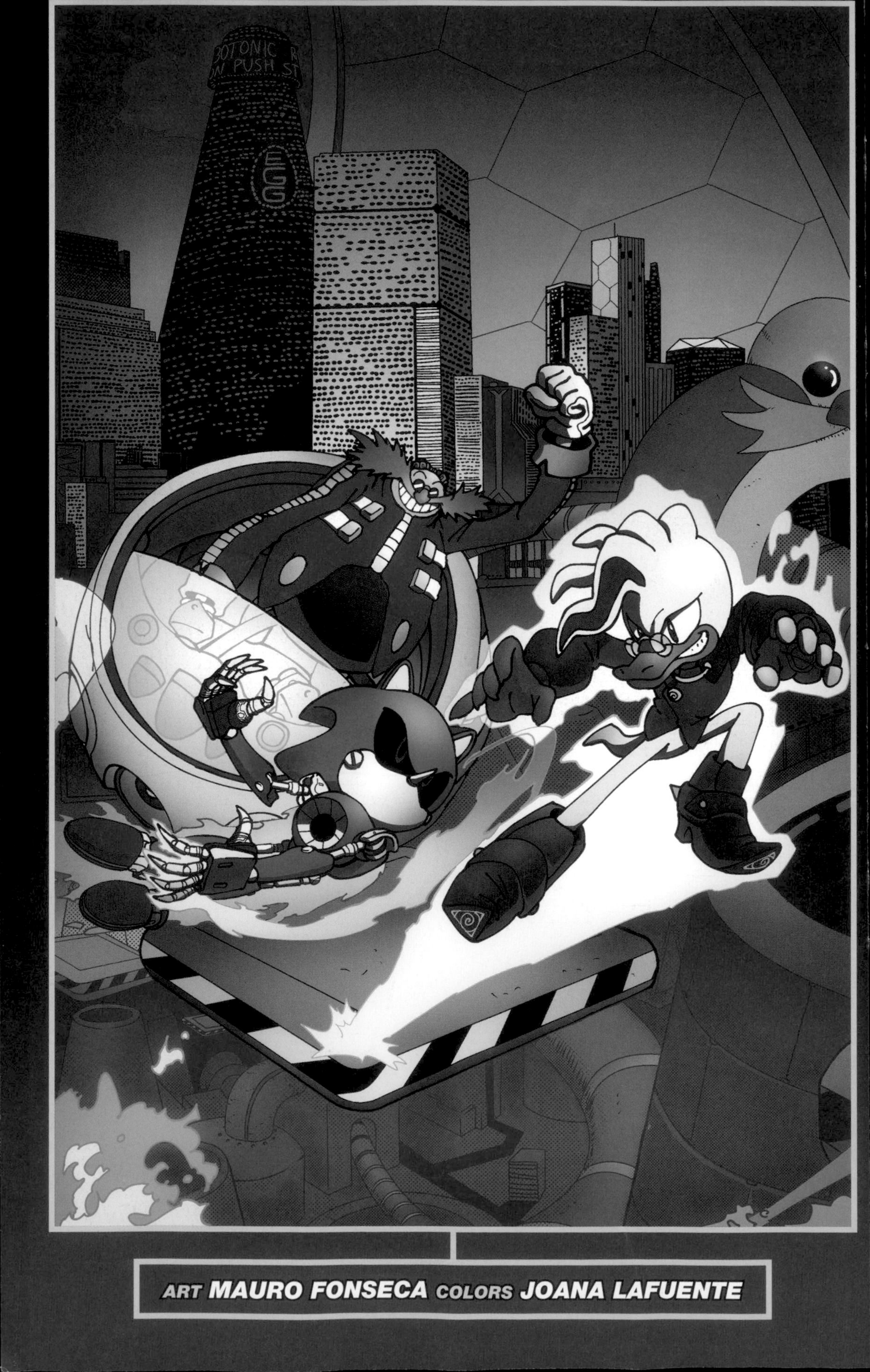
EGG

ART MAURO FONSECA COLORS JOANA LAFUENTE

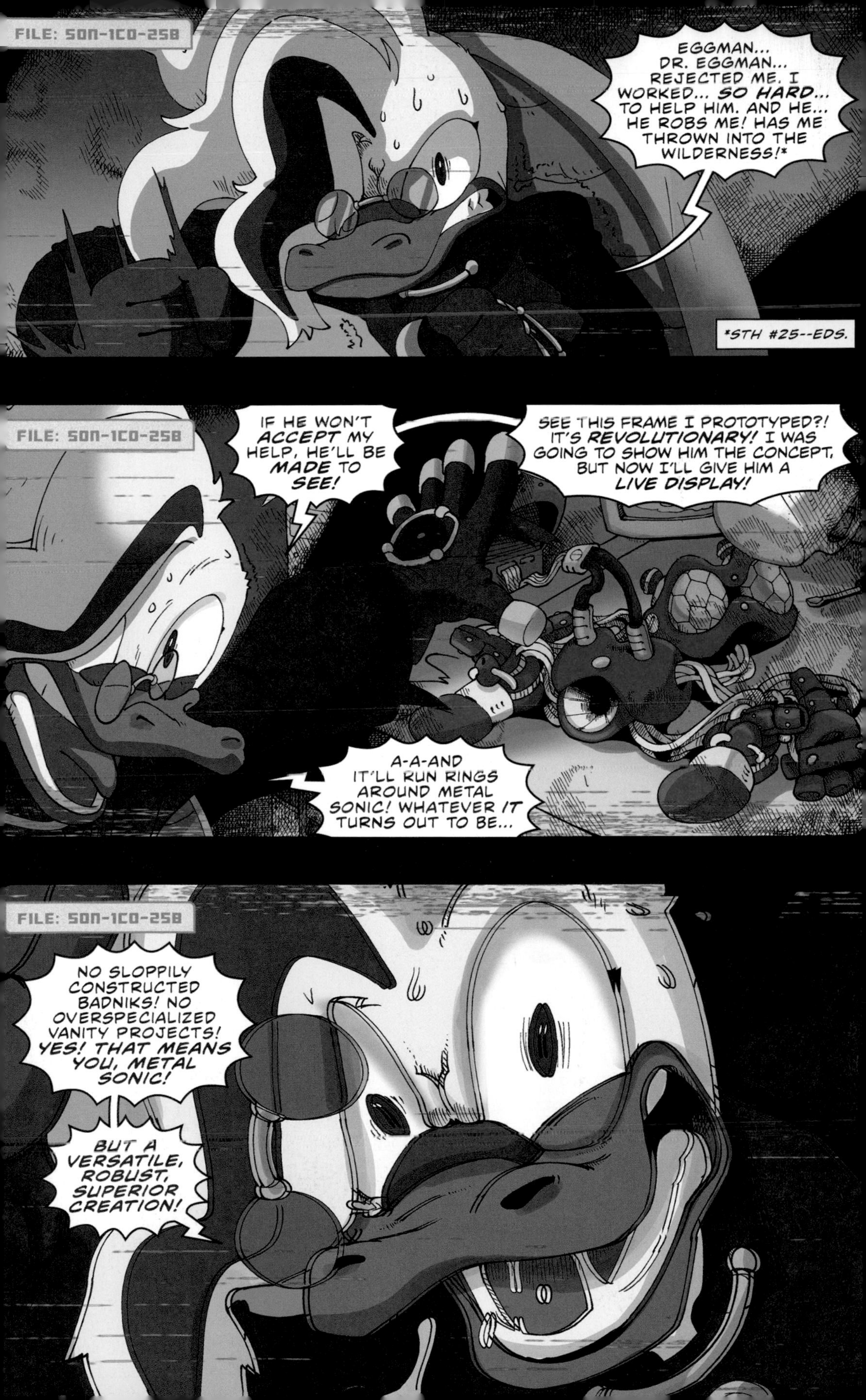
FILE: SON-1CO-258
EGGMAN... DR. EGGMAN... REJECTED ME. I WORKED... SO HARD... TO HELP HIM. AND HE... HE ROBS ME! HAS ME THROWN INTO THE WILDERNESS!*
*STH #25--EDS.
FILE: SON-1CO-258
IF HE WON'T ACCEPT MY HELP, HE'LL BE MADE TO SEE!
SEE THIS FRAME I PROTOTYPED?! IT'S REVOLUTIONARY! I WAS GOING TO SHOW HIM THE CONCEPT, BUT NOW I'LL GIVE HIM A LIVE DISPLAY!
A-A-AND IT'LL RUN RINGS AROUND METAL SONIC! WHATEVER IT TURNS OUT TO BE...
FILE: SON-1CO-258
NO SLOPPILY CONSTRUCTED BADNIKS! NO OVERSPECIALIZED VANITY PROJECTS! YES! THAT MEANS YOU, METAL SONIC!
BUT A VERSATILE, ROBUST, SUPERIOR CREATION!

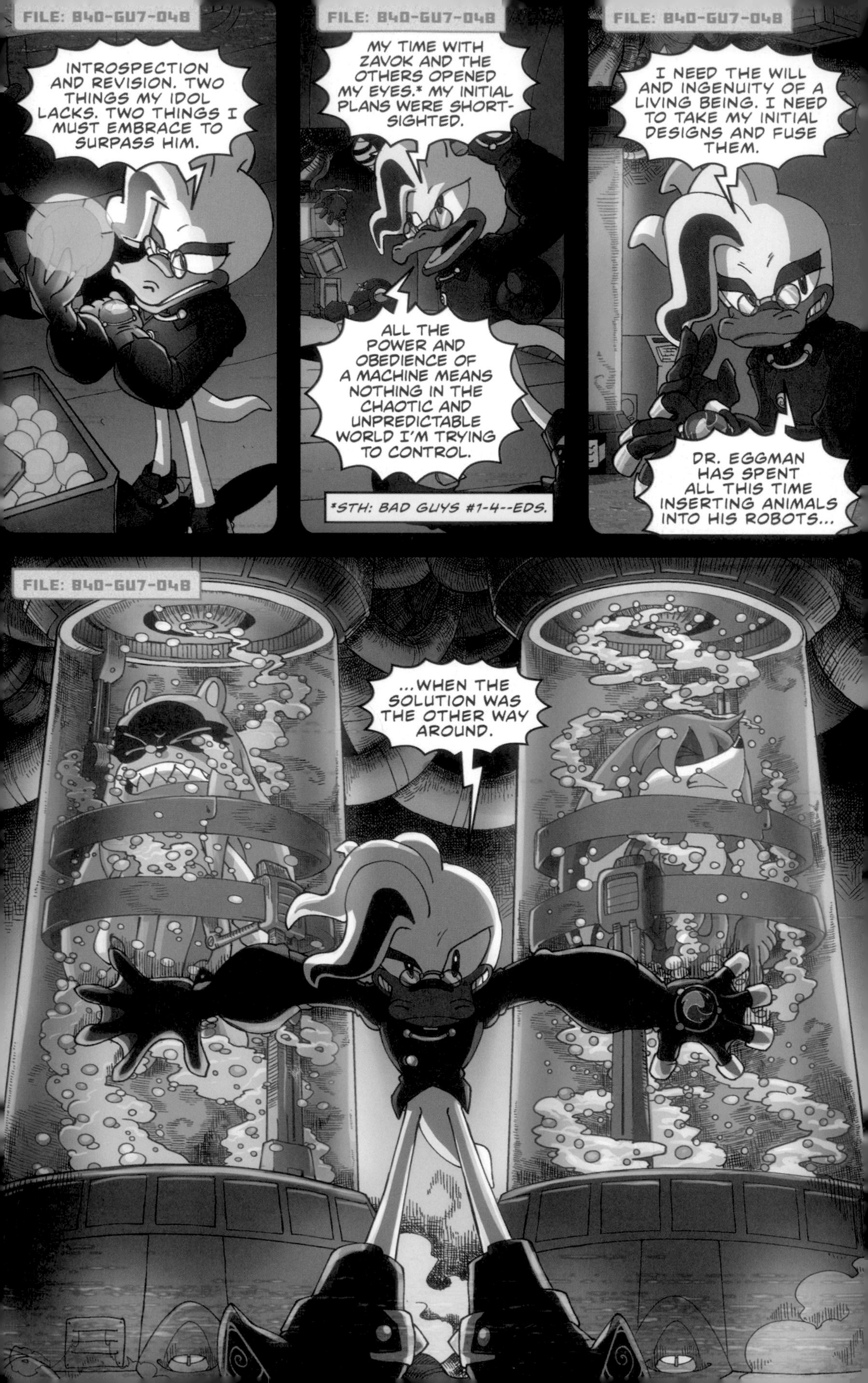
FILE: 840-GU7-048
INTROSPECTION AND REVISION. TWO THINGS MY IDOL LACKS. TWO THINGS I MUST EMBRACE TO SURPASS HIM.
FILE: 840-GU7-048
MY TIME WITH ZAVOK AND THE OTHERS OPENED MY EYES.* MY INITIAL PLANS WERE SHORT-SIGHTED.
ALL THE POWER AND OBEDIENCE OF A MACHINE MEANS NOTHING IN THE CHAOTIC AND UNPREDICTABLE WORLD I'M TRYING TO CONTROL.
*STH: BAD GUYS #1-4--EDS.
FILE: 840-GU7-048
I NEED THE WILL AND INGENUITY OF A LIVING BEING. I NEED TO TAKE MY INITIAL DESIGNS AND FUSE THEM.
DR. EGGMAN HAS SPENT ALL THIS TIME INSERTING ANIMALS INTO HIS ROBOTS...
FILE: 840-GU7-048
...WHEN THE SOLUTION WAS THE OTHER WAY AROUND.

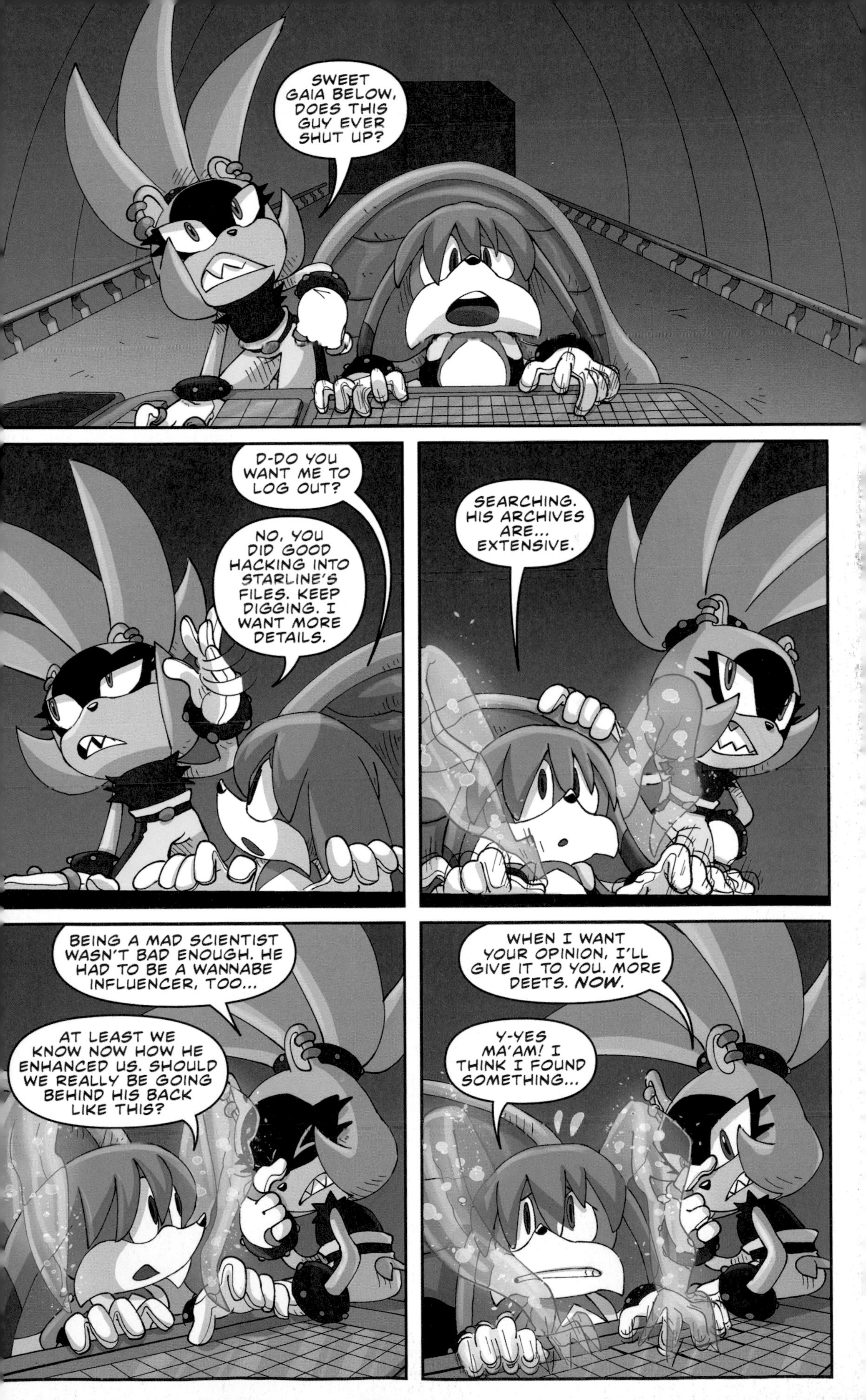
SWEET GAIA BELOW, DOES THIS GUY EVER SHUT UP?
D-DO YOU WANT ME TO LOG OUT?
NO, YOU DID GOOD HACKING INTO STARLINE'S FILES. KEEP DIGGING. I WANT MORE DETAILS.
SEARCHING. HIS ARCHIVES ARE... EXTENSIVE.
BEING A MAD SCIENTIST WASN'T BAD ENOUGH. HE HAD TO BE A WANNABE INFLUENCER, TOO...
AT LEAST WE KNOW NOW HOW HE ENHANCED US. SHOULD WE REALLY BE GOING BEHIND HIS BACK LIKE THIS?
WHEN I WANT YOUR OPINION, I'LL GIVE IT TO YOU. MORE DEETS. NOW.
Y-YES MA'AM! I THINK I FOUND SOMETHING...

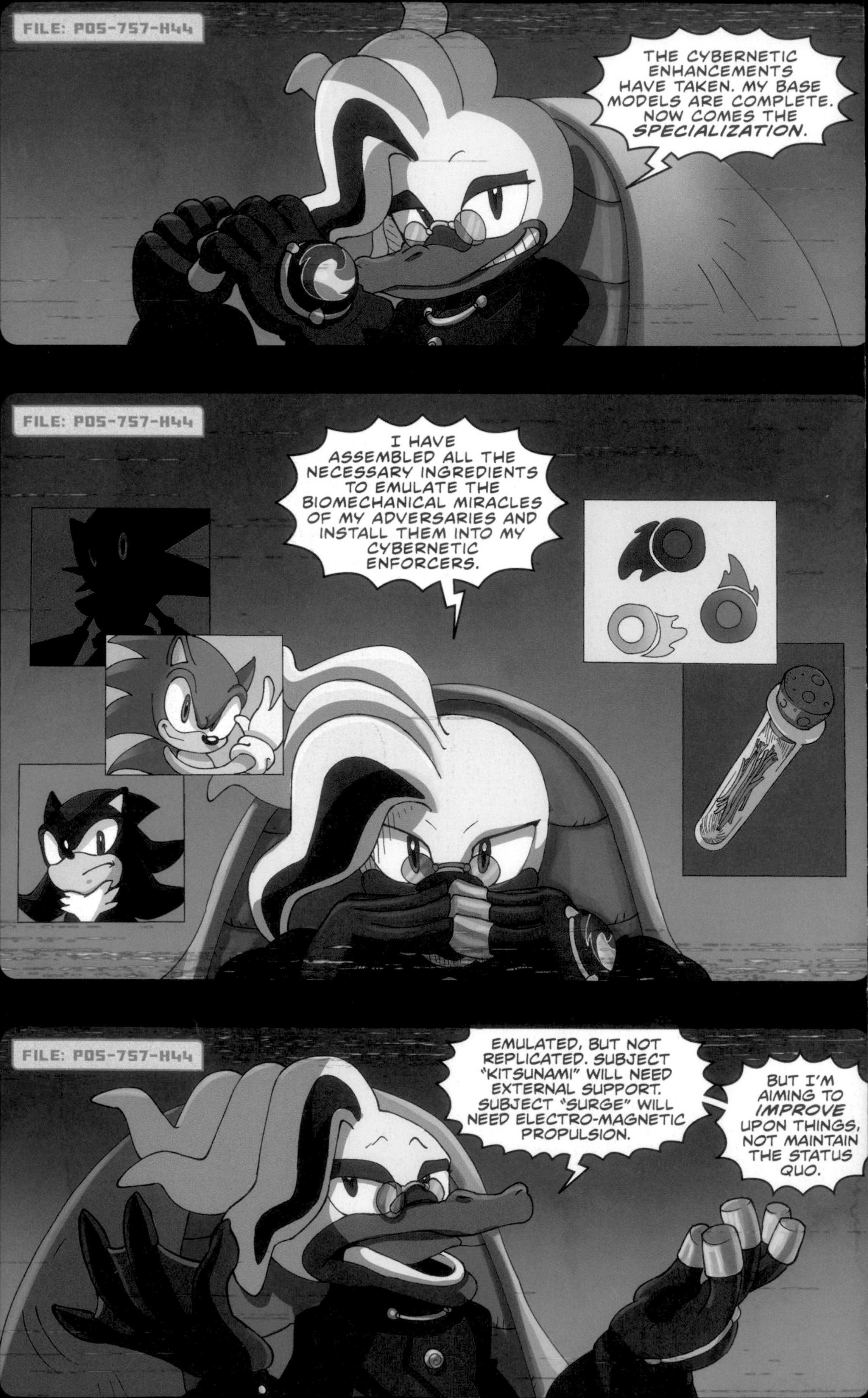
FILE: P05-757-H44
THE CYBERNETIC ENHANCEMENTS HAVE TAKEN. MY BASE MODELS ARE COMPLETE. NOW COMES THE SPECIALIZATION.
FILE: P05-757-H44
I HAVE ASSEMBLED ALL THE NECESSARY INGREDIENTS TO EMULATE THE BIOMECHANICAL MIRACLES OF MY ADVERSARIES AND INSTALL THEM INTO MY CYBERNETIC ENFORCERS.
FILE: P05-757-H44
EMULATED, BUT NOT REPLICATED. SUBJECT "KITSUNAMI" WILL NEED EXTERNAL SUPPORT. SUBJECT "SURGE" WILL NEED ELECTRO-MAGNETIC PROPULSION.
BUT I'M AIMING TO IMPROVE UPON THINGS, NOT MAINTAIN THE STATUS QUO.

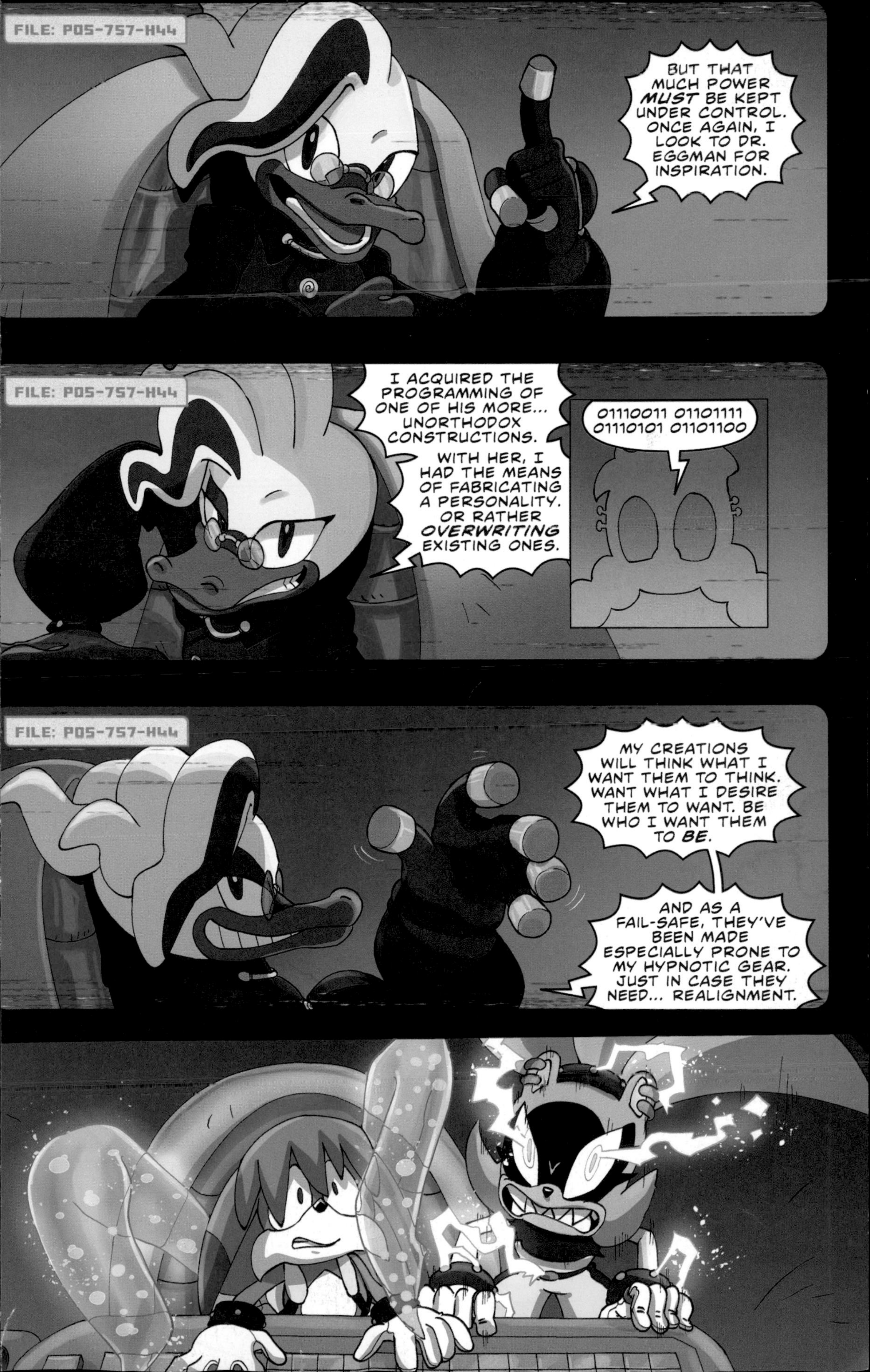

FILE: P05-757-H44
BUT THAT MUCH POWER MUST BE KEPT UNDER CONTROL. ONCE AGAIN, I LOOK TO DR. EGGMAN FOR INSPIRATION.
FILE: P05-757-H44
I ACQUIRED THE PROGRAMMING OF ONE OF HIS MORE... UNORTHODOX CONSTRUCTIONS.
WITH HER, I HAD THE MEANS OF FABRICATING A PERSONALITY. OR RATHER OVERWRITING EXISTING ONES.
01110011 01101111 01110101 01101100
FILE: P05-757-H44
MY CREATIONS WILL THINK WHAT I WANT THEM TO THINK. WANT WHAT I DESIRE THEM TO WANT. BE WHO I WANT THEM TO BE.
AND AS A FAIL-SAFE, THEY'VE BEEN MADE ESPECIALLY PRONE TO MY HYPNOTIC GEAR. JUST IN CASE THEY NEED... REALIGNMENT.

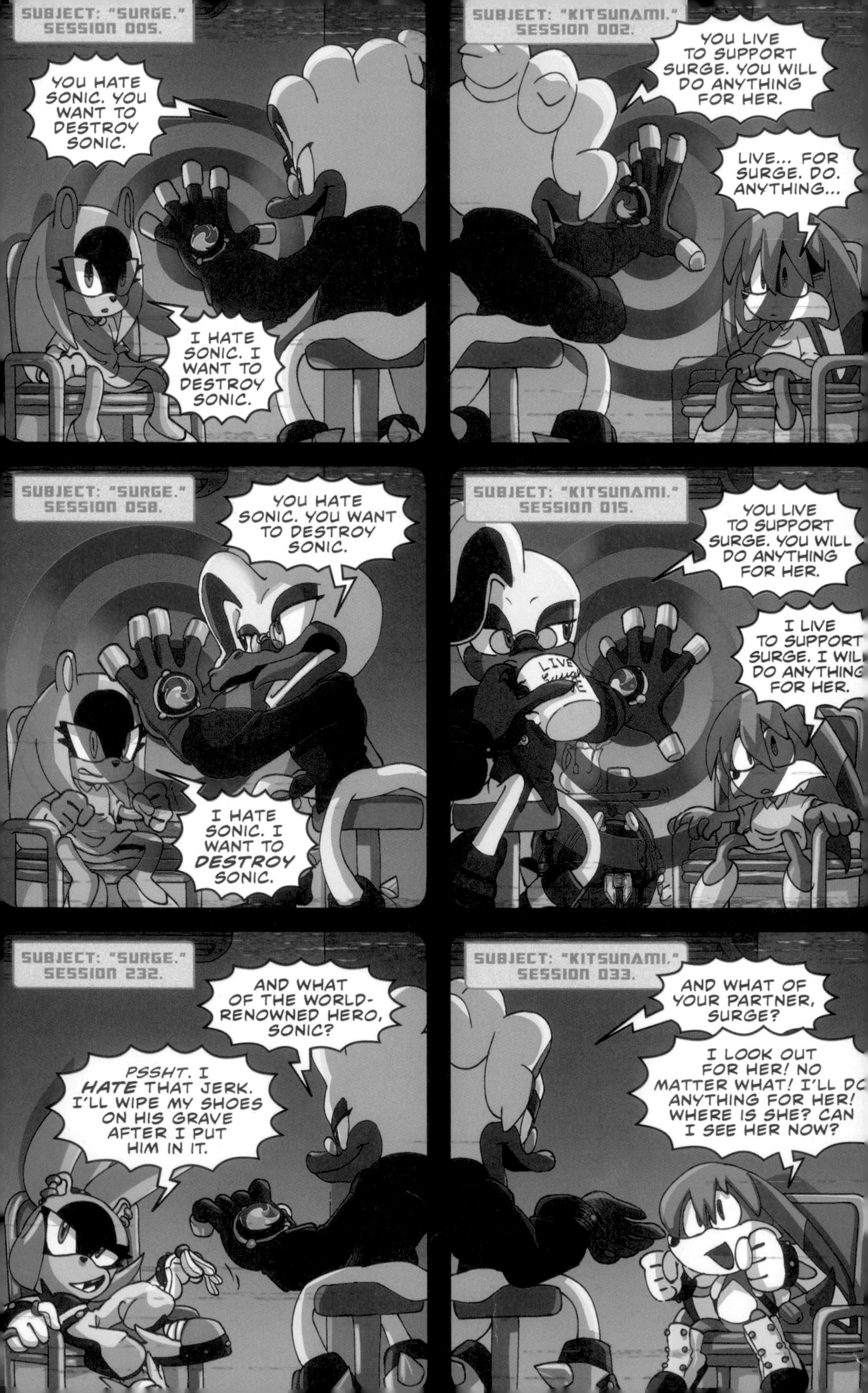
SUBJECT: "SURGE." SESSION 005.
YOU HATE SONIC. YOU WANT TO DESTROY SONIC.
I HATE SONIC. I WANT TO DESTROY SONIC.
SUBJECT: "KITSUNAMI." SESSION 002.
YOU LIVE TO SUPPORT SURGE. YOU WILL DO ANYTHING FOR HER.
LIVE... FOR SURGE. DO. ANYTHING...
SUBJECT: "SURGE." SESSION 058.
YOU HATE SONIC. YOU WANT TO DESTROY SONIC.
I HATE SONIC. I WANT TO *DESTROY* SONIC.
SUBJECT: "KITSUNAMI." SESSION 015.
YOU LIVE TO SUPPORT SURGE. YOU WILL DO ANYTHING FOR HER.
I LIVE TO SUPPORT SURGE. I WIL DO ANYTHING FOR HER.
SUBJECT: "SURGE." SESSION 232.
AND WHAT OF THE WORLD-RENOWNED HERO, SONIC?
PSSHT. I ***HATE*** THAT JERK. I'LL WIPE MY SHOES ON HIS GRAVE AFTER I PUT HIM IN IT.
SUBJECT: "KITSUNAMI." SESSION 033.
AND WHAT OF YOUR PARTNER, SURGE?
I LOOK OUT FOR HER! NO MATTER WHAT! I'LL DO ANYTHING FOR HER! WHERE IS SHE? CAN I SEE HER NOW?

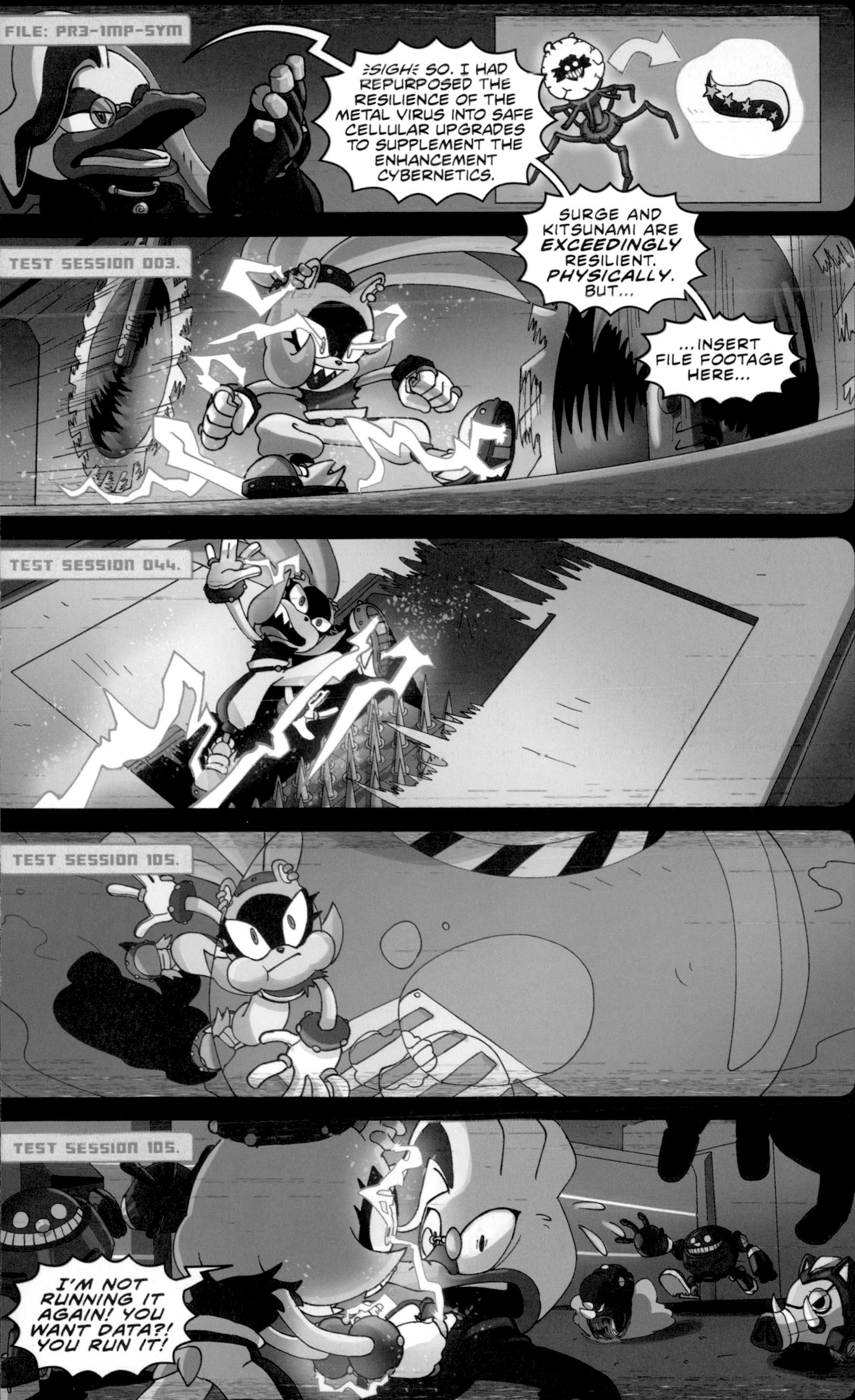
FILE: PR3-1MP-SYM
=SIGH= SO. I HAD REPURPOSED THE RESILIENCE OF THE METAL VIRUS INTO SAFE CELLULAR UPGRADES TO SUPPLEMENT THE ENHANCEMENT CYBERNETICS.
SURGE AND KITSUNAMI ARE EXCEEDINGLY RESILIENT. PHYSICALLY. BUT...
...INSERT FILE FOOTAGE HERE...
TEST SESSION 003.
TEST SESSION 044.
TEST SESSION 105.
TEST SESSION 105.
I'M NOT RUNNING IT AGAIN! YOU WANT DATA?! YOU RUN IT!

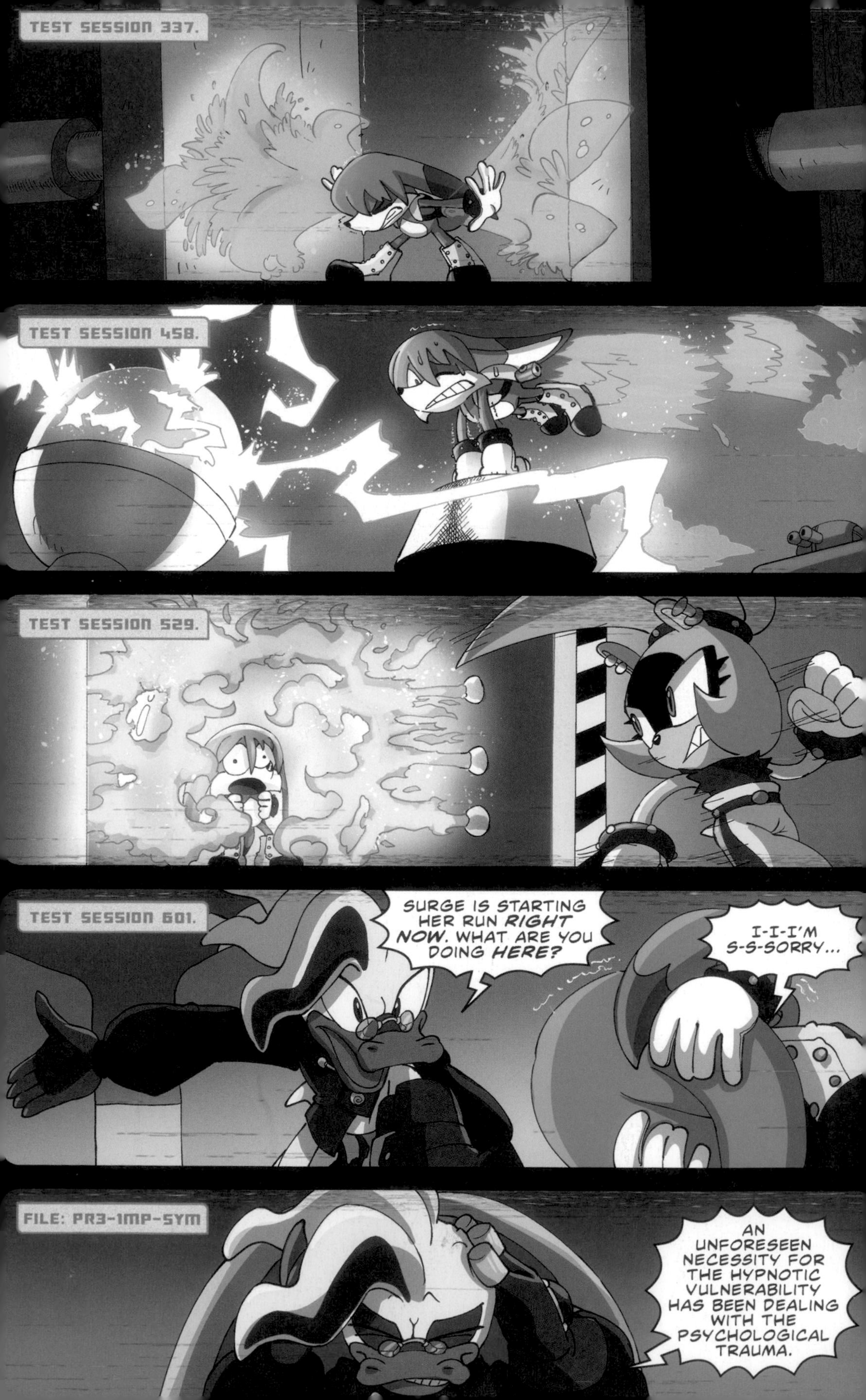
TEST SESSION 337.
TEST SESSION 458.
TEST SESSION 529.
TEST SESSION 601.
SURGE IS STARTING HER RUN *RIGHT NOW*. WHAT ARE YOU DOING *HERE?*
I-I-I'M S-S-SORRY...
FILE: PR3-1MP-SYM
AN UNFORESEEN NECESSITY FOR THE HYPNOTIC VULNERABILITY HAS BEEN DEALING WITH THE PSYCHOLOGICAL TRAUMA.

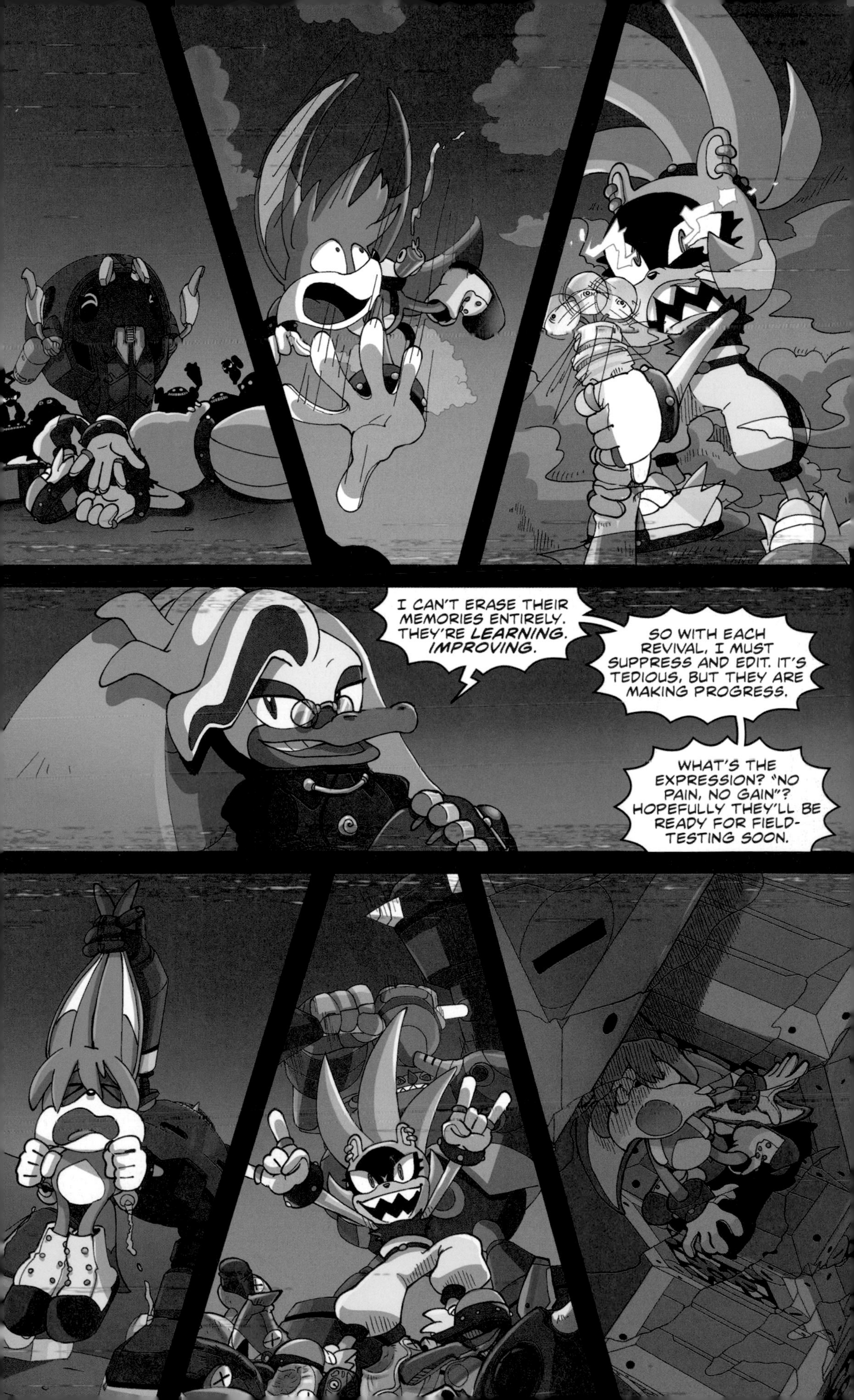
I CAN'T ERASE THEIR MEMORIES ENTIRELY. THEY'RE *LEARNING. IMPROVING.*
SO WITH EACH REVIVAL, I MUST SUPPRESS AND EDIT. IT'S TEDIOUS, BUT THEY ARE MAKING PROGRESS.
WHAT'S THE EXPRESSION? "NO PAIN, NO GAIN"? HOPEFULLY THEY'LL BE READY FOR FIELD-TESTING SOON.

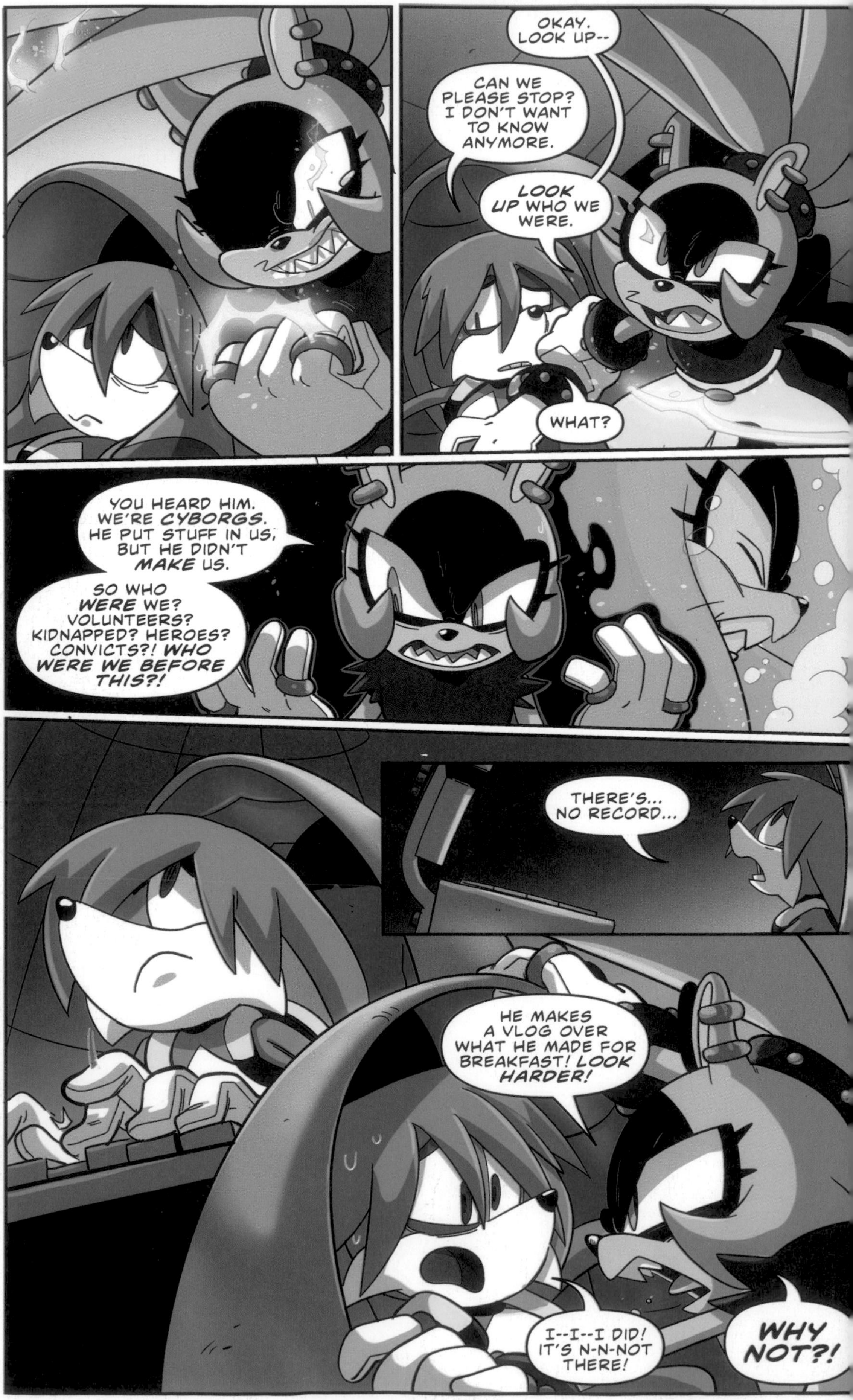
OKAY. LOOK UP--
CAN WE PLEASE STOP? I DON'T WANT TO KNOW ANYMORE.
LOOK UP WHO WE WERE.
WHAT?
YOU HEARD HIM. WE'RE CYBORGS. HE PUT STUFF IN US, BUT HE DIDN'T MAKE US.
SO WHO WERE WE? VOLUNTEERS? KIDNAPPED? HEROES? CONVICTS?! WHO WERE WE BEFORE THIS?!
THERE'S... NO RECORD...
HE MAKES A VLOG OVER WHAT HE MADE FOR BREAKFAST! LOOK HARDER!
I--I--I DID! IT'S N-N-NOT THERE!
WHY NOT?!

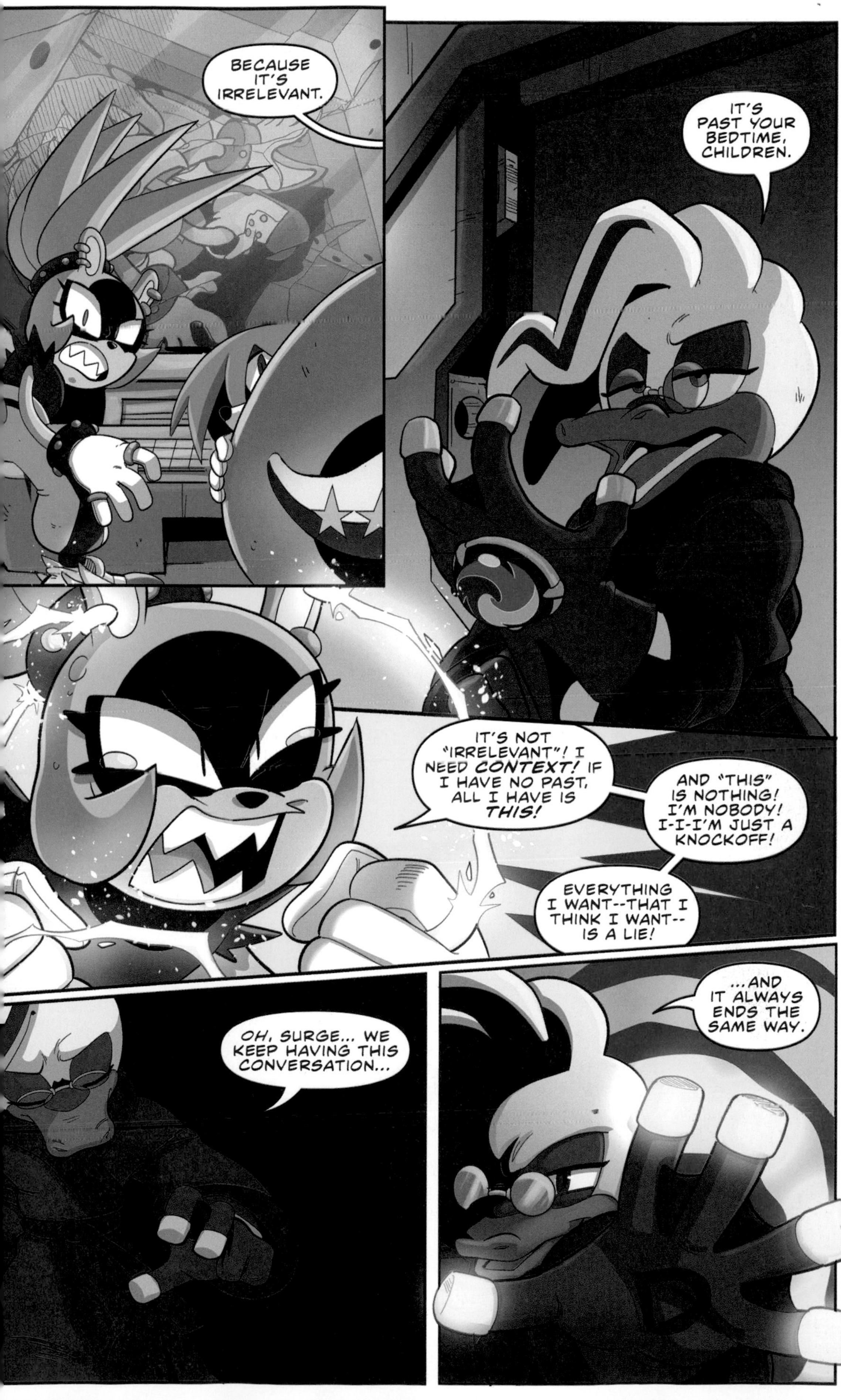
BECAUSE IT'S IRRELEVANT.
IT'S PAST YOUR BEDTIME, CHILDREN.
IT'S NOT "IRRELEVANT"! I NEED *CONTEXT!* IF I HAVE NO PAST, ALL I HAVE IS *THIS!*
AND "THIS" IS NOTHING! I'M NOBODY! I-I-I'M JUST A KNOCKOFF!
EVERYTHING I WANT--THAT I THINK I WANT--IS A LIE!
OH, SURGE... WE KEEP HAVING THIS CONVERSATION...
...AND IT ALWAYS ENDS THE SAME WAY.

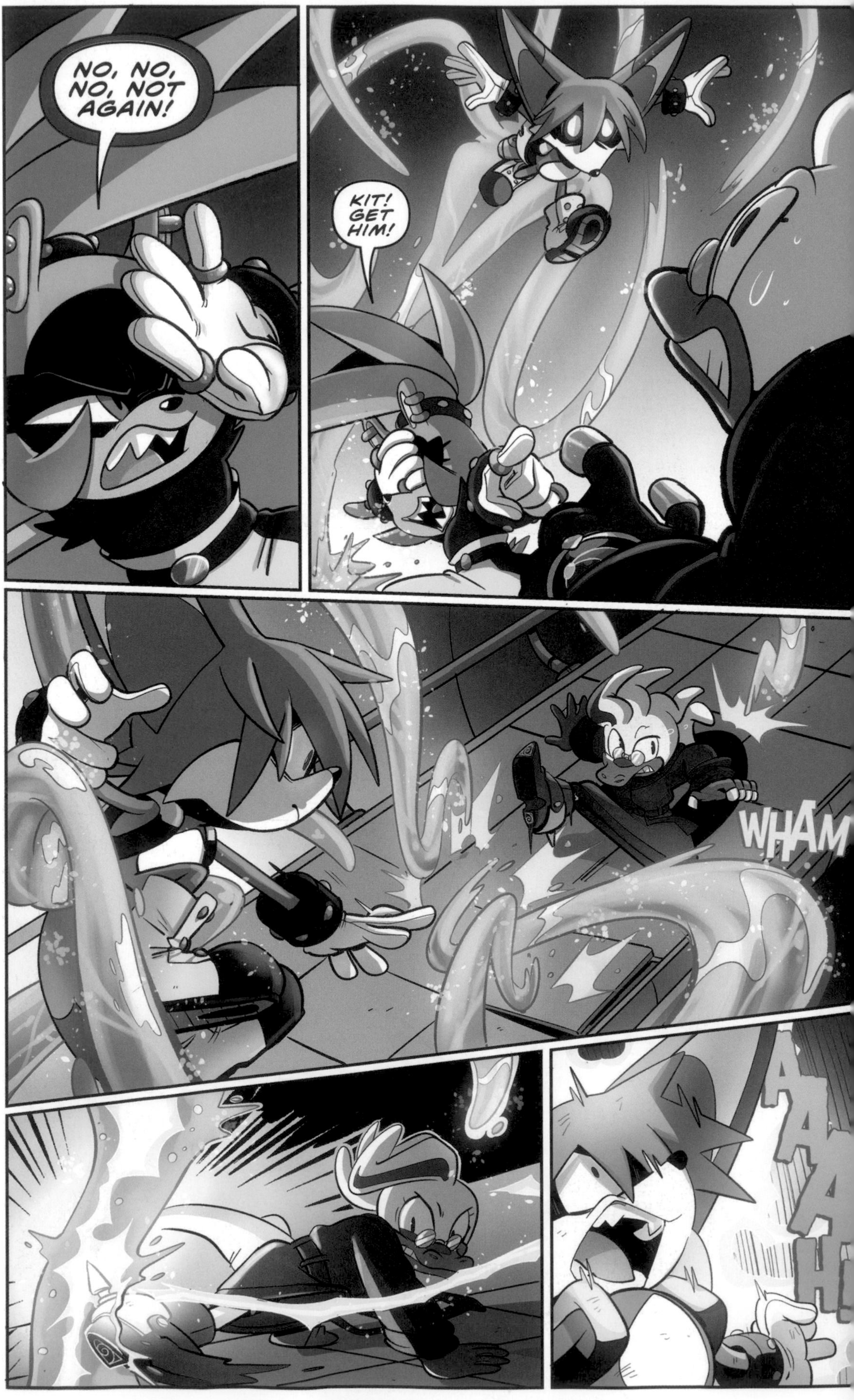
NO, NO, NO, NOT AGAIN!
KIT! GET HIM!
WHAM
AAAH

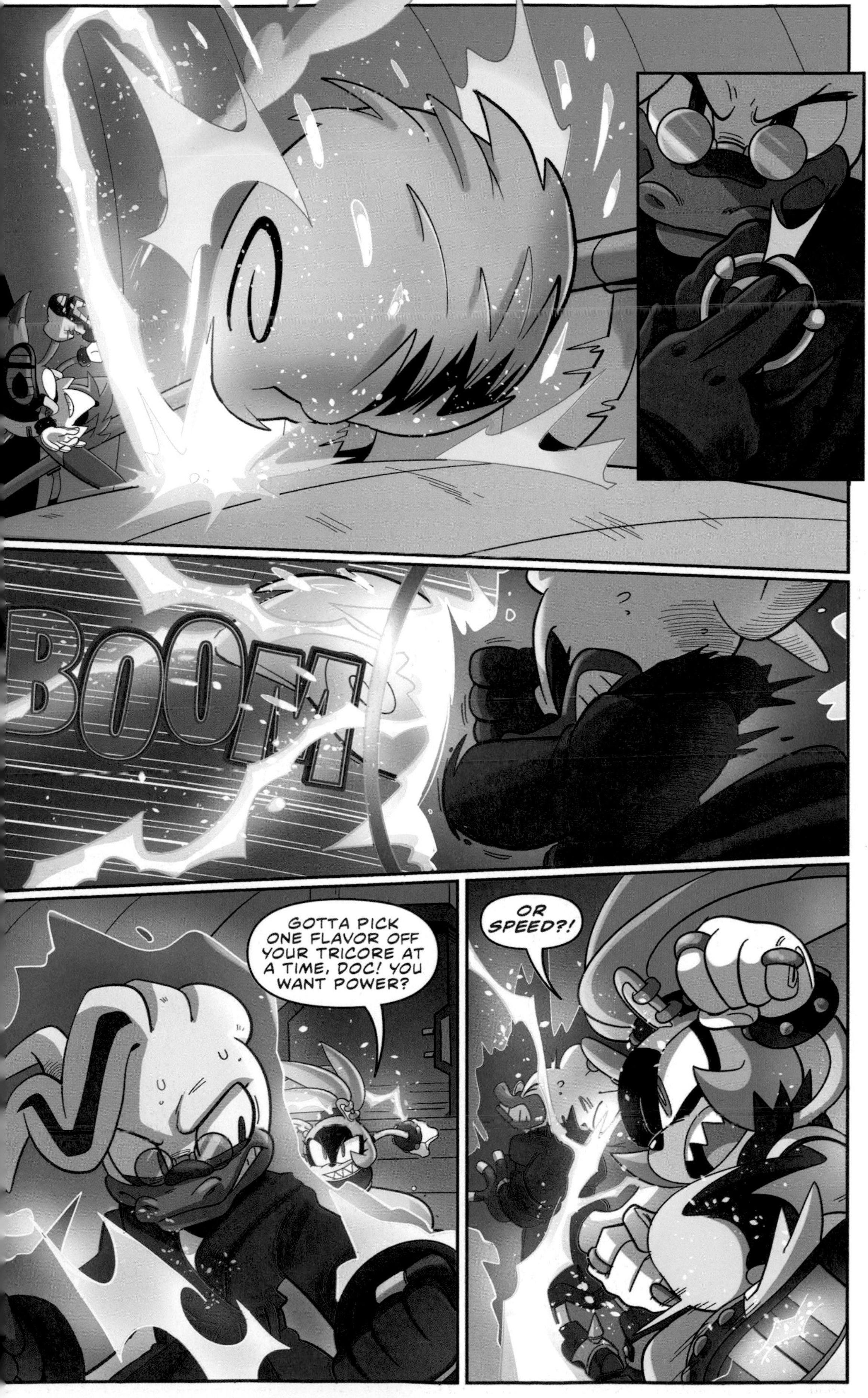
BOOM
GOTTA PICK ONE FLAVOR OFF YOUR TRICORE AT A TIME, DOC! YOU WANT POWER?
OR SPEED?!

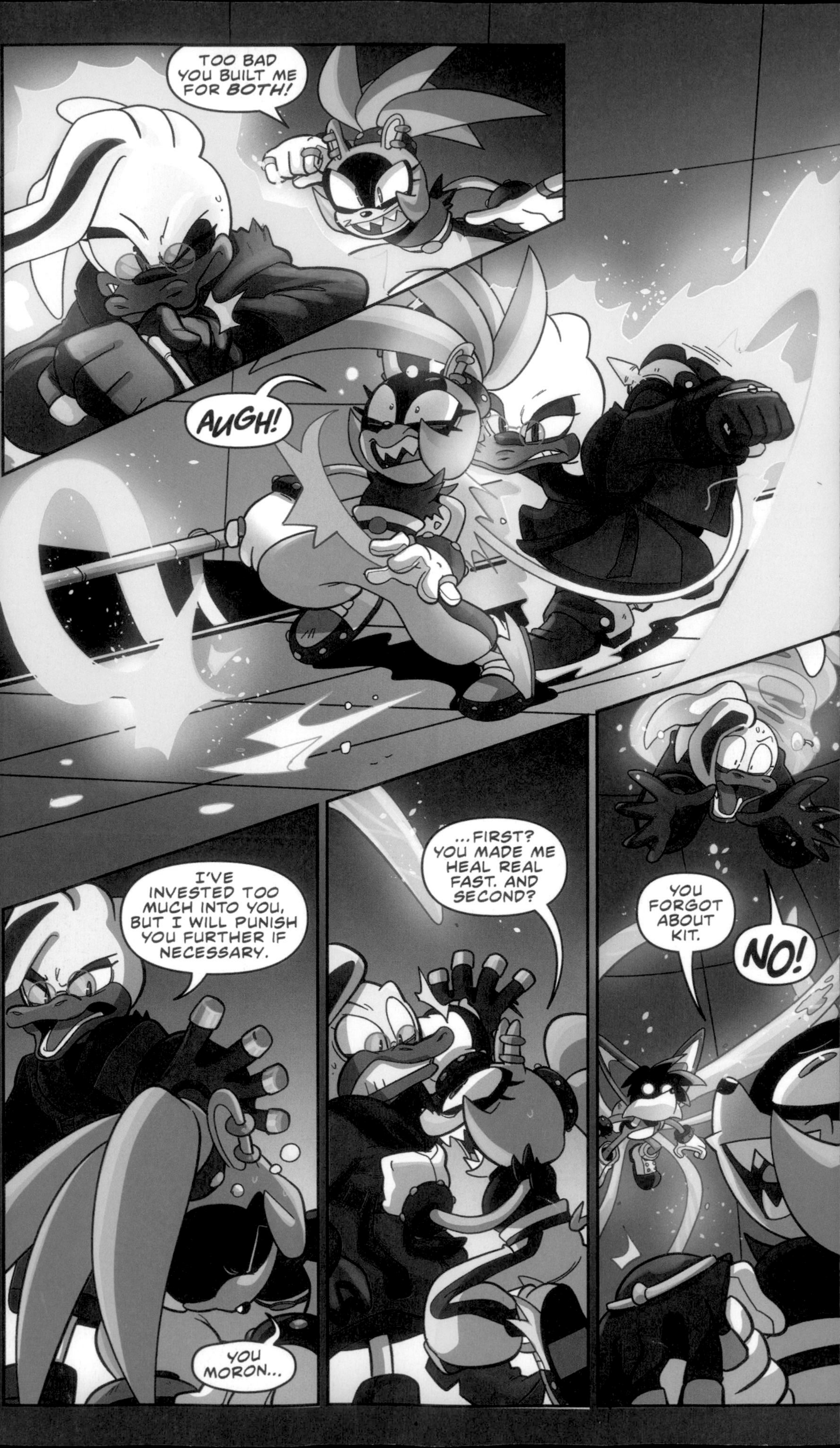
TOO BAD YOU BUILT ME FOR BOTH!
AUGH!
I'VE INVESTED TOO MUCH INTO YOU, BUT I WILL PUNISH YOU FURTHER IF NECESSARY.
YOU MORON...
...FIRST? YOU MADE ME HEAL REAL FAST. AND SECOND?
YOU FORGOT ABOUT KIT.
NO!

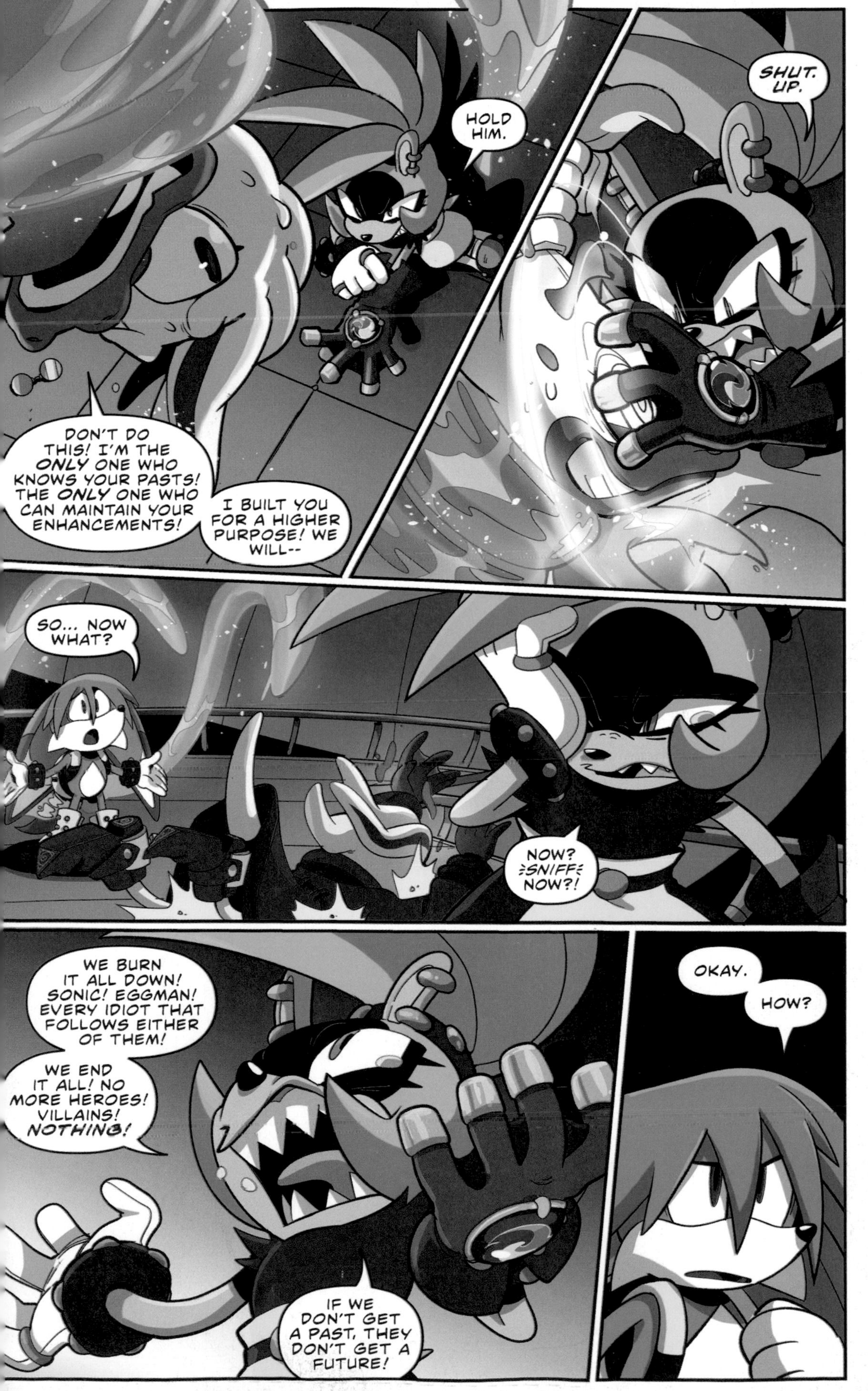
HOLD HIM.
DON'T DO THIS! I'M THE ONLY ONE WHO KNOWS YOUR PASTS! THE ONLY ONE WHO CAN MAINTAIN YOUR ENHANCEMENTS!
I BUILT YOU FOR A HIGHER PURPOSE! WE WILL--
SHUT. UP.
SO... NOW WHAT?
NOW? ≈SNIFF≈ NOW?!
WE BURN IT ALL DOWN! SONIC! EGGMAN! EVERY IDIOT THAT FOLLOWS EITHER OF THEM!
WE END IT ALL! NO MORE HEROES! VILLAINS! NOTHING!
IF WE DON'T GET A PAST, THEY DON'T GET A FUTURE!
OKAY.
HOW?

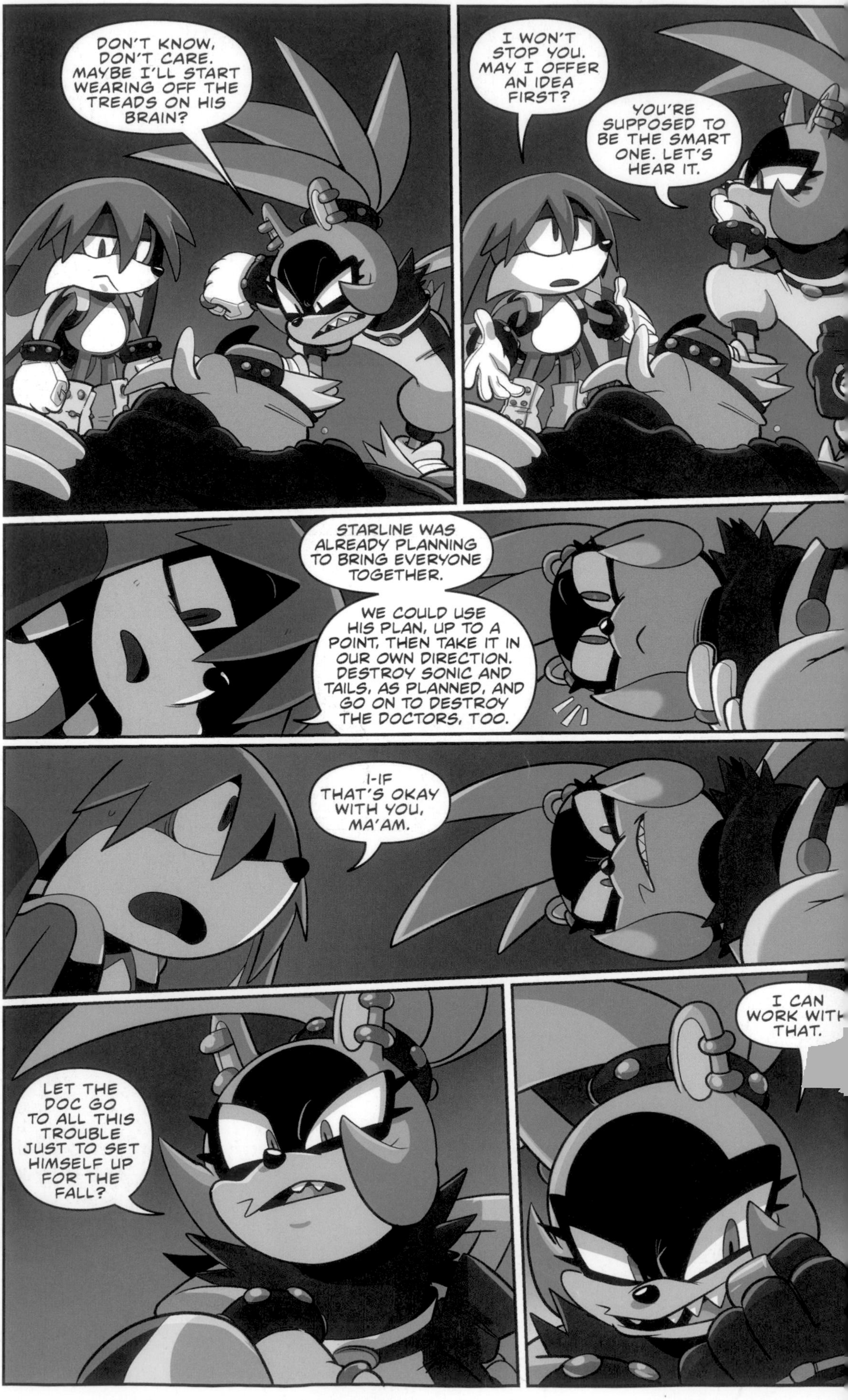
DON'T KNOW, DON'T CARE. MAYBE I'LL START WEARING OFF THE TREADS ON HIS BRAIN?
I WON'T STOP YOU. MAY I OFFER AN IDEA FIRST?
YOU'RE SUPPOSED TO BE THE SMART ONE. LET'S HEAR IT.
STARLINE WAS ALREADY PLANNING TO BRING EVERYONE TOGETHER.
WE COULD USE HIS PLAN, UP TO A POINT, THEN TAKE IT IN OUR OWN DIRECTION. DESTROY SONIC AND TAILS, AS PLANNED, AND GO ON TO DESTROY THE DOCTORS, TOO.
I-IF THAT'S OKAY WITH YOU, MA'AM.
LET THE DOC GO TO ALL THIS TROUBLE JUST TO SET HIMSELF UP FOR THE FALL?
I CAN WORK WITH THAT.

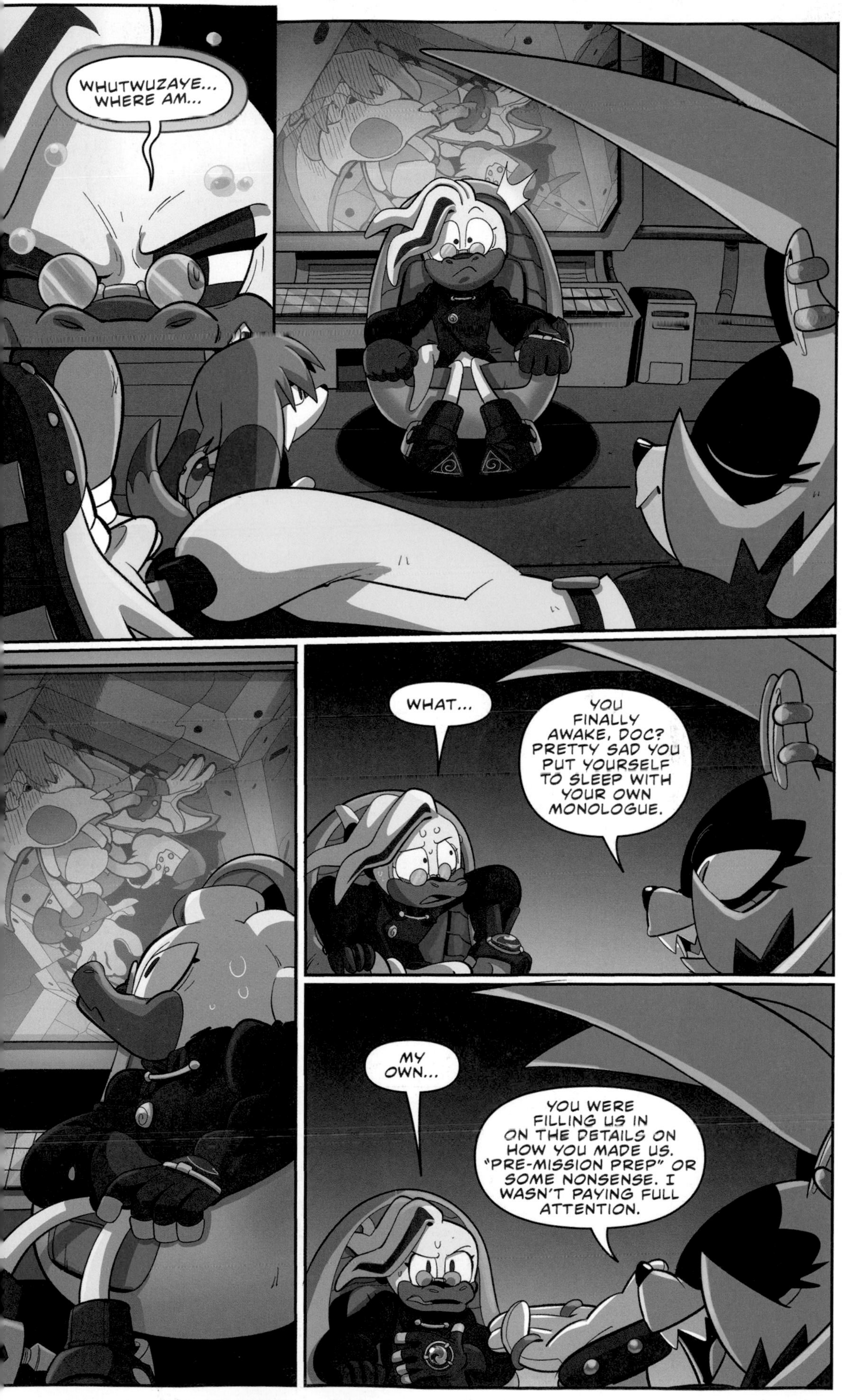
WHUTWUZAYE... WHERE AM...
WHAT...
YOU FINALLY AWAKE, DOC? PRETTY SAD YOU PUT YOURSELF TO SLEEP WITH YOUR OWN MONOLOGUE.
MY OWN...
YOU WERE FILLING US IN ON THE DETAILS ON HOW YOU MADE US. "PRE-MISSION PREP" OR SOME NONSENSE. I WASN'T PAYING FULL ATTENTION.

I DID?

SURE DID.

AND YOU'RE... FINE WITH THIS?

WELL, IF I WASN'T BEFORE, I'M PRETTY SURE YOU WIPED THAT OUTTA MY BRAIN.

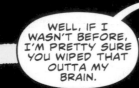

YOU MADE US POWERHOUSES. WHO AM I TO COMPLAIN?

ALL I HAVE TO DO TO GET A LIFETIME OF HERO WORSHIP IS DUST SOME EGO-DRIVEN JERK, RIGHT?

EASY SELL.

KIT'S COOL WITH IT, TOO. RIGHT, KID?

YES, MA'AM.

HE IS BECAUSE I SAY HE IS.

YES, MA'AM.

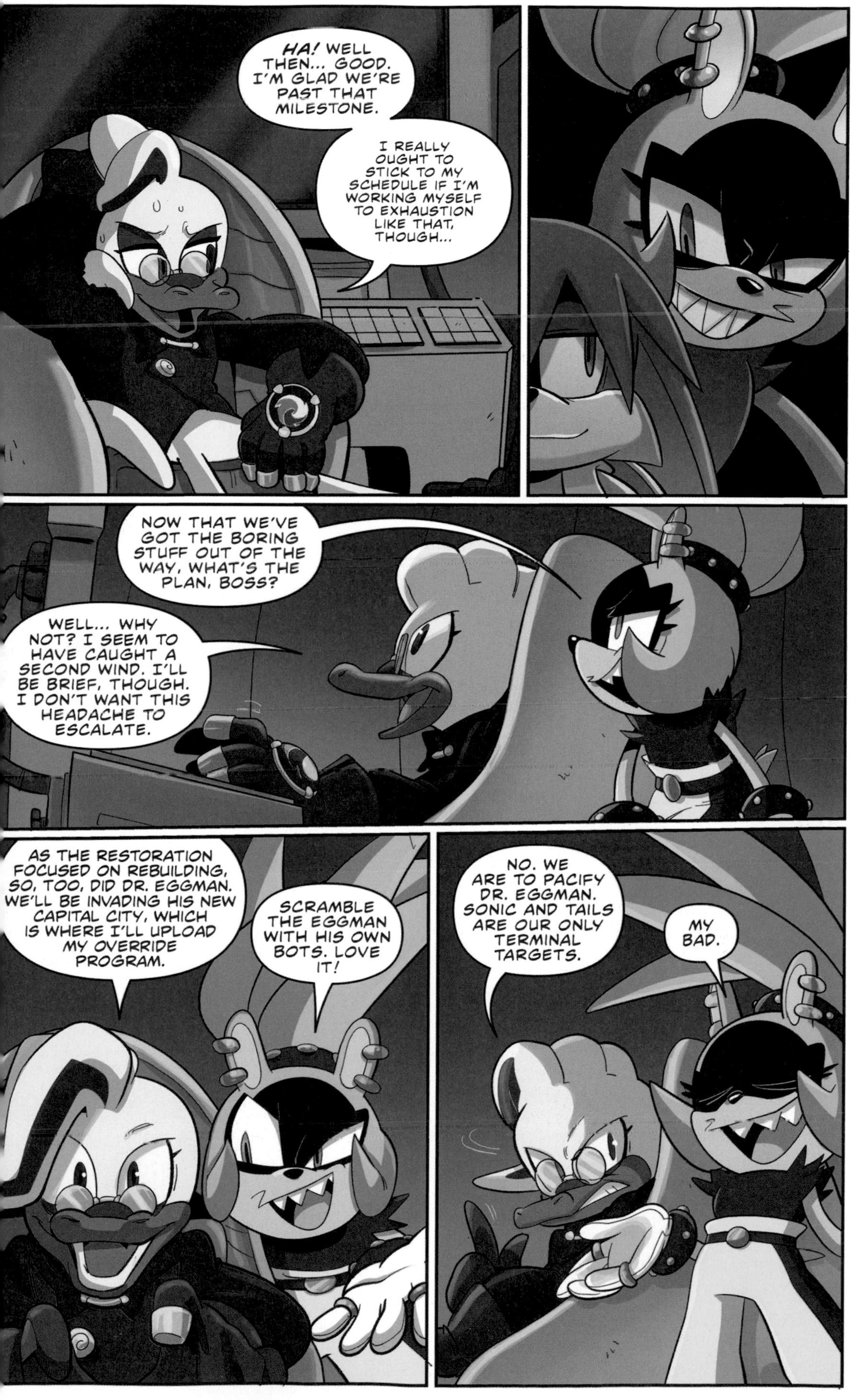
HA! WELL THEN... GOOD. I'M GLAD WE'RE PAST THAT MILESTONE.
I REALLY OUGHT TO STICK TO MY SCHEDULE IF I'M WORKING MYSELF TO EXHAUSTION LIKE THAT, THOUGH...
NOW THAT WE'VE GOT THE BORING STUFF OUT OF THE WAY, WHAT'S THE PLAN, BOSS?
WELL... WHY NOT? I SEEM TO HAVE CAUGHT A SECOND WIND. I'LL BE BRIEF, THOUGH. I DON'T WANT THIS HEADACHE TO ESCALATE.
AS THE RESTORATION FOCUSED ON REBUILDING, SO, TOO, DID DR. EGGMAN. WE'LL BE INVADING HIS NEW CAPITAL CITY, WHICH IS WHERE I'LL UPLOAD MY OVERRIDE PROGRAM.
SCRAMBLE THE EGGMAN WITH HIS OWN BOTS. LOVE IT!
NO. WE ARE TO PACIFY DR. EGGMAN. SONIC AND TAILS ARE OUR ONLY TERMINAL TARGETS.
MY BAD.

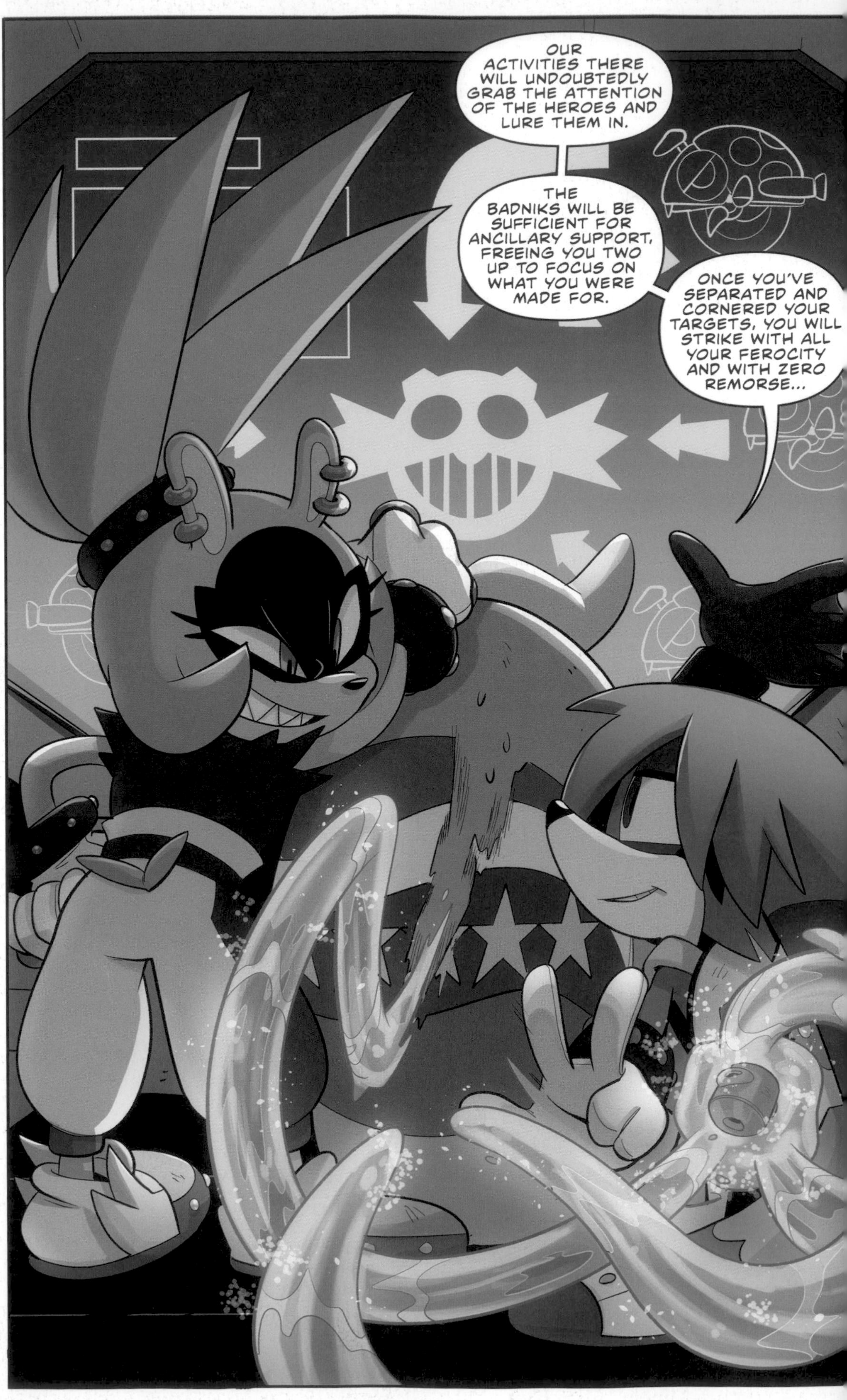
OUR ACTIVITIES THERE WILL UNDOUBTEDLY GRAB THE ATTENTION OF THE HEROES AND LURE THEM IN.
THE BADNIKS WILL BE SUFFICIENT FOR ANCILLARY SUPPORT, FREEING YOU TWO UP TO FOCUS ON WHAT YOU WERE MADE FOR.
ONCE YOU'VE SEPARATED AND CORNERED YOUR TARGETS, YOU WILL STRIKE WITH ALL YOUR FEROCITY AND WITH ZERO REMORSE...

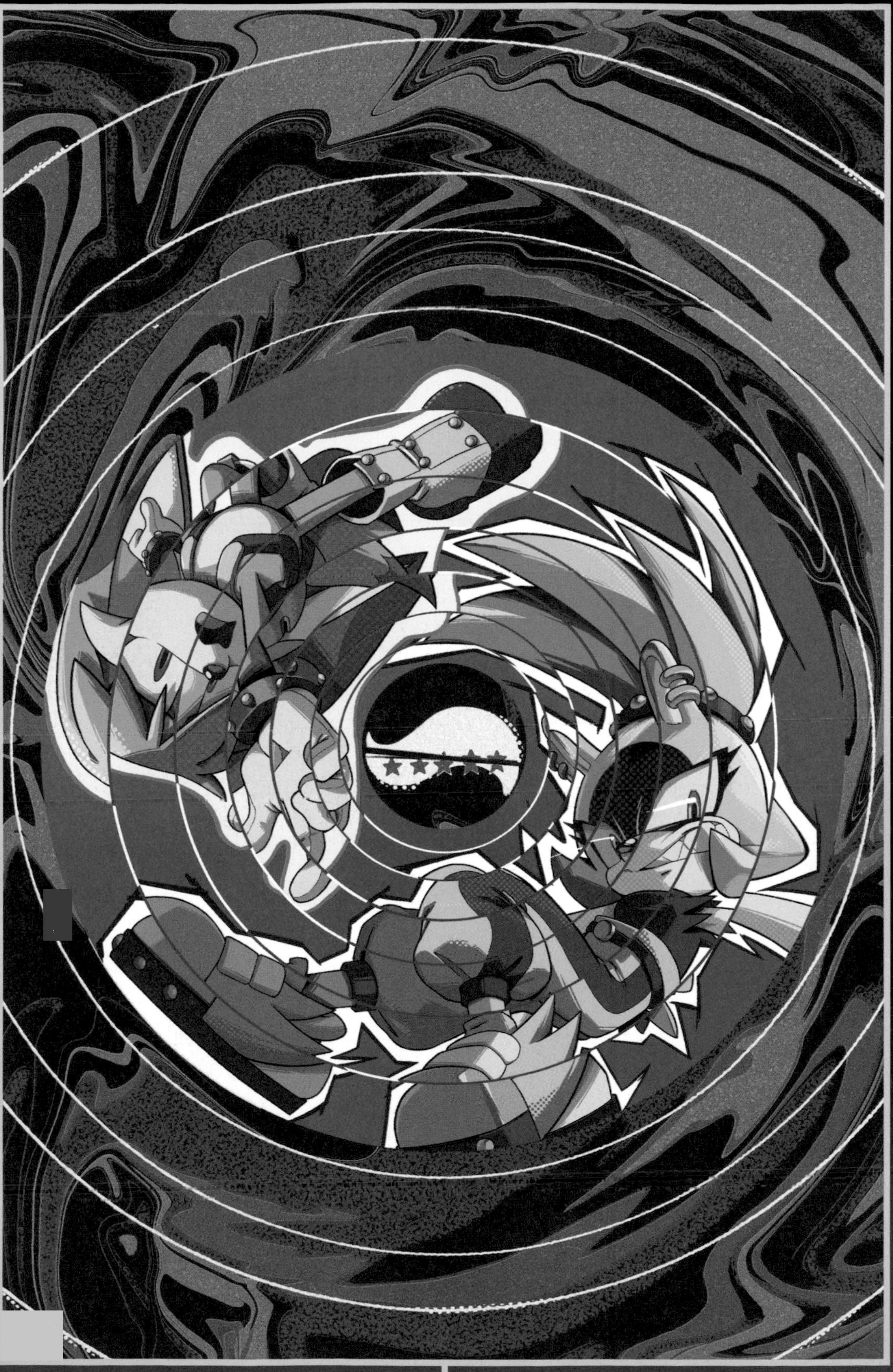

ART BRACARDI CURRY

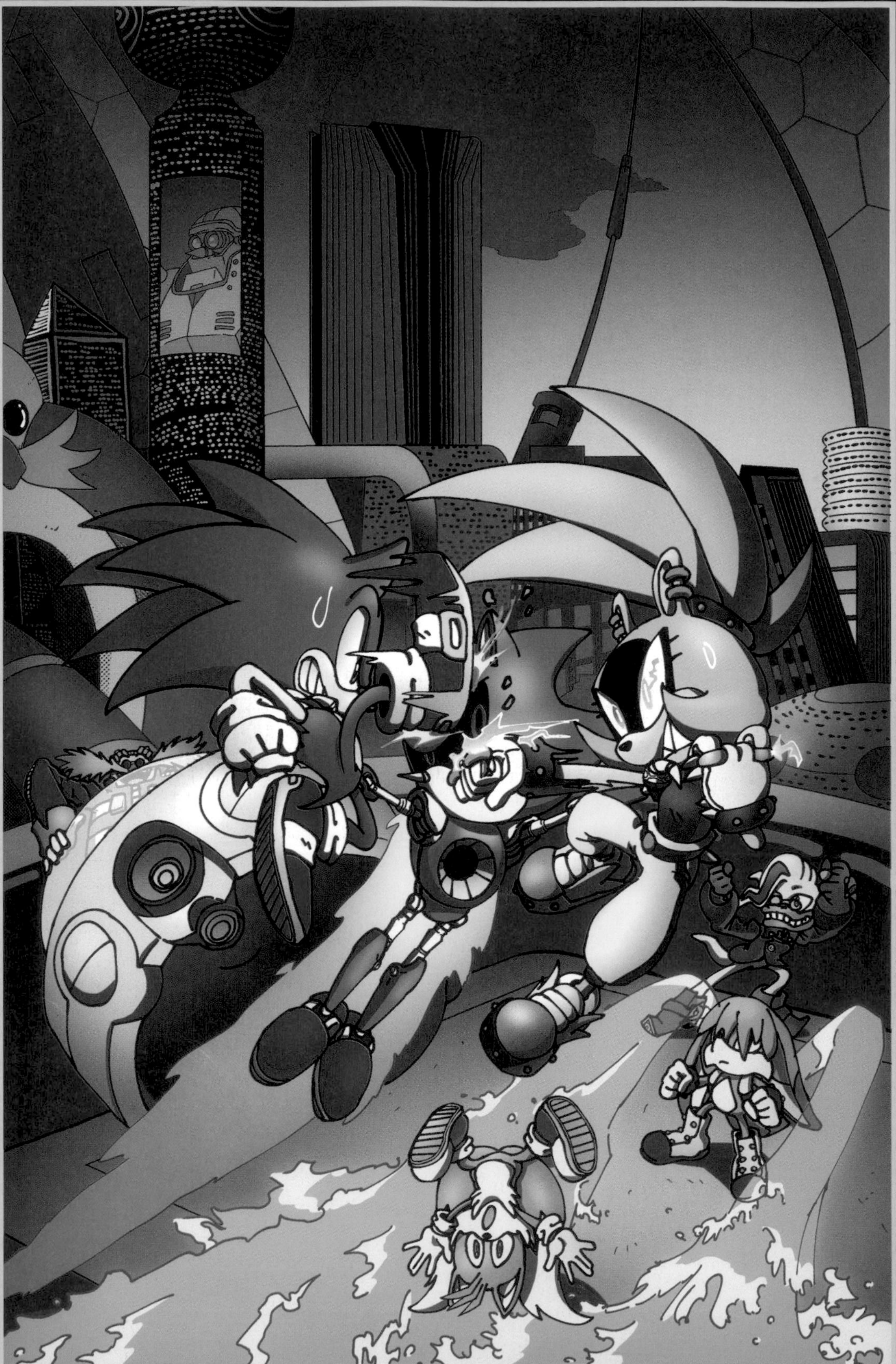

ART MAURO FONSECA COLORS JOANA LAFUENTE

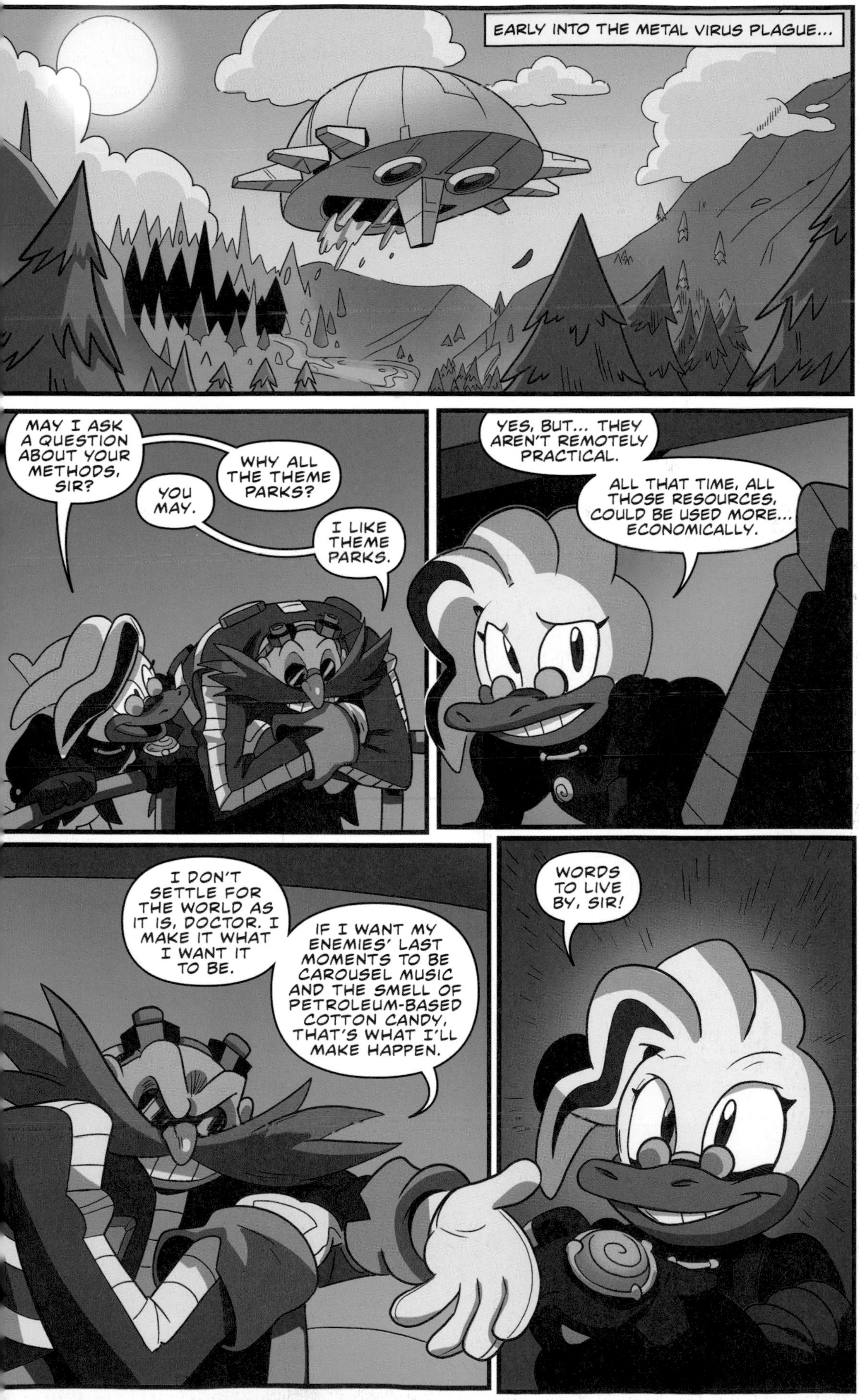
EARLY INTO THE METAL VIRUS PLAGUE...
MAY I ASK A QUESTION ABOUT YOUR METHODS, SIR?
YOU MAY.
WHY ALL THE THEME PARKS?
I LIKE THEME PARKS.
YES, BUT... THEY AREN'T REMOTELY PRACTICAL.
ALL THAT TIME, ALL THOSE RESOURCES, COULD BE USED MORE... ECONOMICALLY.
I DON'T SETTLE FOR THE WORLD AS IT IS, DOCTOR. I MAKE IT WHAT I WANT IT TO BE.
IF I WANT MY ENEMIES' LAST MOMENTS TO BE CAROUSEL MUSIC AND THE SMELL OF PETROLEUM-BASED COTTON CANDY, THAT'S WHAT I'LL MAKE HAPPEN.
WORDS TO LIVE BY, SIR!

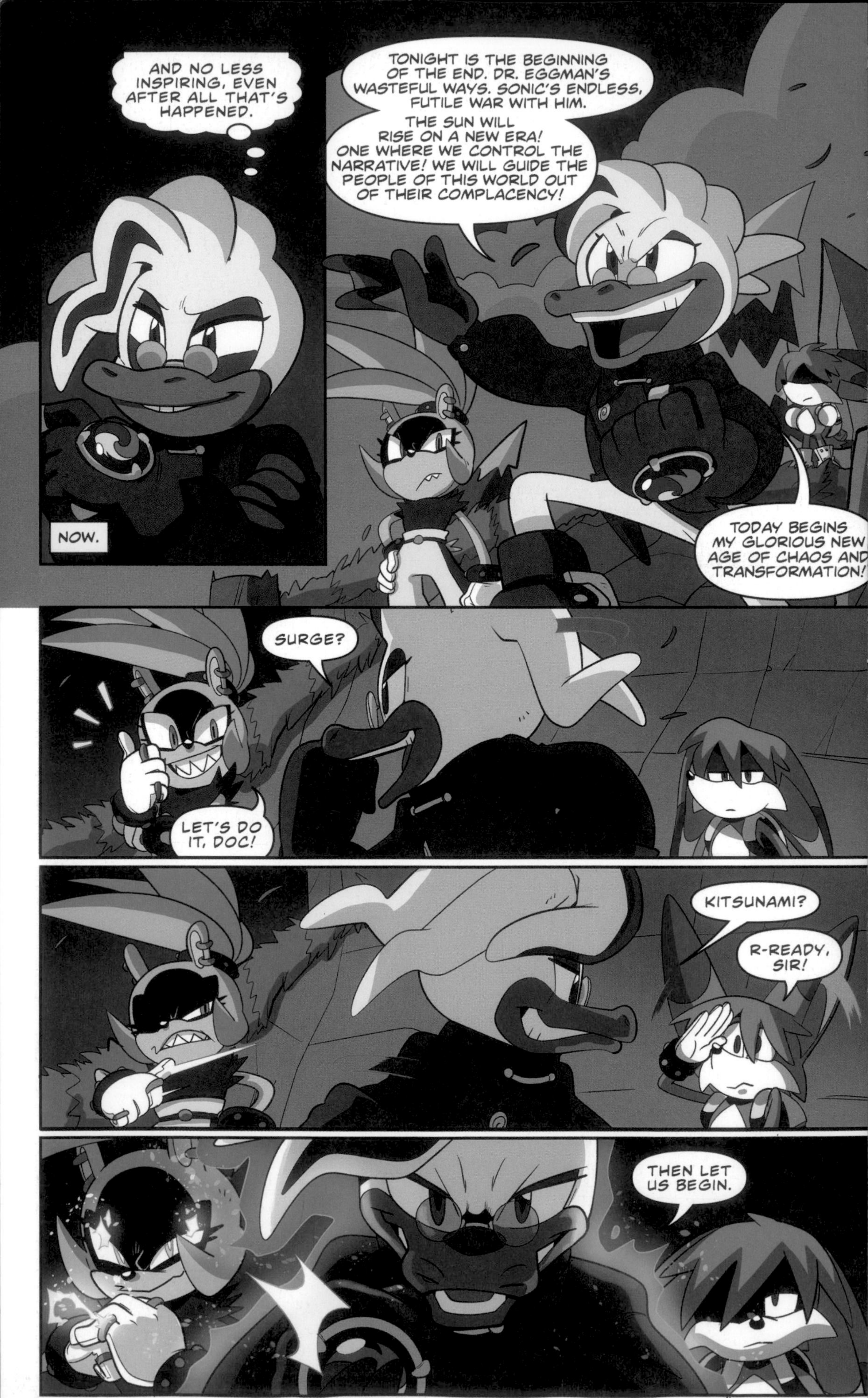
AND NO LESS INSPIRING, EVEN AFTER ALL THAT'S HAPPENED.
NOW.
TONIGHT IS THE BEGINNING OF THE END. DR. EGGMAN'S WASTEFUL WAYS. SONIC'S ENDLESS, FUTILE WAR WITH HIM.
THE SUN WILL RISE ON A NEW ERA! ONE WHERE WE CONTROL THE NARRATIVE! WE WILL GUIDE THE PEOPLE OF THIS WORLD OUT OF THEIR COMPLACENCY!
TODAY BEGINS MY GLORIOUS NEW AGE OF CHAOS AND TRANSFORMATION!
SURGE?
LET'S DO IT, DOC!
KITSUNAMI?
R-READY, SIR!
THEN LET US BEGIN.

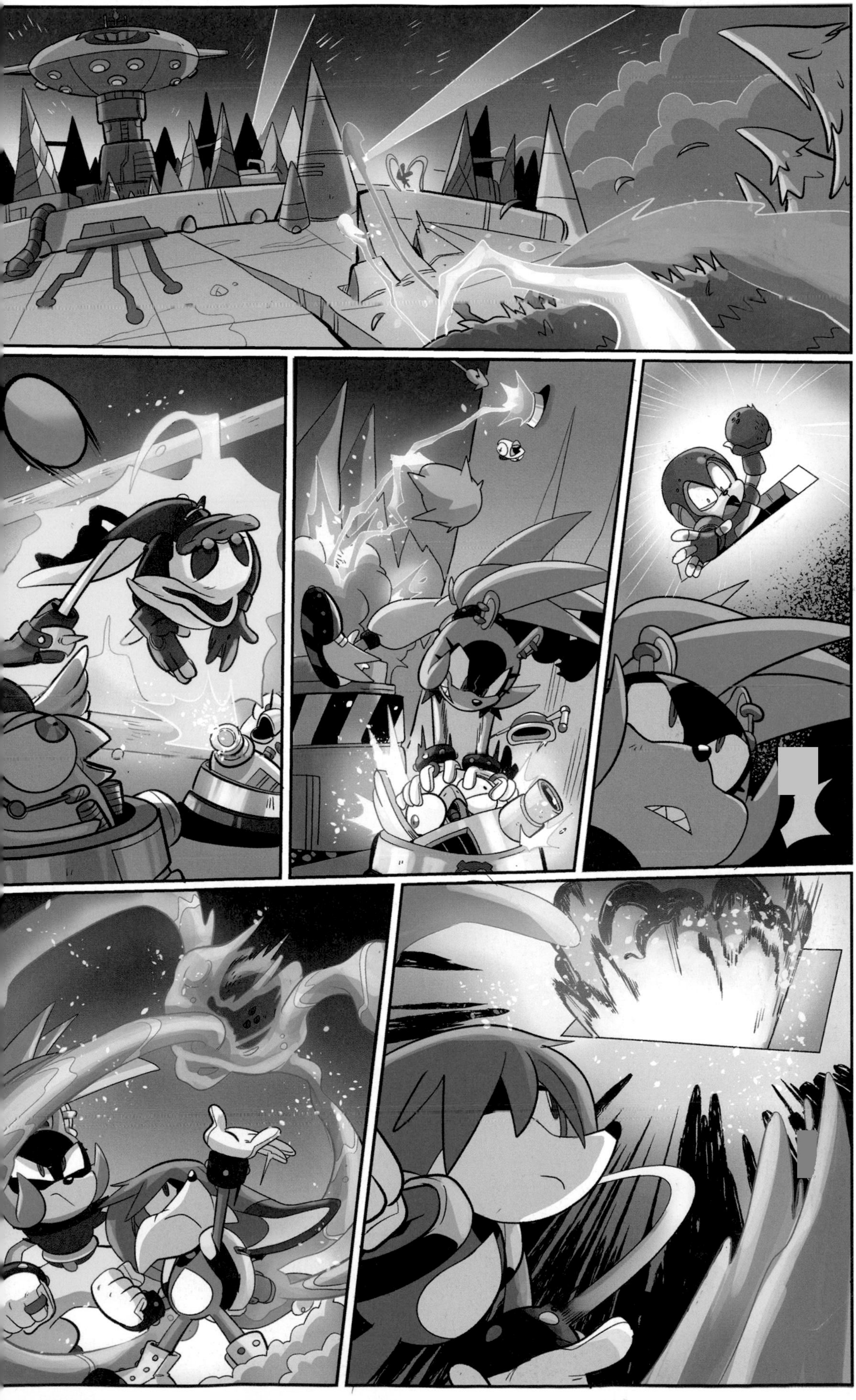

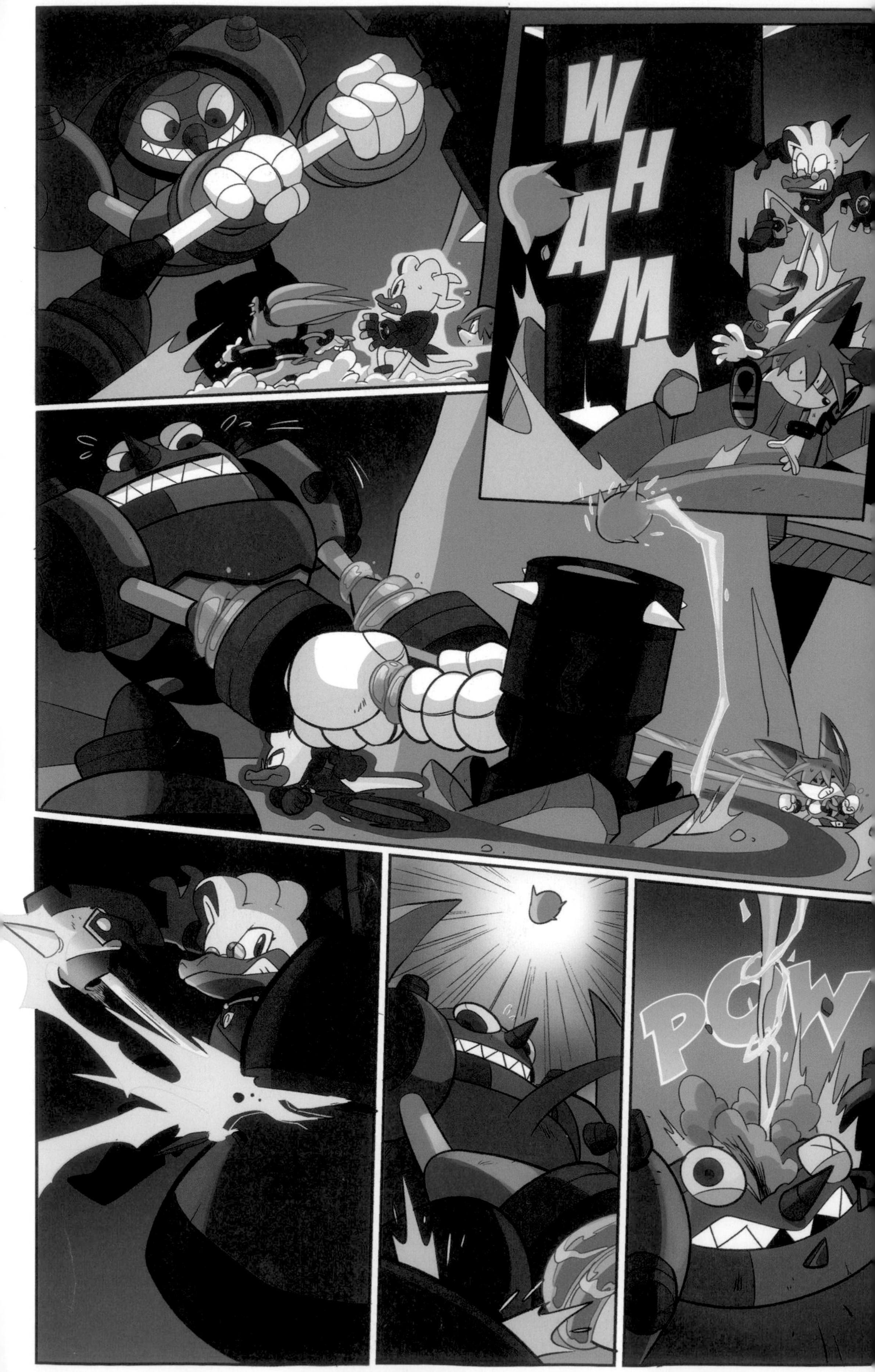
WHAM
POW

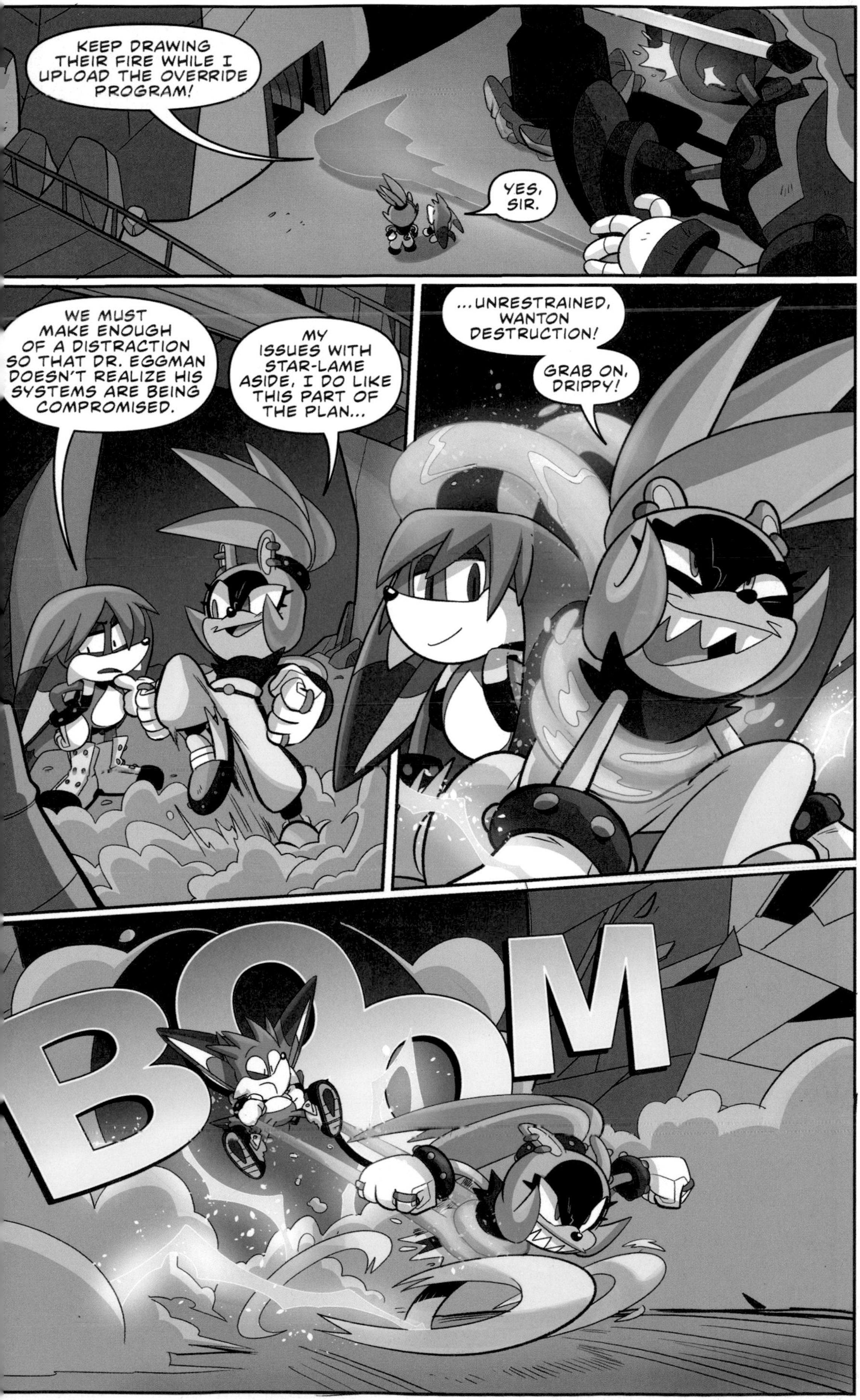
KEEP DRAWING THEIR FIRE WHILE I UPLOAD THE OVERRIDE PROGRAM!
YES, SIR.
WE MUST MAKE ENOUGH OF A DISTRACTION SO THAT DR. EGGMAN DOESN'T REALIZE HIS SYSTEMS ARE BEING COMPROMISED.
MY ISSUES WITH STAR-LAME ASIDE, I DO LIKE THIS PART OF THE PLAN...
...UNRESTRAINED, WANTON DESTRUCTION!
GRAB ON, DRIPPY!
BOOM

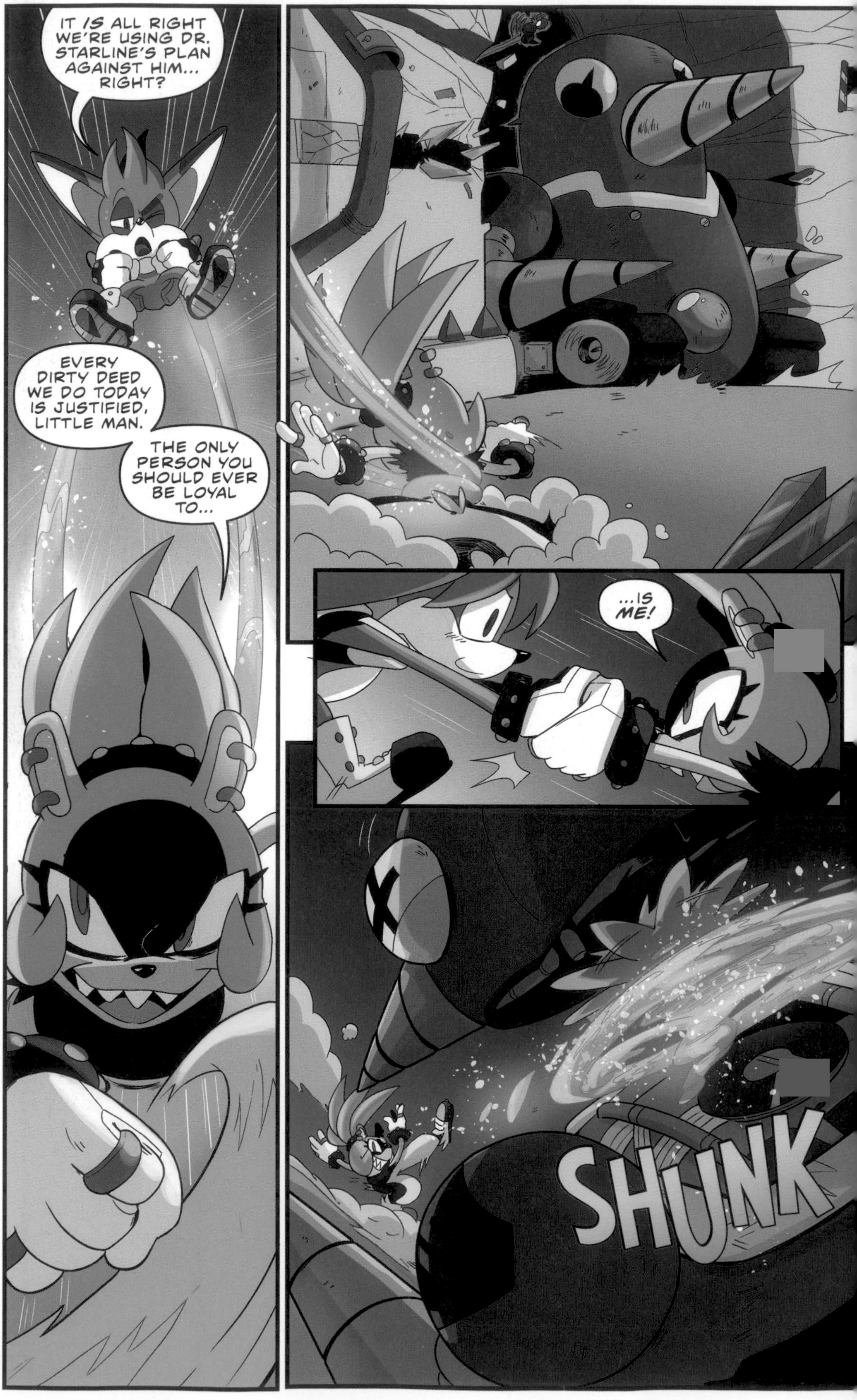
IT *IS* ALL RIGHT WE'RE USING DR. STARLINE'S PLAN AGAINST HIM... RIGHT?
EVERY DIRTY DEED WE DO TODAY IS JUSTIFIED, LITTLE MAN.
THE ONLY PERSON YOU SHOULD EVER BE LOYAL TO...
...IS *ME!*
SHUNK

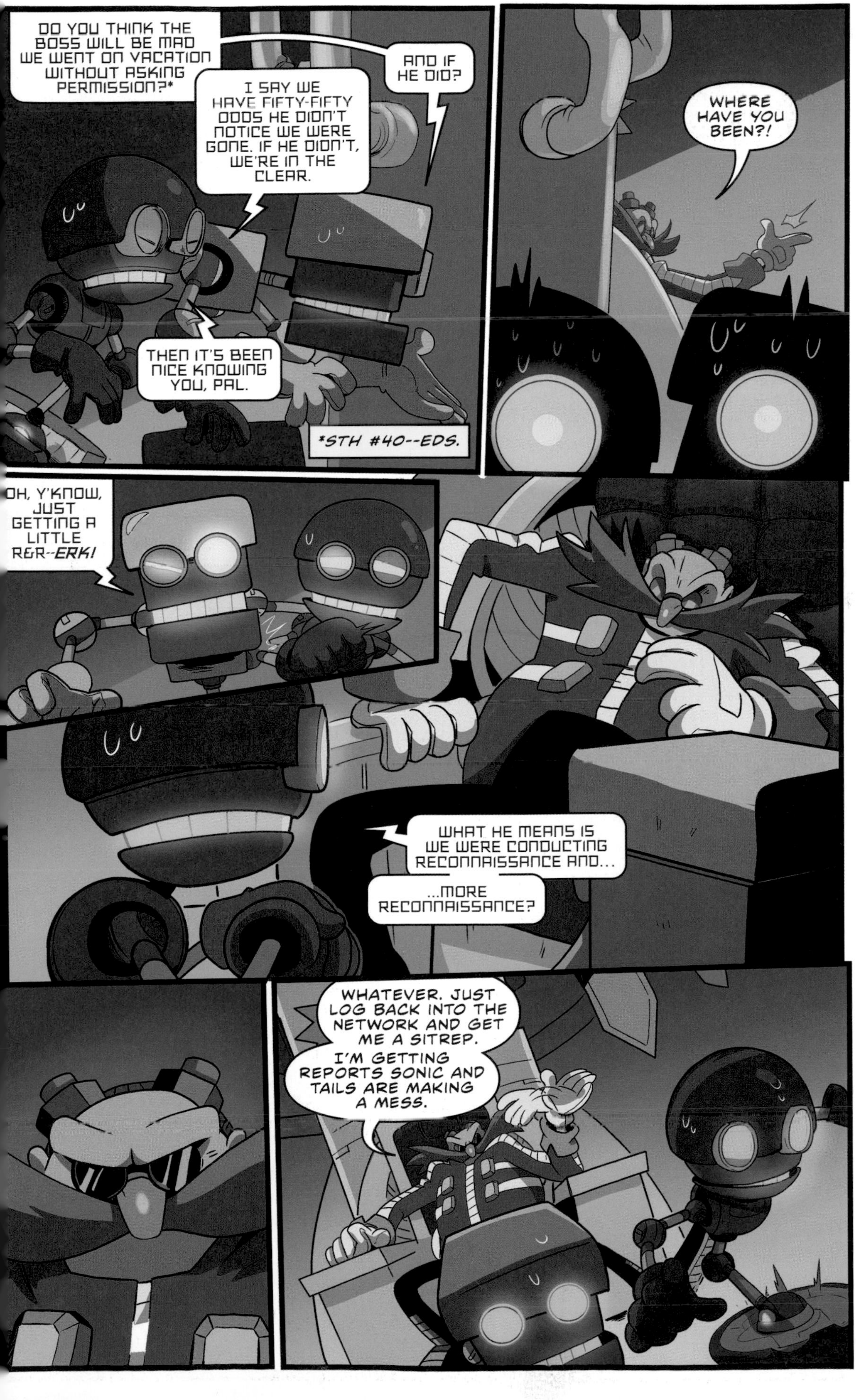
DO YOU THINK THE BOSS WILL BE MAD WE WENT ON VACATION WITHOUT ASKING PERMISSION?*
I SAY WE HAVE FIFTY-FIFTY ODDS HE DIDN'T NOTICE WE WERE GONE. IF HE DIDN'T, WE'RE IN THE CLEAR.
AND IF HE DID?
THEN IT'S BEEN NICE KNOWING YOU, PAL.
*STH #40--EDS.
WHERE HAVE YOU BEEN?!
OH, Y'KNOW, JUST GETTING A LITTLE R&R--ERK!
WHAT HE MEANS IS WE WERE CONDUCTING RECONNAISSANCE AND...
...MORE RECONNAISSANCE?
WHATEVER. JUST LOG BACK INTO THE NETWORK AND GET ME A SITREP.
I'M GETTING REPORTS SONIC AND TAILS ARE MAKING A MESS.

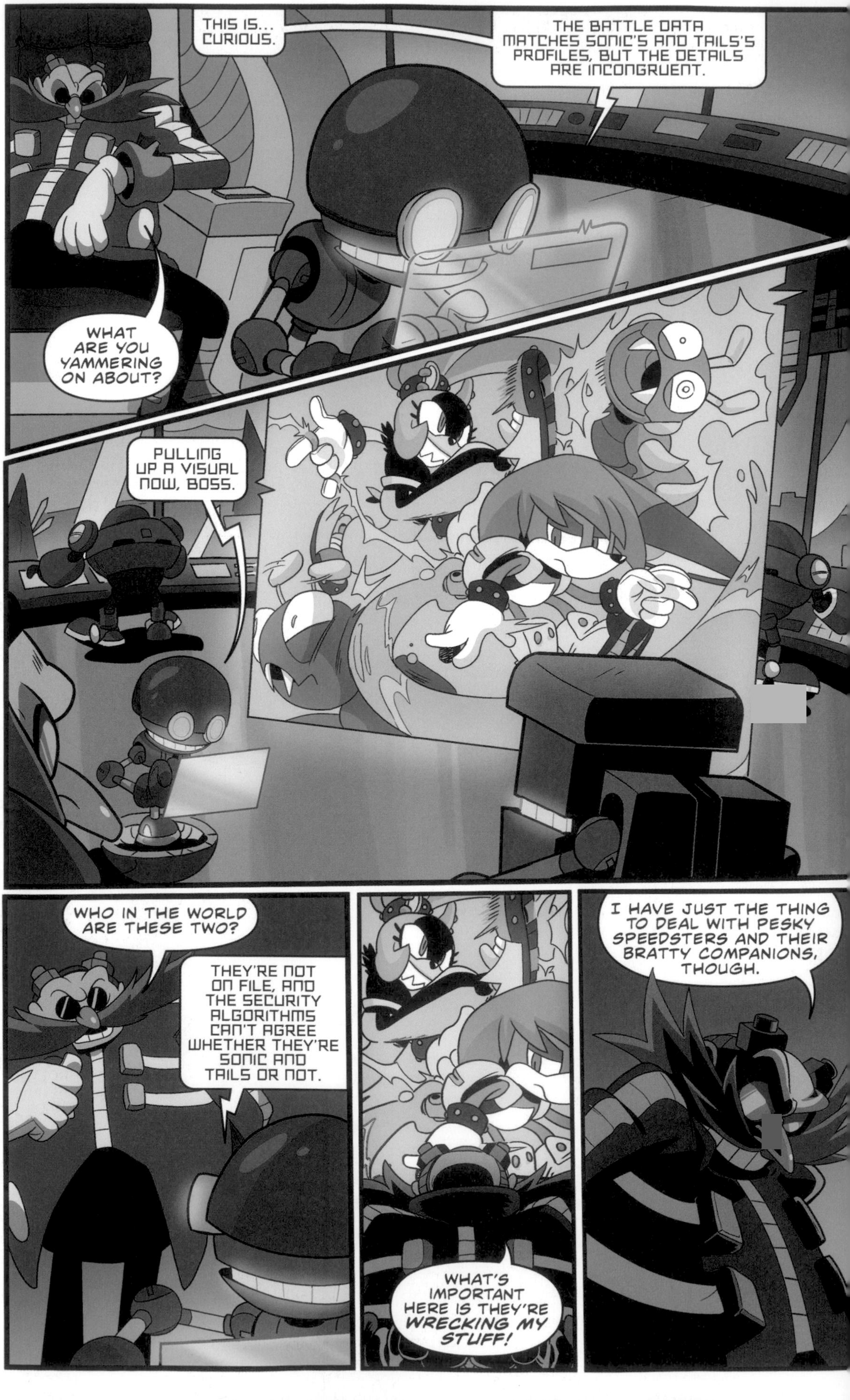
THIS IS... CURIOUS.
THE BATTLE DATA MATCHES SONIC'S AND TAILS'S PROFILES, BUT THE DETAILS ARE INCONGRUENT.
WHAT ARE YOU YAMMERING ON ABOUT?
PULLING UP A VISUAL NOW, BOSS.
WHO IN THE WORLD ARE THESE TWO?
THEY'RE NOT ON FILE, AND THE SECURITY ALGORITHMS CAN'T AGREE WHETHER THEY'RE SONIC AND TAILS OR NOT.
WHAT'S IMPORTANT HERE IS THEY'RE *WRECKING MY STUFF!*
I HAVE JUST THE THING TO DEAL WITH PESKY SPEEDSTERS AND THEIR BRATTY COMPANIONS, THOUGH.

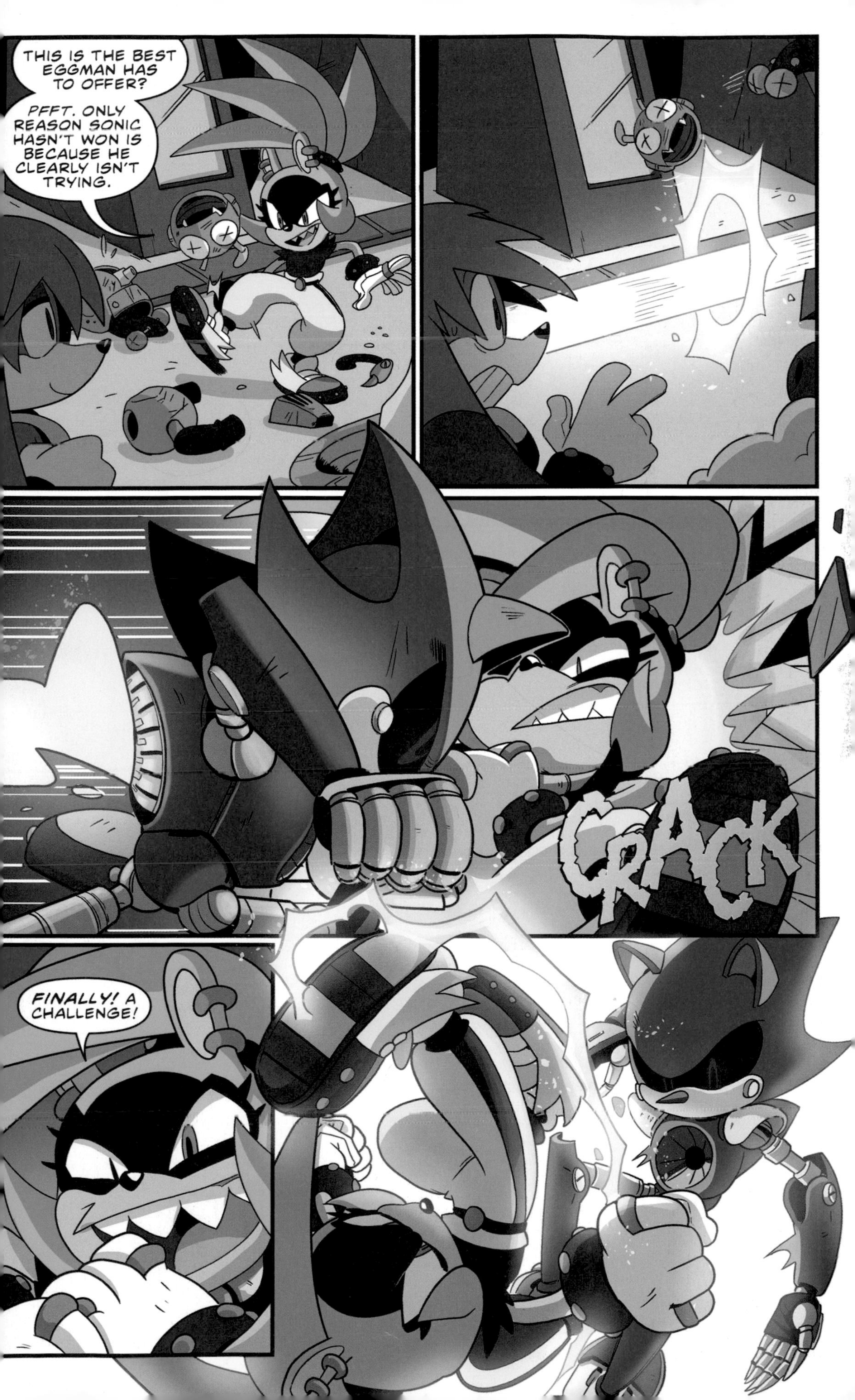
THIS IS THE BEST EGGMAN HAS TO OFFER?
PFFT. ONLY REASON SONIC HASN'T WON IS BECAUSE HE CLEARLY ISN'T TRYING.
CRACK
FINALLY! A CHALLENGE!

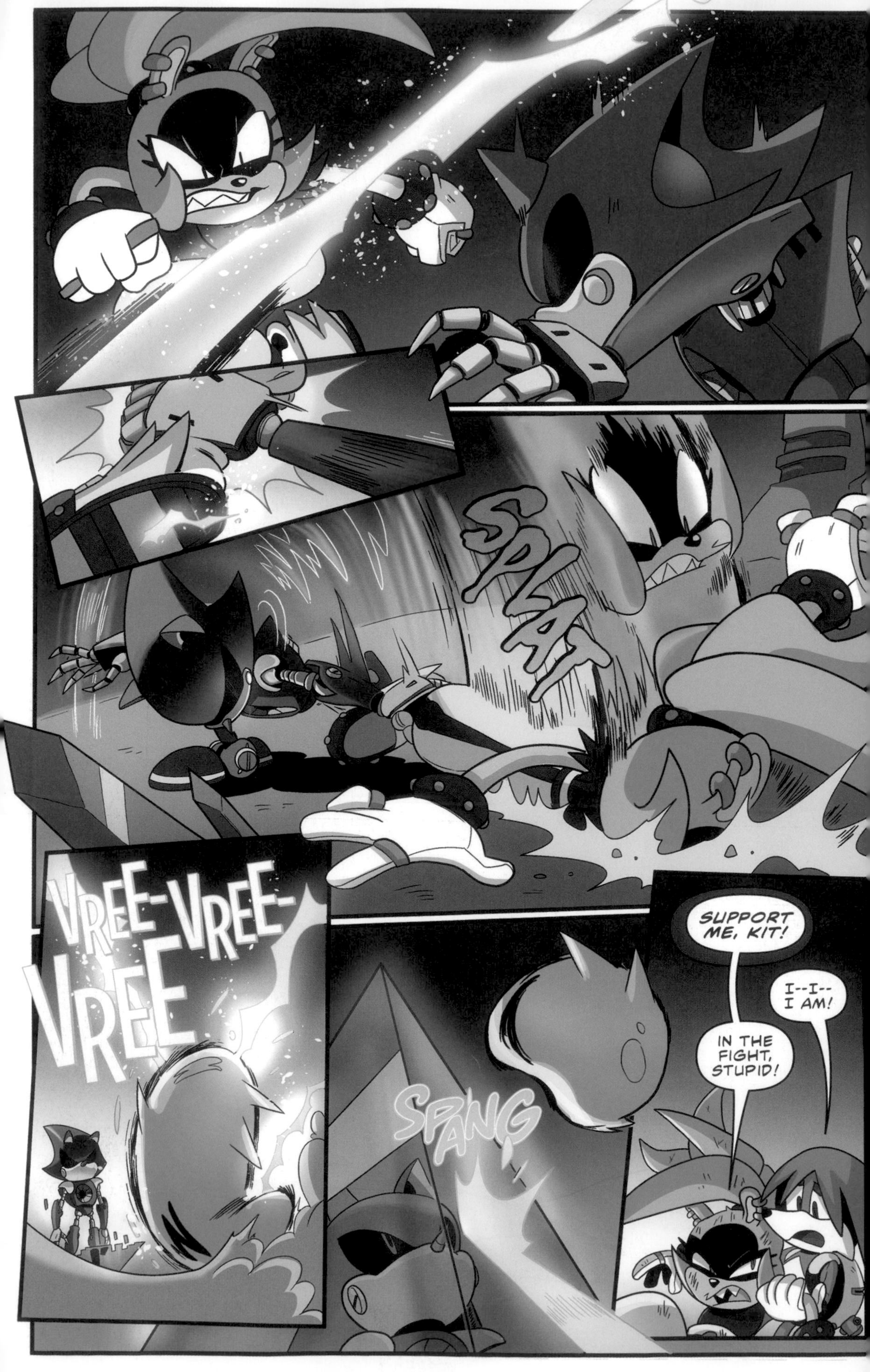
SPLAT
VREE-VREE-VREE
SPANG
SUPPORT ME, KIT!
IN THE FIGHT, STUPID!
I--I--I AM!

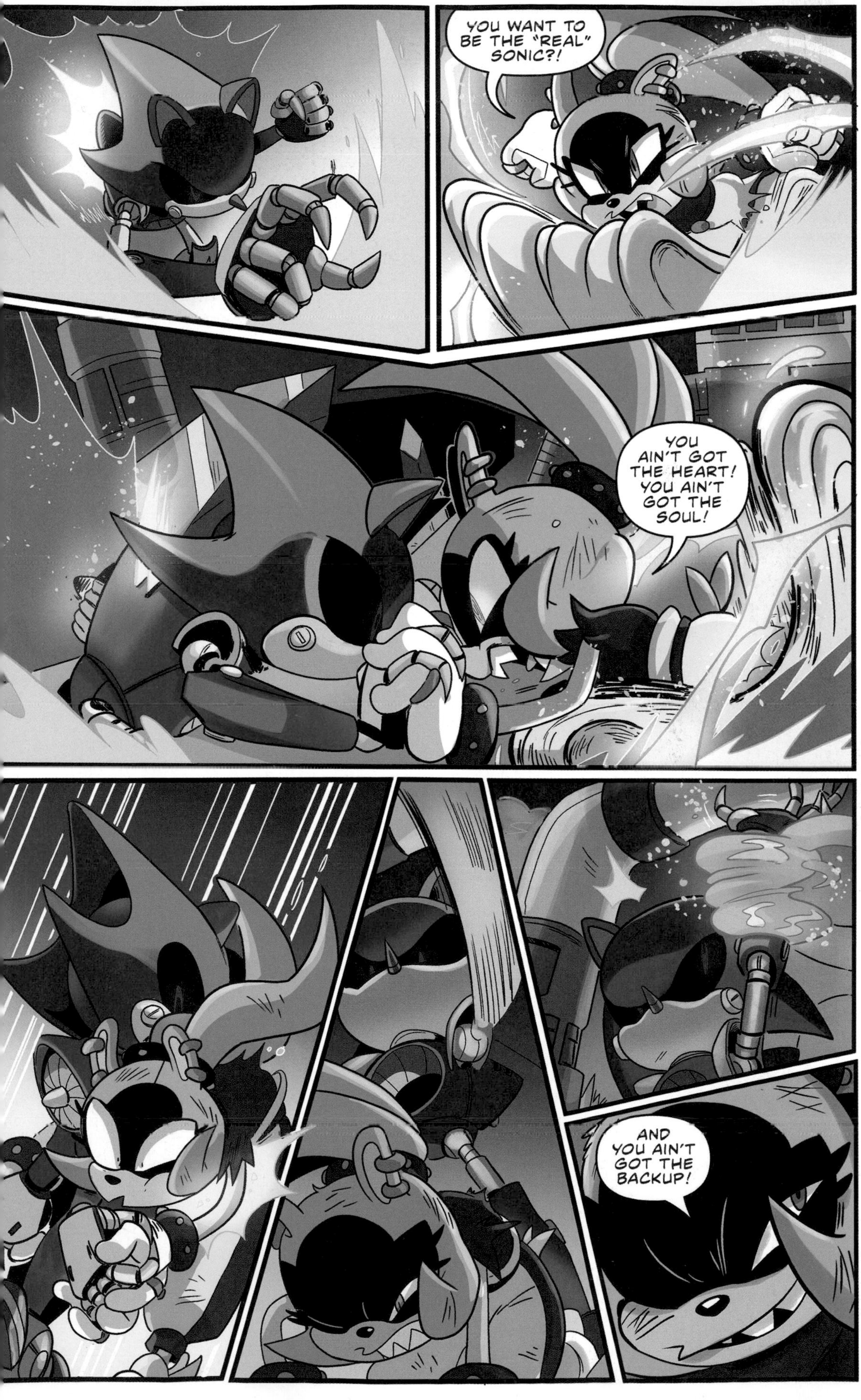
YOU WANT TO BE THE "REAL" SONIC?!
YOU AIN'T GOT THE HEART! YOU AIN'T GOT THE SOUL!
AND YOU AIN'T GOT THE BACKUP!

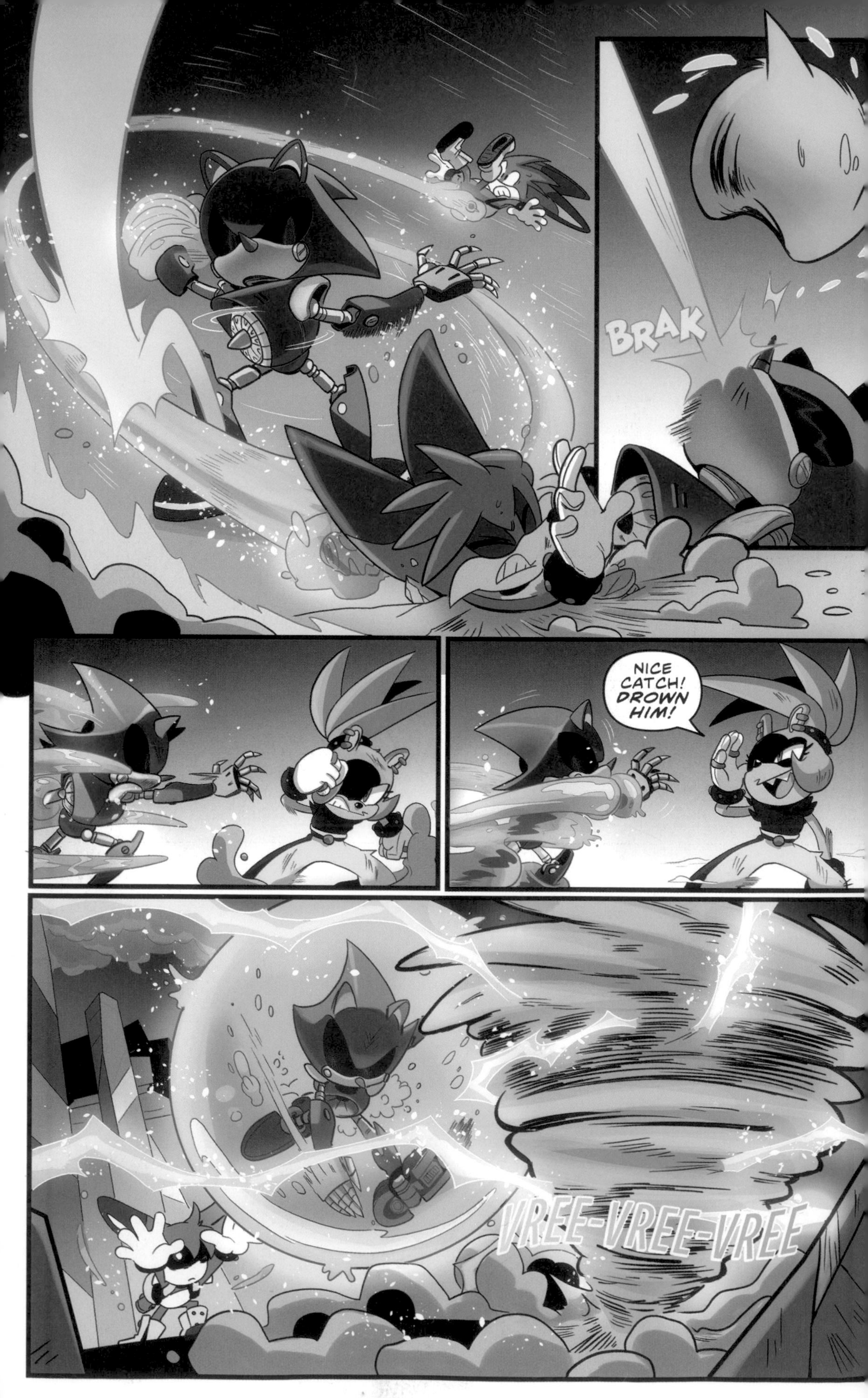
BRAK
NICE CATCH! DROWN HIM!
VREE-VREE-VREE

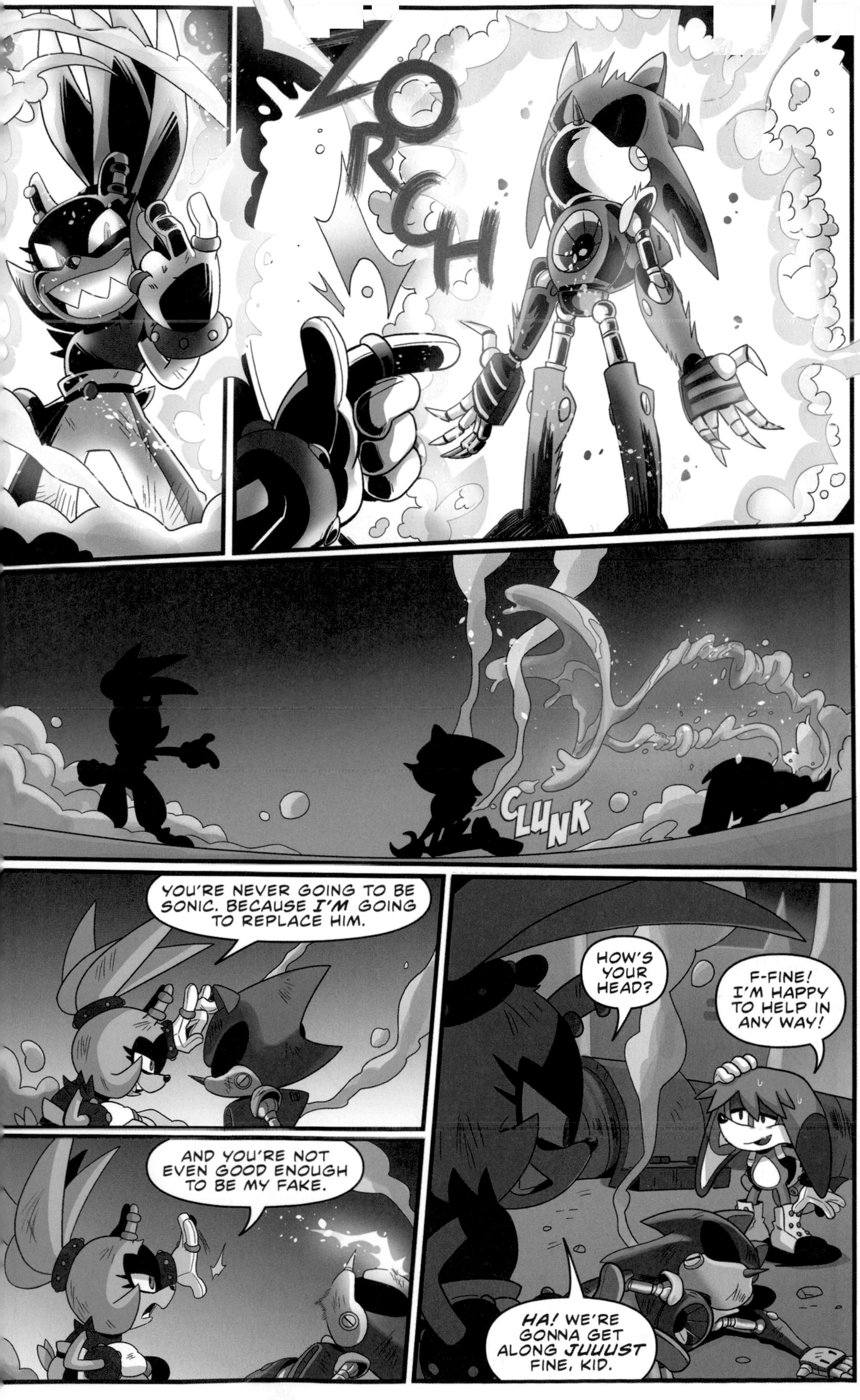
ZORCH
CLUNK
YOU'RE NEVER GOING TO BE SONIC. BECAUSE *I'M* GOING TO REPLACE HIM.
AND YOU'RE NOT EVEN GOOD ENOUGH TO BE MY FAKE.
HOW'S YOUR HEAD?
F-FINE! I'M HAPPY TO HELP IN ANY WAY!
HA! WE'RE GONNA GET ALONG *JUUUST* FINE, KID.

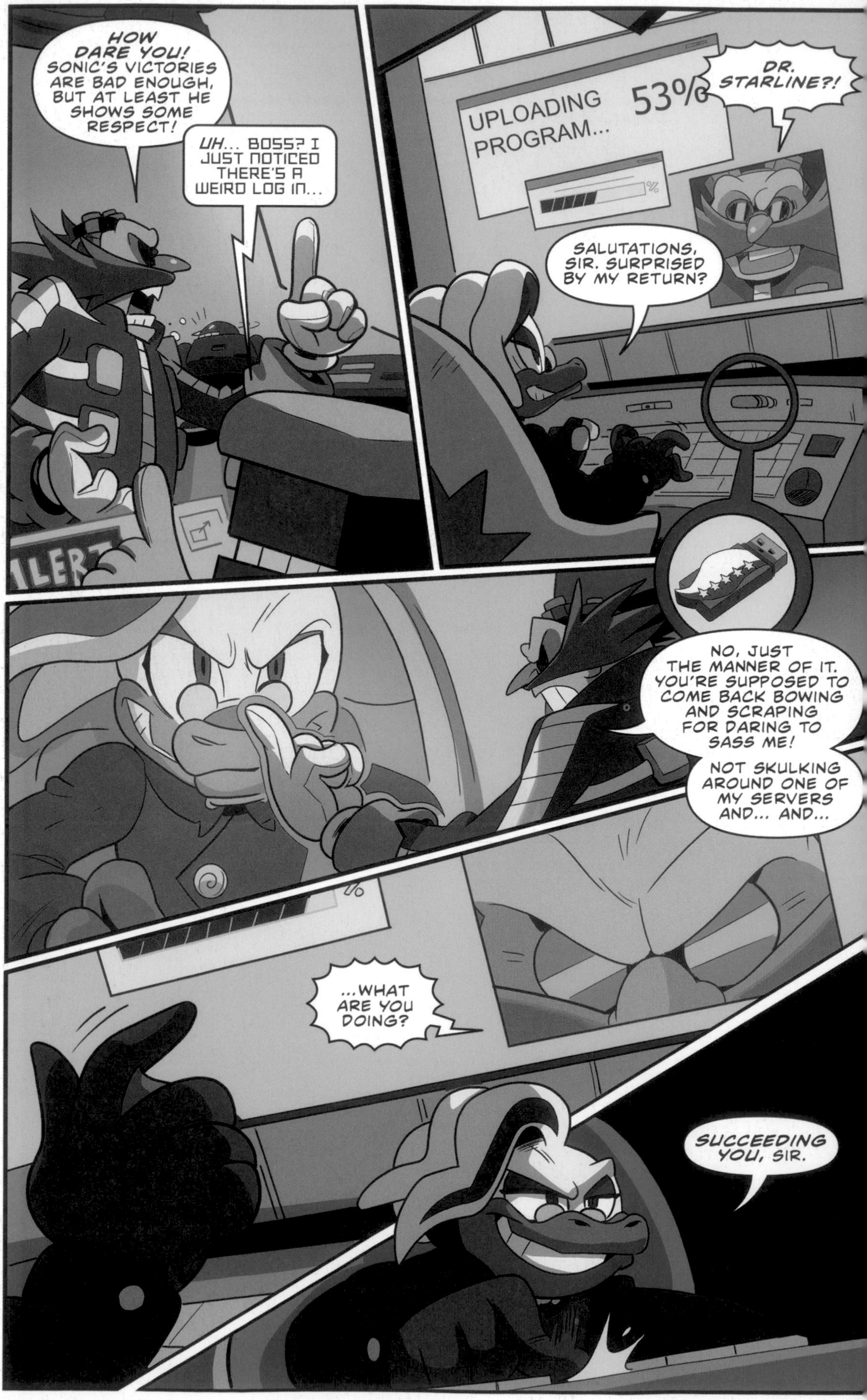
HOW DARE YOU! SONIC'S VICTORIES ARE BAD ENOUGH, BUT AT LEAST HE SHOWS SOME RESPECT!
UH... BOSS? I JUST NOTICED THERE'S A WEIRD LOG IN...
ALERT
UPLOADING PROGRAM...
53%
DR. STARLINE?!
SALUTATIONS, SIR. SURPRISED BY MY RETURN?
NO, JUST THE MANNER OF IT. YOU'RE SUPPOSED TO COME BACK BOWING AND SCRAPING FOR DARING TO SASS ME!
NOT SKULKING AROUND ONE OF MY SERVERS AND... AND...
...WHAT ARE YOU DOING?
SUCCEEDING YOU, SIR.

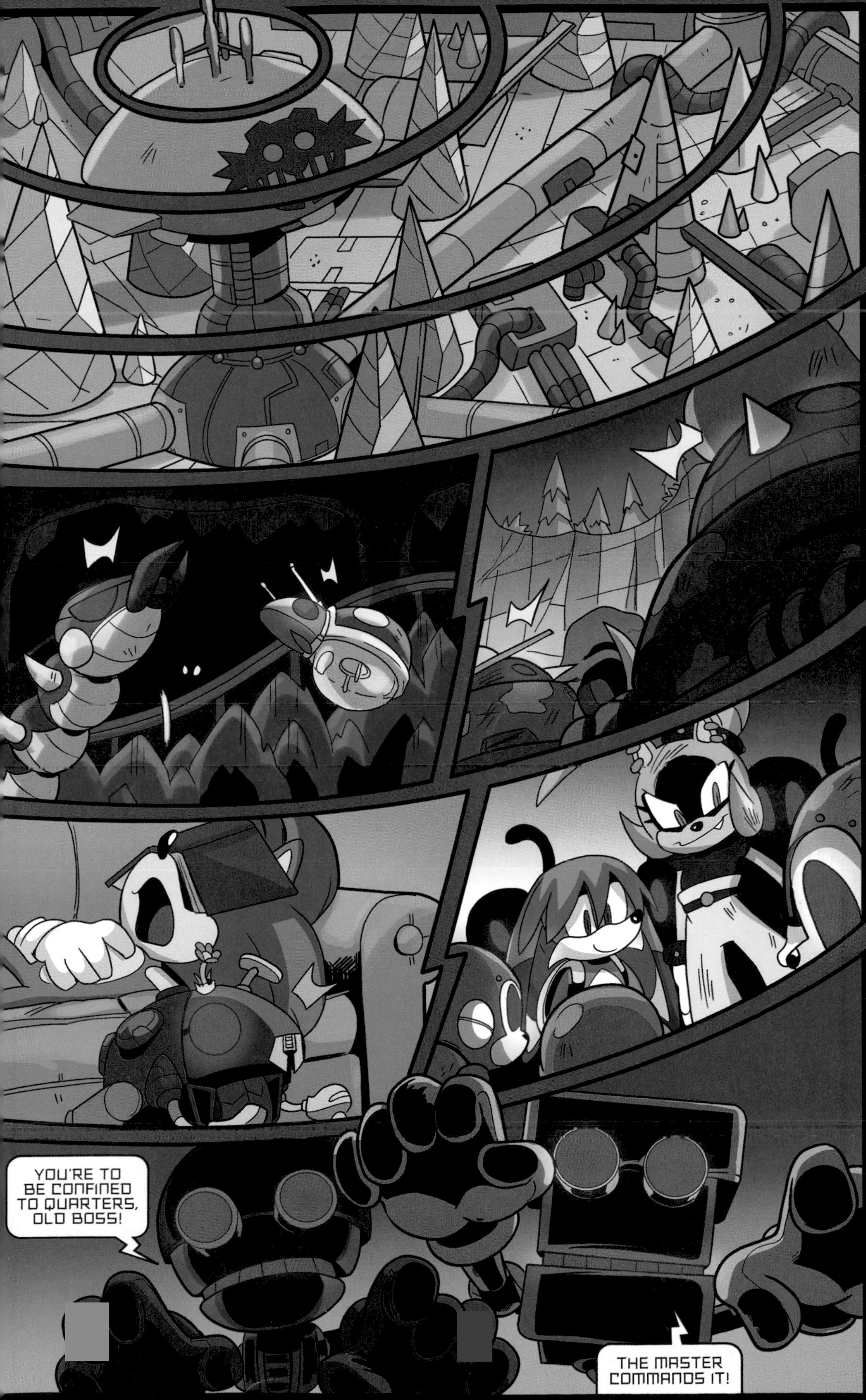
YOU'RE TO BE CONFINED TO QUARTERS, OLD BOSS!
THE MASTER COMMANDS IT!

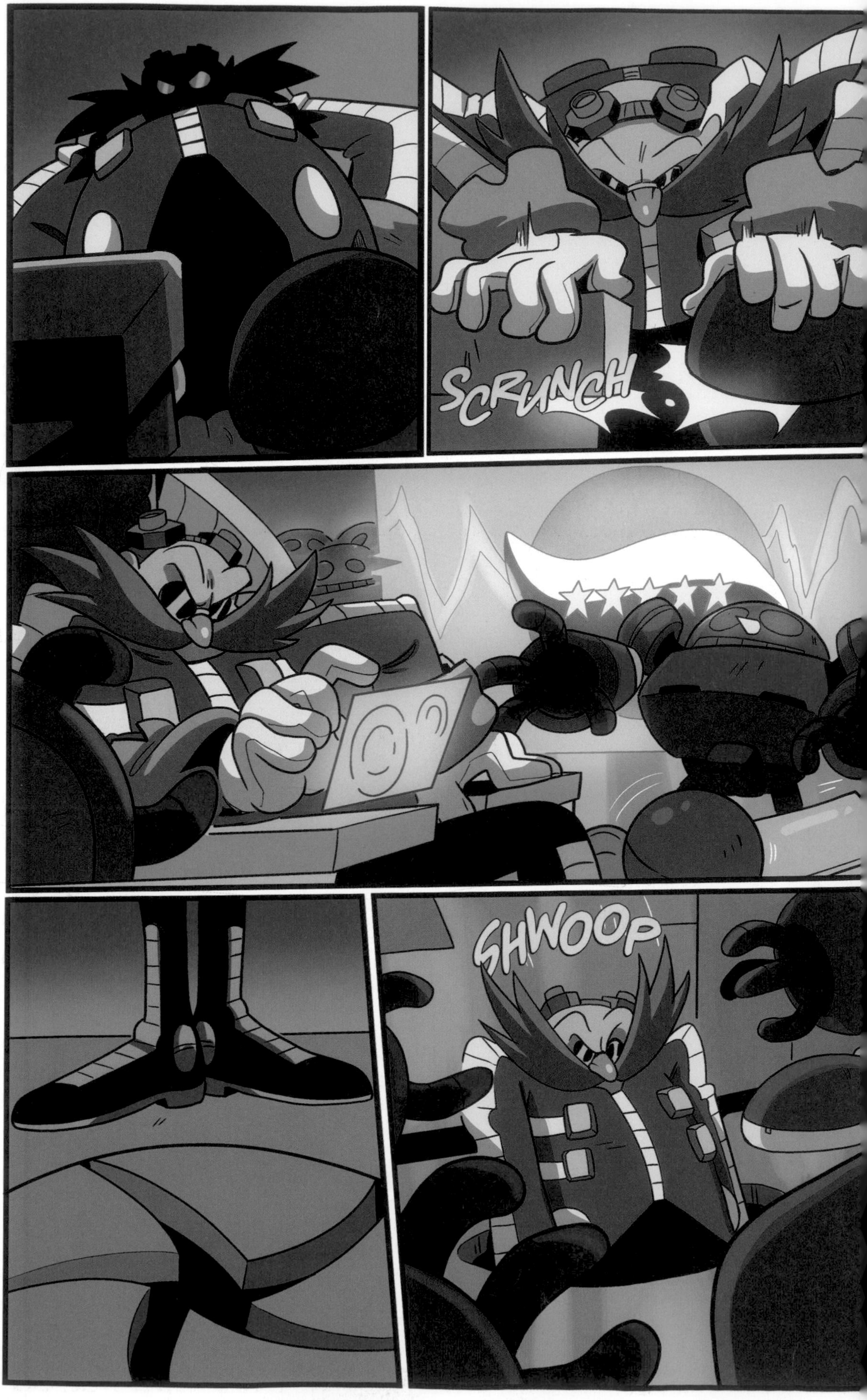
SCRUNCH
SHWOOP

IS IT EVERYTHING YOU HOPED IT WOULD BE, DOC?

BITTERSWEET, AS I IMAGINED...

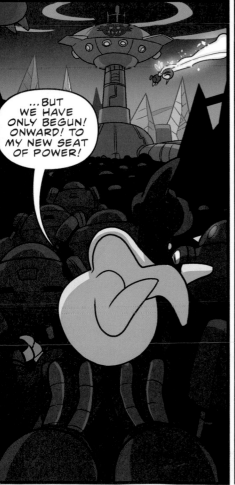

...BUT WE HAVE ONLY BEGUN! ONWARD! TO MY NEW SEAT OF POWER!

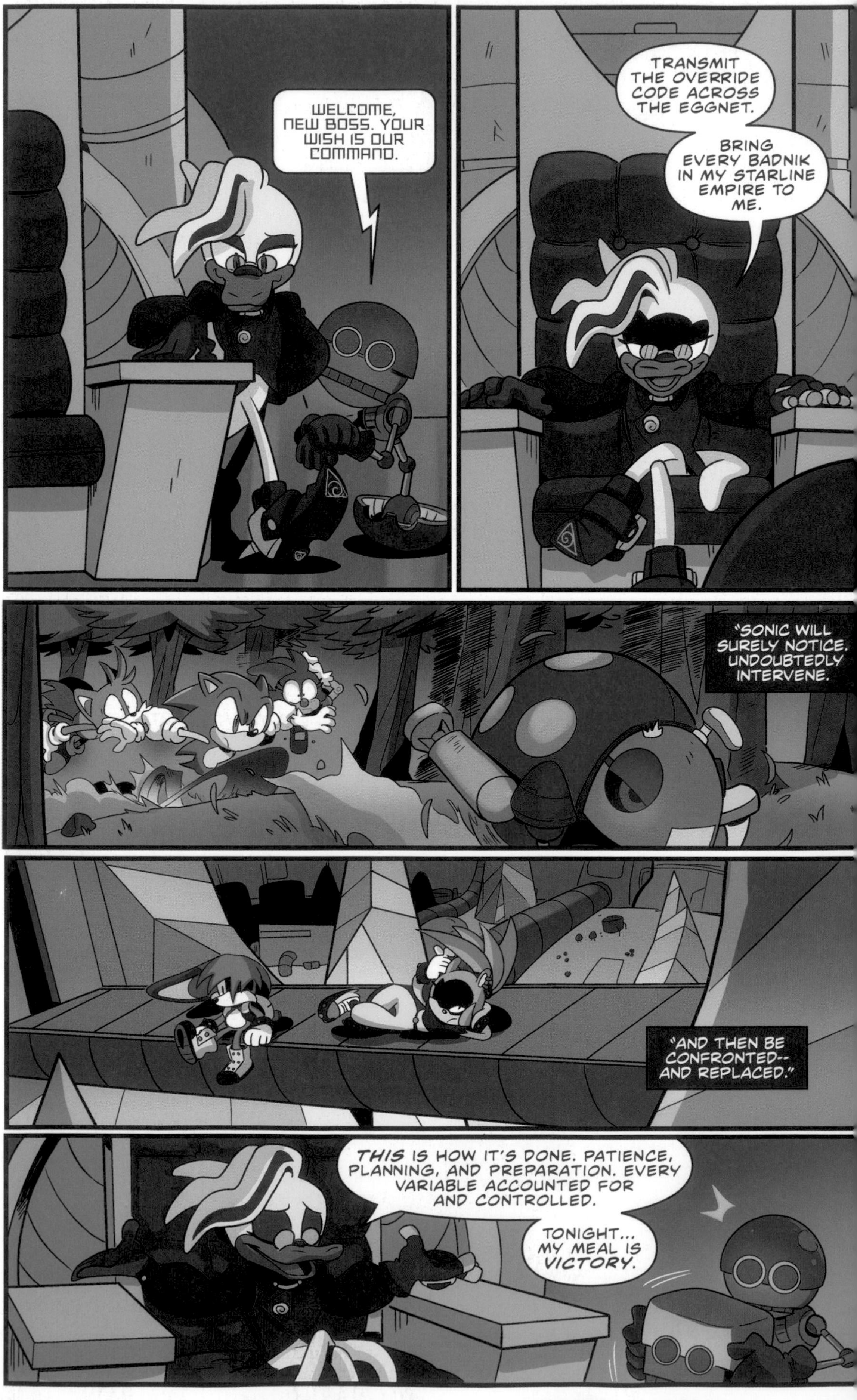
WELCOME, NEW BOSS. YOUR WISH IS OUR COMMAND.
TRANSMIT THE OVERRIDE CODE ACROSS THE EGGNET.
BRING EVERY BADNIK IN MY STARLINE EMPIRE TO ME.
"SONIC WILL SURELY NOTICE. UNDOUBTEDLY INTERVENE.
"AND THEN BE CONFRONTED--AND REPLACED."
THIS IS HOW IT'S DONE. PATIENCE, PLANNING, AND PREPARATION. EVERY VARIABLE ACCOUNTED FOR AND CONTROLLED.
TONIGHT... MY MEAL IS VICTORY.

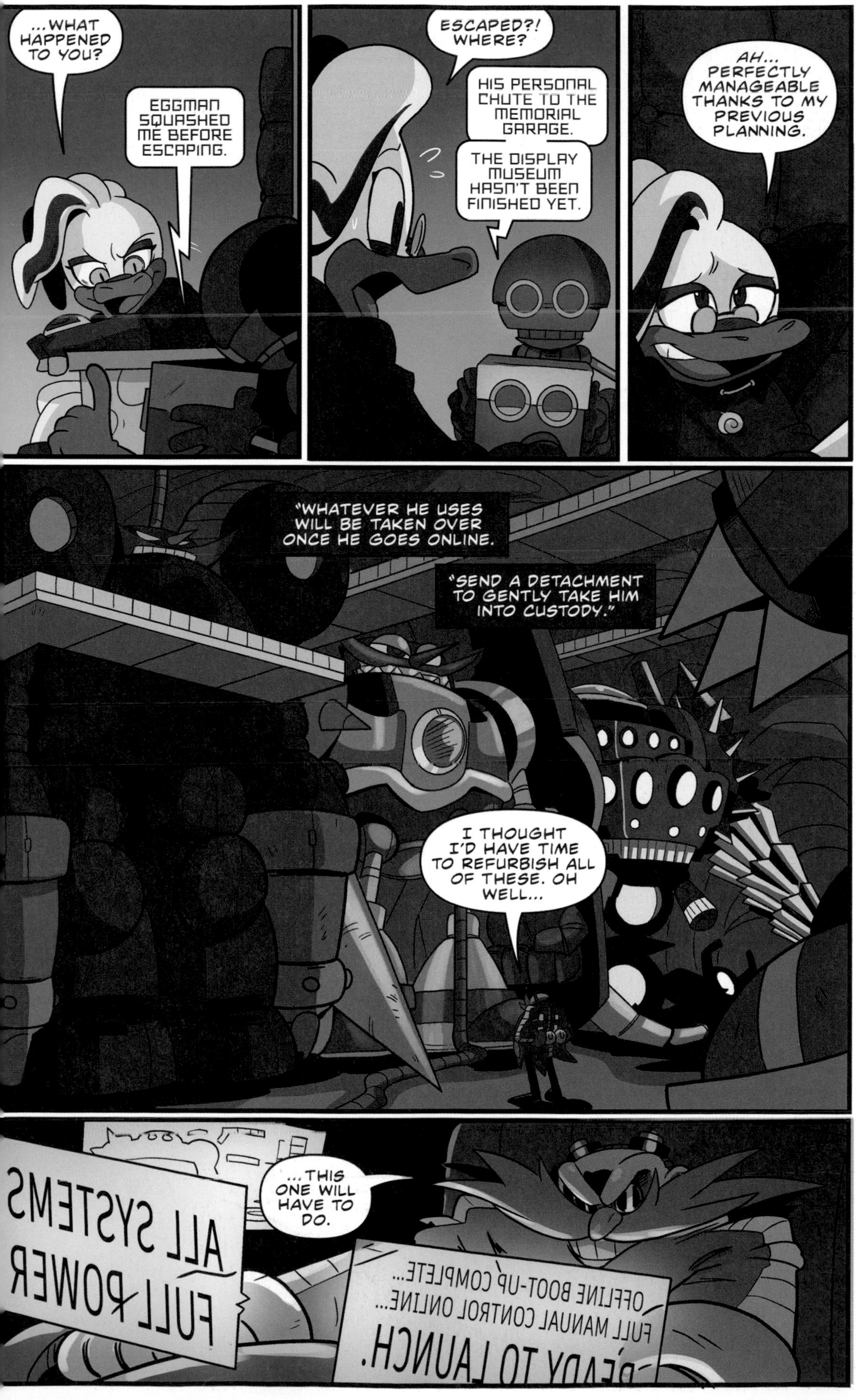
...WHAT HAPPENED TO YOU?
EGGMAN SQUASHED ME BEFORE ESCAPING.
ESCAPED?! WHERE?
HIS PERSONAL CHUTE TO THE MEMORIAL GARAGE.
THE DISPLAY MUSEUM HASN'T BEEN FINISHED YET.
AH... PERFECTLY MANAGEABLE THANKS TO MY PREVIOUS PLANNING.
"WHATEVER HE USES WILL BE TAKEN OVER ONCE HE GOES ONLINE.
"SEND A DETACHMENT TO GENTLY TAKE HIM INTO CUSTODY."
I THOUGHT I'D HAVE TIME TO REFURBISH ALL OF THESE. OH WELL...
...THIS ONE WILL HAVE TO DO.
ALL SYSTEMS FULL POWER
OFFLINE BOOT-UP COMPLETE...
FULL MANUAL CONTROL ONLINE...
READY TO LAUNCH.

THAT'S... AN INCREDIBLE NUMBER OF BADNIKS...

MEH. I COULD TAKE 'EM.

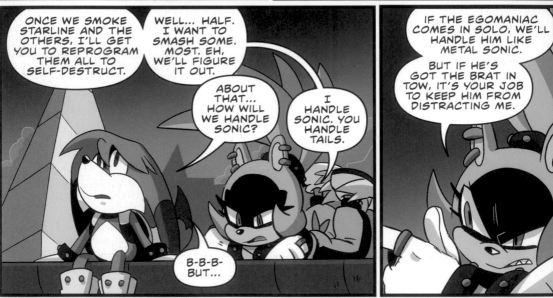

ONCE WE SMOKE STARLINE AND THE OTHERS, I'LL GET YOU TO REPROGRAM THEM ALL TO SELF-DESTRUCT.

WELL... HALF. I WANT TO SMASH SOME. MOST. EH, WE'LL FIGURE IT OUT.

ABOUT THAT... HOW WILL WE HANDLE SONIC?

I HANDLE SONIC. YOU HANDLE TAILS.

B-B-B-BUT...

IF THE EGOMANIAC COMES IN SOLO, WE'LL HANDLE HIM LIKE METAL SONIC.

BUT IF HE'S GOT THE BRAT IN TOW, IT'S YOUR JOB TO KEEP HIM FROM DISTRACTING ME.

ONCE THE "HEROES" AND DOCTORS ARE DONE, WE'RE FREE TO PLAY IT BY EAR.

HUNT DOWN ALL THEIR LITTLE FRIENDS, TOPPLE EVERY STUPID CITY THAT THREW 'EM A PARADE, TEAR IT ALL DOWN. JUST YOU AND ME, KID.

SOUND GOOD?

I CAN'T WAIT!

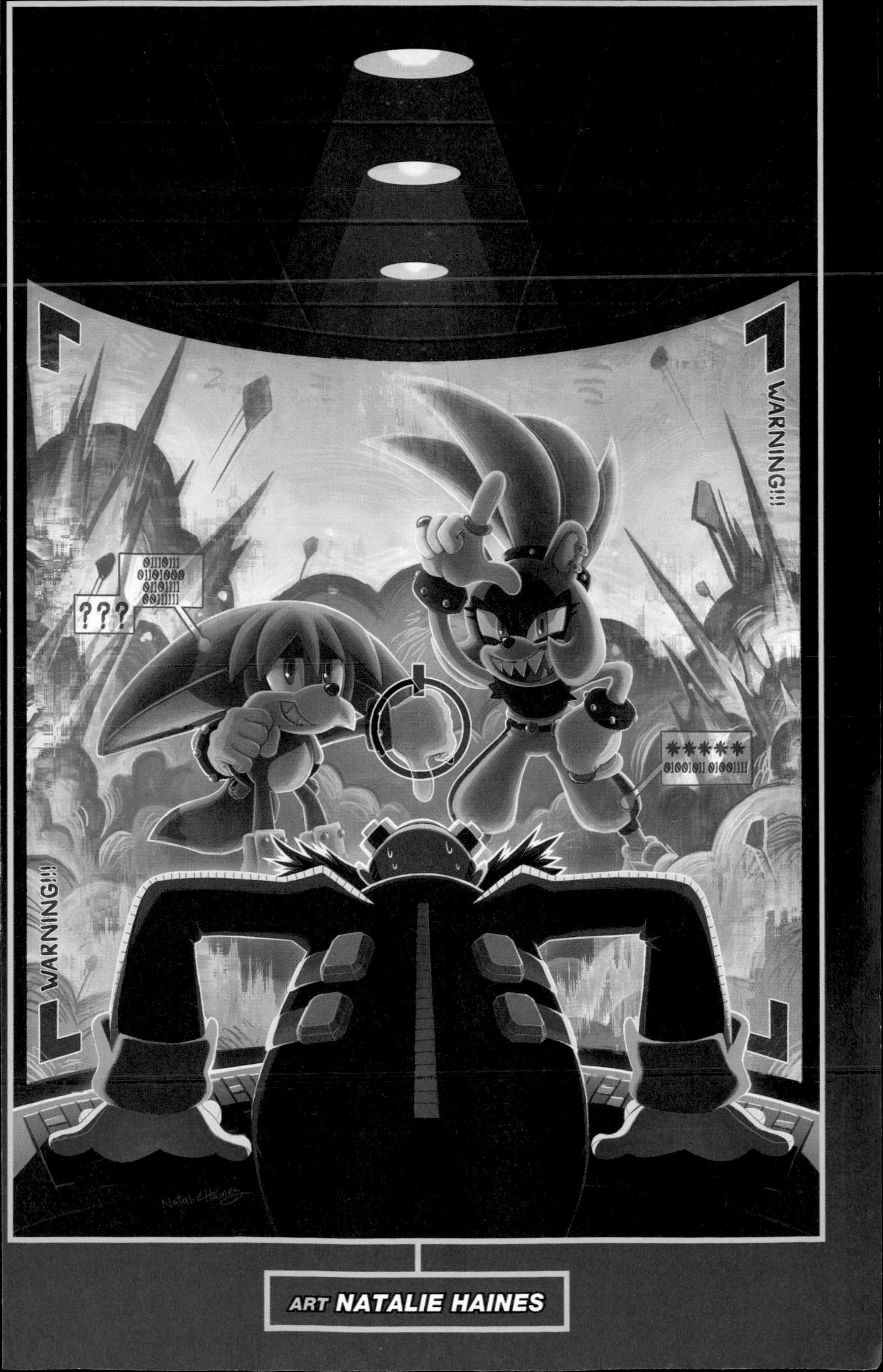
WARNING!!!
01110111
01101000
01101111
00111111
???
*****
01001011 01001111
WARNING!!!
Natalie Haines

ART NATALIE HAINES

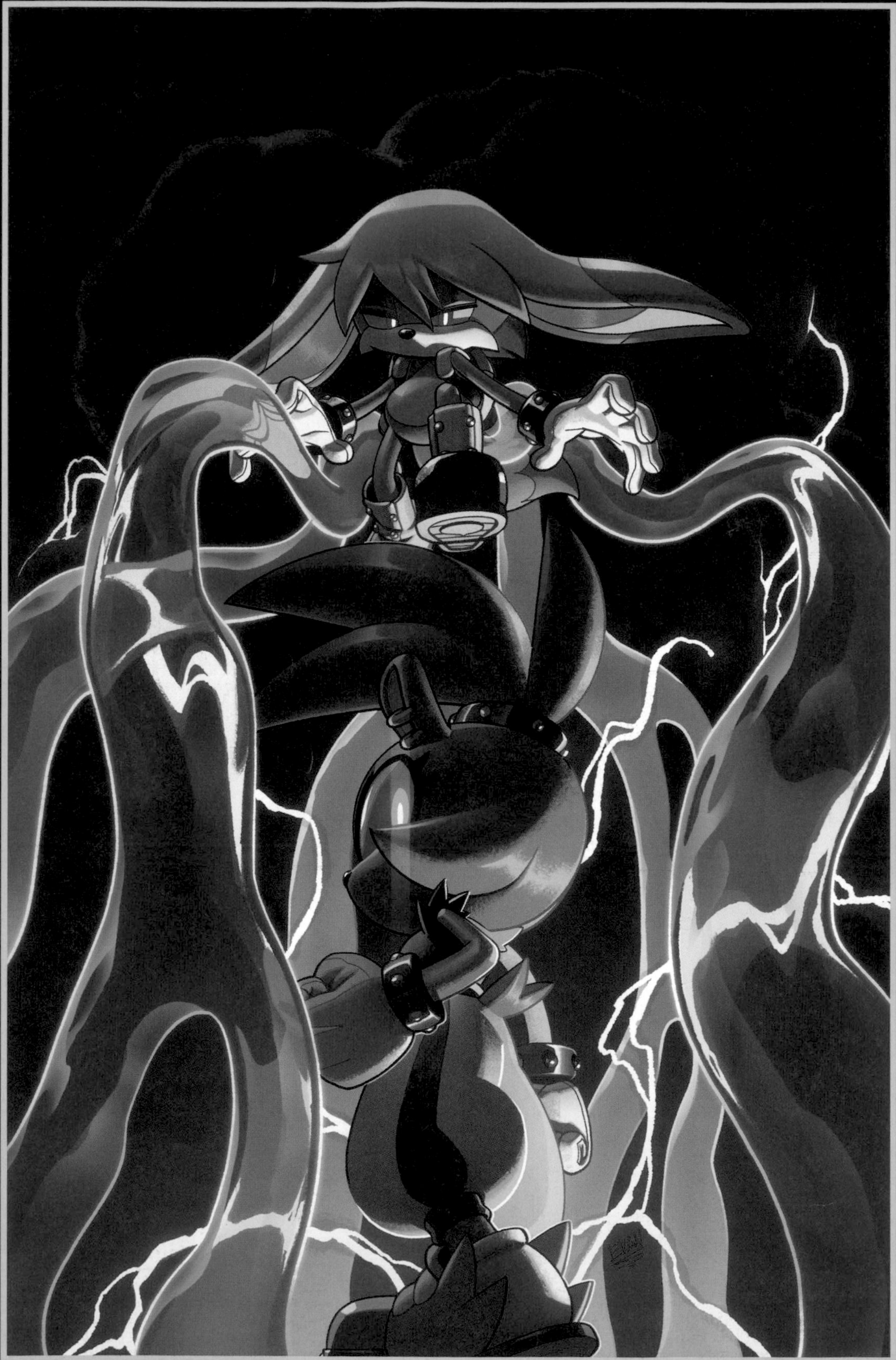

ART EVAN STANLEY

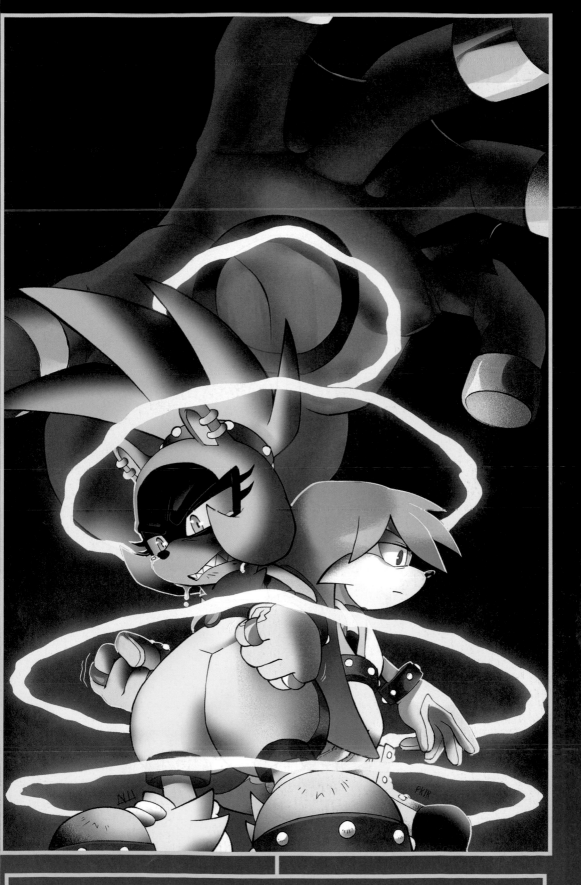

ART **AARON HAMMERSTROM** COLORS **PRISCILLA TRAMONTANO**

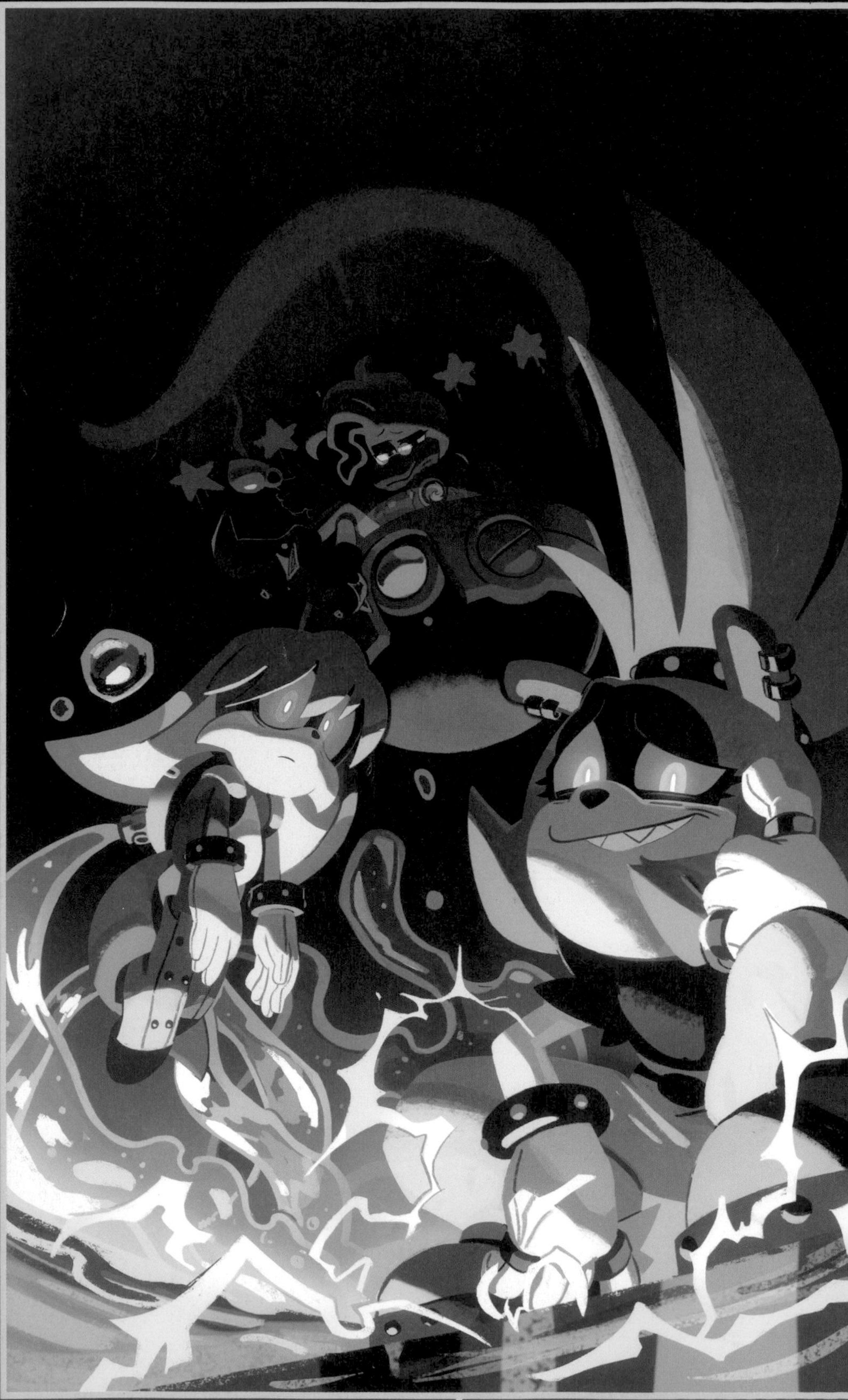

ART NATHALIE FOURDRAINE

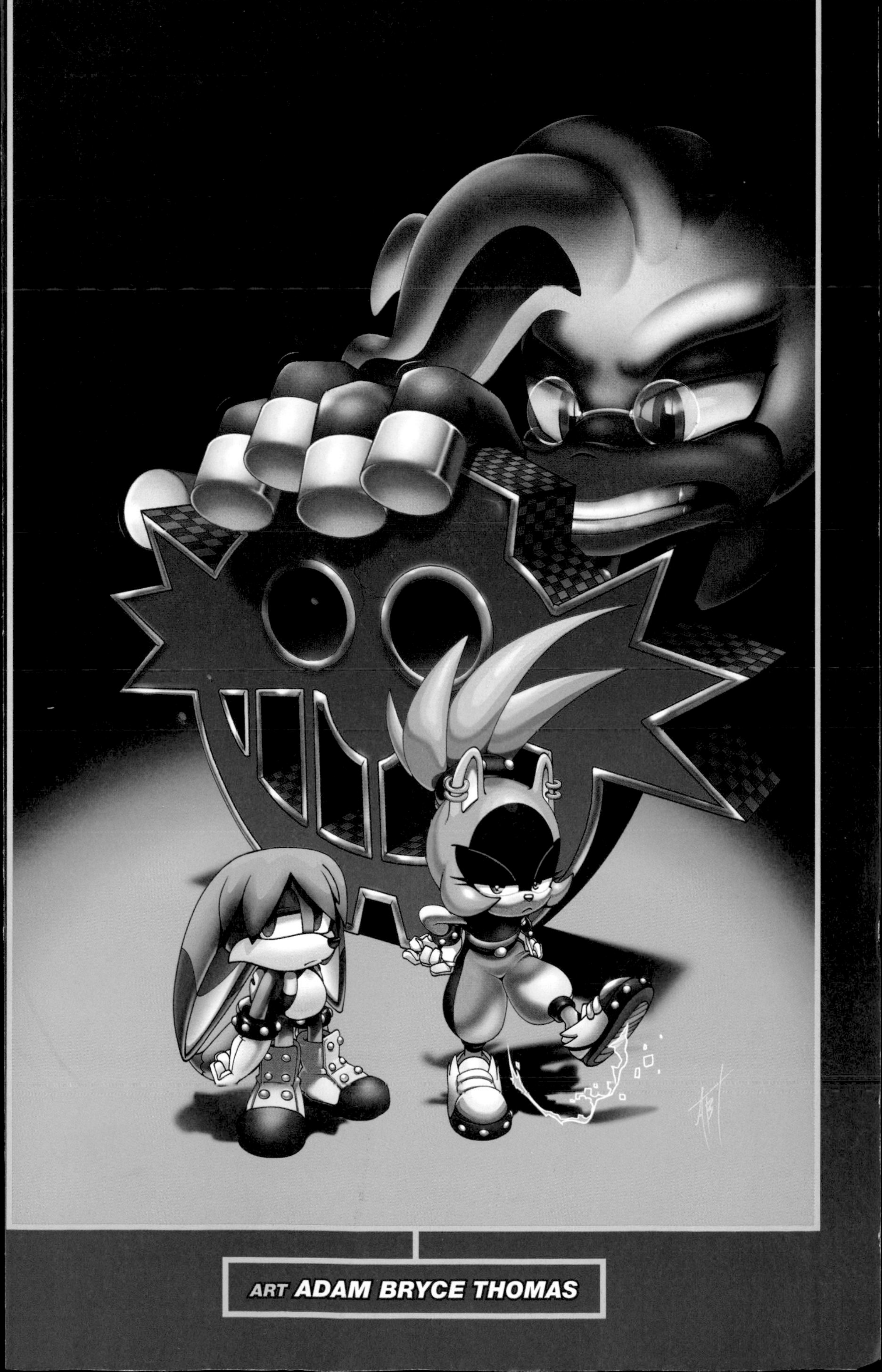
ABT

ART ADAM BRYCE THOMAS

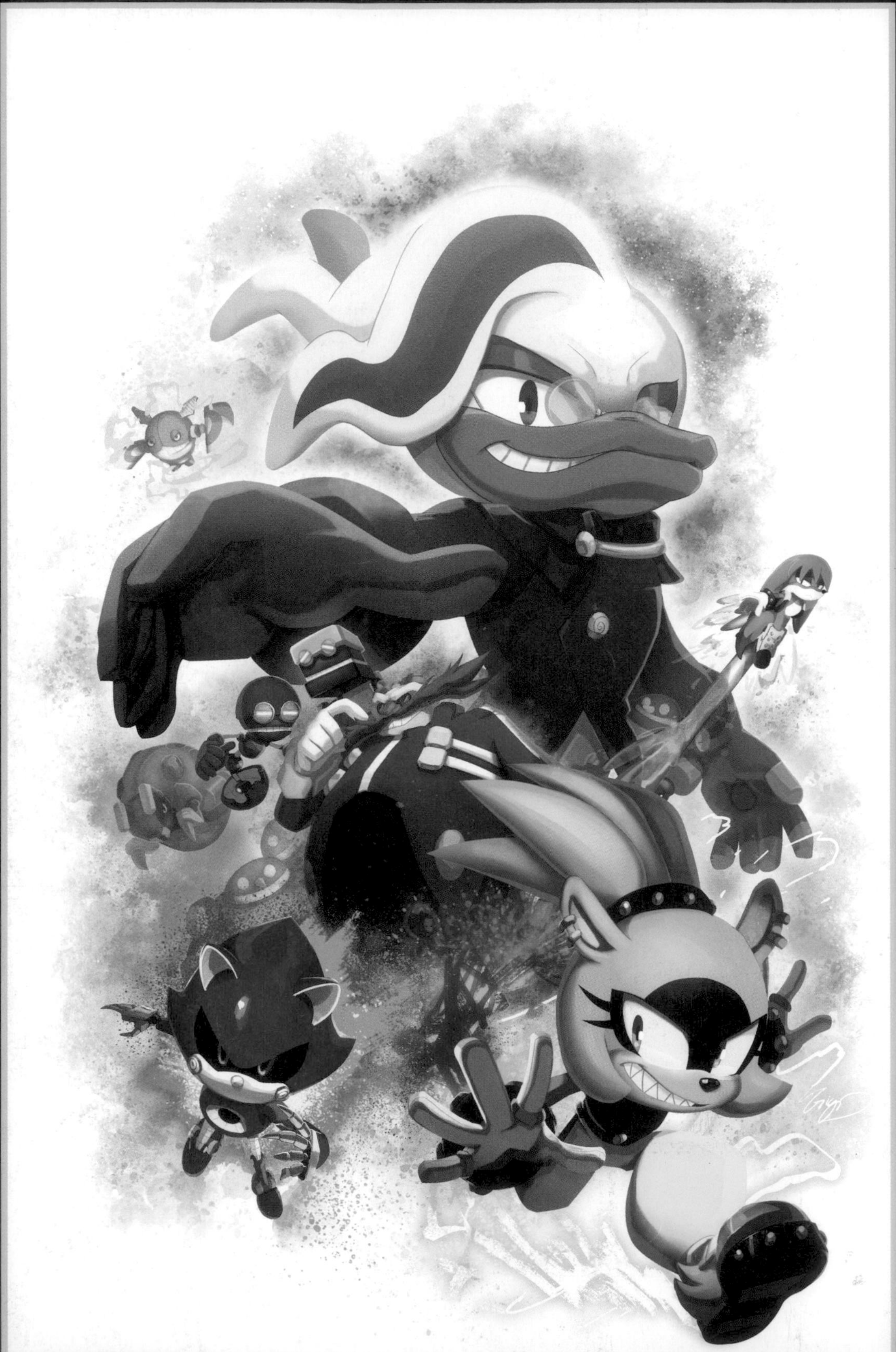

ART GIGI DUTREIX